THE CHINESE EGG

Catherine Storr

McGraw-Hill Book Company

New York   St. Louis   San Francisco
Düsseldorf   Mexico   Toronto

Book Design by Marcy J. Katz

Copyright © 1975 by Catherine Storr

First published in 1975
by Faber and Faber Limited
3 Queen Square London WC 1

First Distribution in
the United States of America
by McGraw-Hill Inc., 1975.

234567 MUBP 789876

Library of Congress Cataloging in Publication Data

Storr, Catherine,
  The Chinese egg.

  SUMMARY: Brought together by a Chinese egg puzzle, three young people become involved in a dangerous search for a missing baby.
  [1. Mystery and detective stories] I. Title.
PZ7.S8857Ch4   [Fic]   75-11575
ISBN 0-07-061794-5
ISBN 0-07-061795-3 lib. bdg.

On a dusty glass shelf in the window of the bits-and-pieces, second-hand, pseudo-antique shop, lay the egg.

It had been shaped by hand from a single block of wood. The block of hard, close, finely grained wood had been delicately divided into pieces that interlocked; each fitting close to its neighbors, cheek to cheek, the jutting wedge of this section sliding smoothly into the angle between the two arms of that. As long as the pieces were put together in the right order by sensitive fingers which could feel the balance of the whole, they held together and made up the perfect egg. Polished outside so that it glowed like burnished bronze, the egg, whole and yet divisible, shone among the junk in Mr. McGovern's shop on the corner of Printing House Lane and the High Street.

Stephen saw it on his way home from school. He often chose to go that way and have a look, fascinated, at Mr. McGovern's collection. So many things that you'd think no one would ever want, even new and whole and clean, and that surely no one would ever buy now, tattered, chipped and worn. Looking in the blurry window now he saw draggled feather boas, dirty books lacking spines, cracked plates, cups without handles, sad, meaningless pictures in flamboyant frames, clocks which had stopped years ago and which would never mark any real time again. He saw mirrors, cracked lamps, dingy lace, half-backed chairs; and in the side window, where the small objects were displayed, he saw tarnished paste buckles, dusty velvet, the chipped sheen of imitation pearls, a string of child's colored beads, gilt brooches, Woolworth jewelry discolored by age. Among them, different because it was real and had been made with skill and with love, he saw the egg.

He went in and bought it. Mr. McGovern who was elderly and, in spite of his name not at all British, would have liked to haggle, but Stephen wasn't interested. He was also embarrassed. He wanted the egg and he didn't want to have to pretend that he wasn't going to pay for it. When Mr. McGovern said "Two pounds," perhaps believing that a boy at school wouldn't have so much, Stephen agreed at once.

"I'll have to go home to fetch it."

"I can't keep anything for you. The peoples come in and say, 'Keep, keep,' then they don't come back, I lose the money."

"You still have the thing."

"Other peoples want and I don't sell because of the first peoples. So I lose."

"I'll be back in five minutes. It's only around the corner."

"So everyone tells me, then they don't come back."

"You could keep it five minutes."

"Five then, by my watch." Extraordinarily his watch was going. All those dead clocks in the shop brooded, stopped forever at different hours, anything from one to twelve, but Mr. McGovern's nickel-plated modern wristwatch told the right time. Stephen ran home, let himself in, collected the notes from the purse in his desk, and was back before the nickel-plated five minutes were past. By the grandfather clock just inside the shop door his errand had taken no time at all.

"Is a beautiful piece of workship," the old man said, now apparently unwilling to part with the egg.

"How many pieces?" Stephen asked. He could just slide a fingernail between two.

"I haven't counted. Twenty? Twenty-five? Is very difficult puzzle. You separate, maybe you never put her together again."

"Isn't there a plan? Instructions?" asked Stephen, child of his age, accustomed to explanations and printed instructions, diagrams and the scientific approach to every sort of mystery.

"No plan. Is a secret egg. Is Chinese. You find her out," Mr. McGovern said, and disappeared into the dark recesses of his shop. Stephen, holding the egg carefully in one hand, turned and left.

And then outside, it happened. He tripped, as he stepped out, on an uneven paving-stone, stumbled forwards, saved himself, just didn't go right down. But his hand opened and the egg sprang from it in spite of his desperate, just-too-late grip on its slippery surface. It seemed to rise into the air and fall slowly, in a parabola, a curve like water from a fountain. It hit the ground with a dull thud and burst, like a wooden firework, into pieces. Stephen saw odd-shaped bits of wood lying around his feet, many, meaningless, robbed of all significance by being divided. His egg had disappeared. He was left with a lot of spillikins of different shapes, but of no importance.

He began to collect them. He might even have found all of them immediately if it hadn't been that at that moment the trail began back from the local comprehensive school. Boys and girls of all ages and sizes were surging through the street on their way home at the end of their school day. Stephen had to dodge through them, avoiding their feet, as he searched for the hooked and angled shapes. "Excuse me," he said desperately, rescuing a small mallet-shaped fragment from under the heel of a Brunhild in a gray duffle coat. "Hi! Don't step on that!" to a boy in jeans and Aran-type pullover. He dodged and grabbed, and the chattering, uncaring crowd poured past him like a river in flood. When he finally stood up, dishevelled, hot and angry, he'd collected more than twenty pieces; he couldn't be sure of the exact number. He put them loose in his pocket and went moodily home.

Vicky got home that same Friday evening to find her Mum cutting out all over the kitchen table. Bits of tissue-paper pattern floated off the back of a chair as she opened the door. The table was bright with dark blue polished cotton scattered with little flowers of shocking pink.

"What's it going to be?"

"Dress," her mother said, her mouth full of pins.

"Super! Who for? You?"

"Wait a minute while I get these pins in."

She anchored one of the extraordinary-shaped bits of paper on to the blue. It looked like a pale island in a sea of blue and pink. Then she said, "For you. Summer dress."

"Can I see the pattern?"

She saw it and was pleased. Her Mum generally chose well, and her dressmaking, if not professional, almost always had a sort of style. She never finished the seams off inside as you were supposed to, and sometimes, from not reading the instructions carefully enough, she made silly mistakes. Once she'd made the whole dress back to front, puzzling all the time why the darts came in such funny places. Even so it had turned out all right.

She had a good eye for color, often adding extras, a braiding, big buttons, cuffs of a different material, which turned the clothes she made into something special.

"Are you making one for Chris too?"

"Not out of the same material I'm not."

She never did. Vicky and Chris hadn't been dressed alike ever since they were tiny. It was only sense. They looked quite different. Chris was slender, with mid-brown to reddish hair, and she was pretty. No, she was more than pretty, she was fabulous. Boys took one look at Chris and then pursued her. Vicky was not fat, but beside Chris she looked big. She had big bones, too much nose, too big a mouth, long hands and feet Her hair was dark and absolutely straight. Chris's was just wavy enough never to look untidy, Vicky's always did. Chris's skin was fair, Vicky's was dark. Chris's eyes were a wonderful clear blue, Vicky's were greenery-yellow. People often said in surprise, "Are you really sisters, you aren't a bit alike." Then after they'd seen the girls' father they often said, "Of course, Chris is just like her Mom, isn't she? And Vicky's like her Dad." Sometimes Chris and Vicky agreed and let it go, sometimes they explained. There'd been a time, when Vicky was small, when she'd explained every time, thinking it was fun to surprise them. Now she wasn't so sure.

Chris came into the room and said, exactly as Vicky had done, "What's that you're making?"

"Dress for Vicky."

"Can I see the pattern?"

"Help yourself. And don't upset my pinbox."

"Super!" Chris said, just as Vicky had done.

"Glad you like it."

"Going to make one for me too?"

"If I've time before the summer comes."

"I don't think it ever will. You'll have plenty of time. It's freezing for April."

"Only just April today."

"Spring holidays start next week. It ought to be warmer now."

"May's often a nice month," Mrs. Stanford said hopefully. She pinned a long wedge-shaped piece of tissue paper to a length of the material and said, "That's the three skirt pieces. I'll clear off and get tea."

Tea was high tea. Sometimes Mr. Stanford got back in time for it, sometimes he didn't. This was partly because he worked on shifts, partly because Mrs. Stanford kept irregular hours herself. She was good about getting the girls' breakfasts when they had to get to school on time, but for the rest of the day she pleased herself. It wasn't unusual for them to come back from school at half-past four and find she'd only just got herself lunch. High tea could be any time between five and nine in the evening; it depended on friends, on shopping, on Mrs. Stanford's own appetite, on television programs, on the day of the week. Vicky and Chris were so used to it that when they visited houses where meals were always at fixed hours, they were faintly surprised. If tea was late and they were hungry, there were always biscuits in a battered red tin, coke in the fridge and often bits left over from the night before in the larder. Chris ate everything and never put on an extra pound; Vicky had to watch her weight. She was the one who sometimes rebelled against the endless meals of baked beans, cold sliced ham and sliced white bread, spread with lashings of butter. Not that she didn't like it, but it put pounds on her.

Tea today was tinned red salmon and salad, followed by red jelly. Plus bread and butter, of course. Vicky was ravenous, the school lunch had been more uneatable than ever. She and Chris ate a huge tea, then sat around groaning.

"I'm too full. Wish I hadn't eaten that second lot," Chris said.

"What're you going to write about for English?" Vicky asked.

"They're a rotten lot of subjects. I don't want to do any of them."

"I don't mind the one on Macbeth."

"You must be crazy! It doesn't mean a thing."

"What is it?" Mrs. Stanford asked, licking a thread before putting it into the eye of her needle.

"About how the witches knew Macbeth was going to kill Duncan," Chris said.

"No it isn't. It's whether Macbeth would have done anything about it if he hadn't been told he was going to be king," Vicky said.

"What's the difference? They told him the future, didn't they?"

"But what's interesting is whether he'd have murdered Duncan if they hadn't said anything."

"But he did murder Duncan. He couldn't have been king without," Chris said.

"Only did the witches make him do it by telling him first?"

"Is that what you're going to write about?" Mrs. Stanford asked, half-attending.

"I might. I've got math as well. And history. It's going to take me hours."

She turned her school bag out onto the cleared table. There was a cascade of books, exercise books, three pens, an elderly eraser, two set squares and a pencil, a ruler, a packet of Lifesavers and a piece of wood.

"Can I borrow your eraser? I've gone wrong already," Chris said reaching for it. Her fingers met the piece of wood first, and she said, "What on earth's that? It doesn't look like anything."

"I dunno. Saw it in the gutter. Somehow it looked nice. As if it meant something."

"Funny shape," Chris said, holding it up, a stalk of wood with a wedge-shaped excrescence at each end.

"Piece of something else, if you ask me," their mother said.

"The ends are sort of polished," Chris said.

"What can you do with it? If it's just a piece of something it isn't any good, is it?"

"S'pose not. I just sort of liked it. It looked somehow . . ."

"What, for Pete's sake?"

"I don't know. As if someone had meant it to be that shape. That's all."

"You're crazy," Chris said affectionately.

"It feels nice. Chuck it over. It might bring me luck," Vicky said, frowning at her math. But she didn't have luck with her math. Every single problem she tackled came out hopelessly wrong.

"Why Vicky?" Mr. Stanford said to his wife later that evening, when the girls had gone up to bed, and she was sitting at the sewing-machine, feeding the blue and rosy material through its predatory foot.

"They've both got to have new summer frocks."

"Why Vicky first? Why not Chris for a change?"

"To tell you the truth I bought this material for Chris. Just her color, it is."

"Why make it for Vicky, then?"

"I know it's stupid, but every now and then it comes over me that Chris is ours, and she knows it. Chris is safe. As safe as a child can be. And Vicky isn't. I want to make it up to her."

"That doesn't mean you have to be doing things for Vicky that you don't do for Chris."

"I don't in the ordinary way. I don't think about them like that. It's different too, Chris being so pretty. You know, I feel God's been unfair making Chris the pretty one and Vicky plain. Well, not plain exactly, but she's not like Chris."

"That she's not," Mr. Stanford said.

"She's a nice girl. You love her too," his wife said.

"Of course I do. Only I don't forget she's not mine. Nor yours."

"That's what I mean. However much we look to her as if she was our own, she can't ever be the same. There's always the thinking, 'Perhaps that's her mother coming out,' or, 'Who was her father, when all's said and done?' That's why I feel different about her."

"That's why you give her Chris's summer frock?"

"Maybe. I don't know. I just feel I owe her something, that's all."

"You owe her? I'd say she owed you. There was no call for you to bring her home the way you did."

"Let's not have that again. You agreed at the time, you know you did."

"Right. But I never . . . ."

"And she and Chris make a fine pair, don't they, now?"

"They're all right," Mr. Stanford said without enthusiasm.

"And Chris would have been lonely."

"I won't have you upsetting yourself about that."

"I'm not upsetting myself. And Vicky's a good girl."

"She's all right."

"Clever, too."

"She'll never be a patch on Chris for looks," said Chris's father proudly.

"We couldn't have done without the two of them."

"So you say."

"I couldn't, anyway. Sometimes . . ." But she didn't finish the sentence. She'd been going to say that she couldn't imagine her life without both her own and her adopted daughter, but looking at her husband's face she decided not to say it aloud. She loved them both. That was enough.

When Stephen had got home and tried to fit the bits of the egg together he realized the truth of what Mr. McGovern had said. It was not an easy puzzle. He'd spent longer over it than he should, considering the amount of weekend homework he had in this, his last year, and by dinner he hadn't got anywhere near discovering the lie of the pieces. He ate angrily through one of his mother's experimental dishes, returning the standard "all right" when she asked anxiously whether it was what he liked. He felt furious. He was furious with himself for dropping the egg, furious with himself again for not seeing at once how it should fit together, and furious with his parents for being there, for asking him questions he didn't want to have to answer, for his mother's anxiety and her ineptness with food—why couldn't she just cook roast chicken or beef or warm up frozen food like other people's mothers; why did she have to try out fancy sauces and elaborate French ways of messing up perfectly good food which might have been all right if she'd been better at it, but which always, in her hands, went wrong? His father, fortunately for Stephen, was tired, so he didn't have to answer the endless inquiries into what he'd been doing, what he'd been thinking and why? why? why? all the time. Stephen supposed this went with his profession, and it seemed to have become an inescapable part of his private life as well.

"What are you going to do after dinner, darling?" his mother asked, as she stacked plates for Mrs. Noble to wash up in the morning. Stephen said, "Work, I suppose," wondering what his father would say if he'd answered that he was going to try to mend a broken egg. He could just imagine how his father's expression would change to the alert, watchful look which meant that he thought for once he was going to see into Stephen's mind. He'd say, "That sounds like quite a tricky business. How are you going to set about that?" or, "Now why should you want to do that?" or if he was feeling philosophical, "Interesting concept the egg, as the perfect indivisible whole. . . ." Or something like that, with a string of the names of all the different tribes in the South Seas or somewhere, who worshipped the egg as a god or as a fertility symbol or the token of rebirth or anything else sufficiently far-fetched. Stephen by now knew quite a lot of the jargon, though he couldn't be sure he always got it right. One thing was certain, though, whatever else his father said about it, he wouldn't just see it as an egg. That would be too ordinary and simple. It would have to mean something else. Stephen thought that both his parents really made life much more complicated than it need be, since his father would see the egg not as an egg but as a symbol, and his mother wouldn't just boil it or fry it, but would look up how to turn it into something unrecognizable in one of her foreign cookery books. By the time either of them had finished with it, in fact, no one would ever know it had started life as nothing more than an egg. "Its own mother wouldn't know it," Stephen said aloud in the privacy of his own room, and laughed and felt better.

Probably, just because he felt better, when he looked at the wooden shapes where he'd left them angrily an hour or so earlier, he saw them not as incomprehensible, hostile, separate *things*, but as having meaning, parts of a whole. He forgot his history essay and the intensive reading he should have been doing around the Metaphysical poets, and sat down at his desk, fingering the smooth pieces of wood. He found that without thinking he'd interlocked three of them together, obviously right. There was the beginning of the outside curve, ovoid, polished. The inner surfaces were plain, that was the only help in seeing how the egg was to be put together. Pleased with his progress, he made the mistake of concentrating too hard, trying to work the puzzle out like an algebraic formula, or a problem in geometry, as if it were a proposition in logic. It was better, he found, if he didn't think directly about it, but let his fingers play with the pieces, his eyes wander over them. Then suddenly it jumped at him, how this angle was made to fit into that, how what had seemed an impossible shape to fit in anywhere turned out to be the kingpin that held others together. Before, when the pattern had completely eluded him, he'd been working at it too hard; now he played, allowing his mind to wander, thinking of his friends, school, places he'd been to, girls he'd looked at and longed for, music he'd heard. And while he dreamed and remembered, the egg grew in his fingers. Like any jigsaw—only this was a three-dimensional one—it got simpler as the pieces to be fitted in became fewer. Even so, it wasn't easy. He stuck at it, with a growing feeling of triumph, for over two hours. It was eleven when he'd got all but the last three pieces into place. It wasn't until that moment that he realized that although only three pieces remained on the red leather inside the flap of his desk, this wasn't the total number needed to complete the egg. He fitted them in, with a sort of desperate hope that he'd got it wrong, but there was no doubt. The smooth surface of the egg still showed one or two rectangular gaps where another polished segment should slot in. And though the egg held together, it was doubtfully, hesitantly, without the firm confidence Stephen had sensed in it when he'd first held it in his hand. There was at least one bit still missing; he must have overlooked it in the street. He'd go and look for it first thing next morning. It was a Saturday, fortunately. He was determined to find it. He went to bed angry again, stayed awake longer than usual, raging against the luck that had made him trip just at that psychological moment, and overslept the next morning. He didn't get out to begin his search until after ten.

Chris and Vicky went out shopping every Saturday morning. This Saturday was no different from any other to start with. They did the boring stuff—that meant the household shopping—first, then went to look for the more interesting things. Chris wanted shoes. Vicky wanted a barrette to keep her straggling hair off her face; astonishingly she found immediately exactly what she wanted, made of pale fine cane, woven into a sort of flat knot. "Marvelous, you're so dark. Keep it on, Vicky, it's great," Chris said. Looking in the mirror Vicky saw that it was true. The barrette, the way Chris had looped her hair off her face, made a new, different Vicky. Not pretty, not ravishingly pretty like Chris, but a girl with a style of her own. She almost smiled at her reflection, then her eyes took in the sloppy pullover she'd been wearing for the last year and the faded jeans stretched a little too tight. Beside her, Chris, in almost equally old clothes, but somehow looking finished and put together just right, was sure of herself in the way that perhaps only a girl who has been pretty, without effort, from babyhood, can be. Vicky scowled at her own reflection, then cheered up and bought the barrette. It was miraculously cheap. She came out of the boutique saying, "Lucky! We've both been lucky, your shoes and now this."

Chris said, "Your silly bit of wood you found. Think it really works?" Vicky put her hand in her pocket. She'd forgotten it, but it was there. She started to say, "That wasn't the sort of luck I meant," when the thing happened.

They were on the pavement outside the delicatessen, just by the pedestrian crossing, the one that Mum always said was dangerous; the road was too wide, a driver coming up on the outside couldn't see who'd stepped off the pavement. Vicky wasn't really looking at it, but it flashed suddenly before her eyes. The funny thing was that what she saw was in a sort of frame, like a small bright picture surrounded by odd, dark, angled shapes like the top of a tower, like battlements. In the bright picture, she saw the crossing and an old lady starting to walk across in front of a blue van that had stopped for her. In that instant she heard two sounds. A voice, a boy's voice, cried out, "Look out!" and brakes screamed. She thought she saw a car coming up much too fast on the further side of the van; she wasn't sure if the old lady fell. She clutched Chris's arm and shut her eyes, she didn't want to see the accident.

"What's the matter?" Chris said.

Vicky opened her eyes. She saw the boy who had called out, his mouth still open, staring, shocked.

"What's the matter? You're hurting," Chris said.

"The old lady," Vicky said.

"What old lady?"

"On the crossing."

"There isn't anyone on the crossing. What's the matter? You're seeing things," Chris said.

"But I saw her. And a blue van. She was going to be hit."

"You're crazy. There isn't anything like that. Look!" Chris said.

Vicky looked. Chris was right. Traffic was flowing smoothly up the High Street, buses, vans and cars. Three small children with their mother stood on the curb waiting correctly until some kind-hearted driver should stop. No old lady, no blue van. No accident.

"I saw her," Vicky said again.

"You've gone all white. You're shaking. We'd better go back," Chris said.

"Wait a minute," Vicky said. The boy was still there. He was standing quite still, looking at the pedestrian crossing, as if he couldn't believe his eyes.

He had called out. He must have seen it too.

Vicky felt peculiar. She was cold, but she was sweating.

Sound roared in her ears, she couldn't see properly. She took three steps away from Chris toward the boy, meaning to ask him something, she didn't know what, but when she'd reached him all she said was, "Chris!" desperately before blackness fell on her like a shower of soft dark feathers.

"Help me," Chris said to the boy, who stood there staring at nothing as far as she could see and looking, she thought, a bit daft. "Into the café," Chris said, pointing to it with her head, and they half-carried, half-dragged Vicky to a table just inside the door. "Get her head down on her knees. She'll come around in a second," Chris said, competently holding Vicky on the chair with one hand and with the other forcing her head down. "It's only a faint. She used to do it in school prayers all the time, but she hasn't for ages now."

If she hadn't been the prettiest girl Stephen had ever seen, he wouldn't have stayed. He wanted to get away and try to sort out what had happened. Since that wasn't possible, he ordered three coffees and waited while the other girl, the not pretty one, sighed and sat up. She looked awful, dead white, with black shadows around her eyes and the hair on her forehead damp with sweat. He preferred to look at her friend.

"Drink your coffee, Vicky. You'll feel better then," the pretty one said, and the other girl obeyed without speaking, as if she hadn't the will to do anything else. "Gosh, I needed that! Thanks," the pretty one said to Stephen. When she smiled she was prettier than ever.

"What happened?" Vicky asked Chris.

"You fainted. Well, nearly. He helped me get you in here."

"There was something else. I saw something." She shivered suddenly and said to Stephen, "Why did you call out?"

He'd hoped no one had heard above the noise of the traffic. He said, "What do you mean?"

She didn't answer. She had taken a handkerchief out of her pocket and was wiping her forehead with it. She put her hand into her pocket again and took out something else. She held it out to the pretty girl and said, "There was a shape like that around what I saw." She held the thing up and looked past it at Stephen. He saw, incredulously, an angled piece of wood with a polished surface at either end. He said, "Where did you find it?"

"In the road."

He said, "It's mine!"

"What d'you mean, it's yours?"

In order to keep the egg in its perilous, incomplete shape, Stephen had wrapped it in a plastic bag. He took it out of his pocket now, extracted it from the bag and laid it on the table.

"You see? It's a piece out of this."

"How'd it get into the road, then?"

"I dropped it. I couldn't find all the pieces when I looked for them."

"I only found it yesterday," Vicky said.

"That's when I lost it."

"It is his. You ought to give it back to him," Chris said.

Vicky didn't either offer Stephen the piece or put it back in her pocket. Looking at him hard, she said, "You did call out just now. You said, 'Look out!' Why?"

"I heard too," Chris said, not liking it.

"I suppose I thought . . . I thought there was someone on the crossing."

"That's what Vicky said. Some old lady, she said. I couldn't see anyone."

"The blue van was right by us," Vicky said.

"No, it wasn't. It was a bus, when you said that."

"It was a blue van. Like that one," Vicky said, pointing through the window at a van standing stationary farther down the street. As she spoke, it pulled out and came toward them. It slowed as it approached the crossing. This time the picture wasn't nearly so bright, the sky was gray and there was beginning to be a thin drizzle, but again Stephen had cried, "Look out!" and the brakes screamed again, and Vicky's eyes shut in a convulsive effort not to know. But this time when she opened them all the traffic had come to a standstill, people were running, there was already a crowd around something lying in the middle of the road.

"Come on. Let's get out of here," Chris said, as white and shaking as the other two.

Stephen said, "I'd better see you back." They left their coffees half-drunk and made for the open door. The ambulance came ringing its urgent warning before they had left the busy street.

"I don't like it," Chris said, back at home. They were sitting in the kitchen after a dinner that neither of them had been able to touch.

"You don't think I do?"

"Did you really see the blue van that first time?"

"Yes, I did. And it was a car just like the one that—that did it, the first time too."

"A Jag."

"I don't know. You know I'm no good at cars."

"And you saw an old lady. It was an old lady that got knocked down. I heard them say so."

"Do you know how bad she was?" Vicky asked.

"They must've taken her away in the ambulance."

"Perhaps she was just stunned."

"I don't know."

They sat and looked at each other.

"D'you think that boy saw it too?"

"I don't know."

"He didn't want to say why he'd said, 'Look out,' did he?"

"I don't know," Vicky said again.

"You never did give him that bit of the thing he said he'd lost and you found on the road."

Vicky took it out of her pocket and put it on the table.

"What did you mean when you said there was a shape like it around what you saw?" Chris said.

"Sort of jagged bits, like this, only dark. In the middle I saw the accident."

"Suppose you really could see what's going to happen next?"

"I don't want to. It was a lousy thing to happen."

"But suppose you could see something nice? Like who won the Derby. We'd all get rich. That wouldn't be bad."

"It won't happen again."

"You mean you hope it won't."

"It won't."

Mrs. Stanford came in and sat down.

"Might just as well not have cooked any dinner for all the appetite you two had. Three-quarters of it gone into the dustbin."

"You didn't, Mum! Waste," Chris said.

"Shepherd's Pie's never the same warmed up. And don't you say waste to me. You should have eaten it, if you didn't want it thrown away."

"Couldn't. Not if you'd paid me."

"Upsetting, seeing an accident," Mrs. Stanford agreed.

"Vicky saw it twice."

"What do you mean, saw it twice?"

"Saw it before it happened."

"You didn't, did you?" her Mum asked Vicky.

"I don't know."

"But Vicky, you said. . . ."

"I could have made a mistake, couldn't I?"

Chris always knew when Vicky didn't want to go on talking about something. She got up now from the table and said, "All right if I wash my hair now, Mum? Will you come up and rinse me when I'm ready?"

"You washed your hair two days ago. What're you doing it again for now?"

"Wasn't two days. Was Wednesday. That's three."

"Once a week used to be good enough for me when I was a girl."

"'Friday night's Amami night. Take me out and make me tight,'" Chris sang. Adding in her ordinary voice, "Laurie's coming to take me out tonight, that's why I've got to wash my hair." She ducked her mother's pretended swipe and left the kitchen laughing.

"Well, I don't know," Mrs. Stanford said. She looked again at Vicky, sitting across the table and said, "What's up, love?"

"Nothing."

There was a pause, then Mrs. Stanford said, "It was the accident, was it?"

"Made me feel shaky, a bit."

"Is that all?"

"Mm."

A pause.

"Vicky? There's something wrong, isn't there?"

"I just don't feel too good, that's all," Vicky said, looking at the table instead of at her mother.

"Is it the old thing?"

"What old thing?"

"You know. Worrying about your father?"

"Not especially. Not more than usual."

"I've often thought he very likely didn't know."

"Didn't know what?"

"About you. Your mother might not have told him."

"Why wouldn't she?"

"Girls don't always. Not if they're not seeing the fellow any more, I mean."

"She didn't tell you?"

"Not really. There wasn't all that time. She went so suddenly. That morning she'd been all right, as far as anyone could see. That evening she'd gone. Hemorrhage, it was. They put six pints of blood into her, but they couldn't save her."

"Did she think about what was going to happen to me?"

"She did once say that she wished someone like me could look after the baby. Not thinking it would be me, I don't think."

"Was it because you and she were in bed next to each other?"

"I s'pose that's how we started talking. And she liked the way I made a fuss of Chris. Cuddled and talked to her. Silly, I suppose. Some of the mothers in there, they hardly used to look at their babies. Couldn't wait to get out of hospital, put them on the bottle and hand them over to someone else. Perhaps it was because Chrissie was my first, I acted like I did."

"Did my mother cuddle me?" Vicky asked. She'd often nearly asked this question before, but never quite. Now it came out easily. That was the sort of person her Mum was, warm and easy.

"As if she could eat you. You were what I'd call good-looking for a baby. Neat little face, you had, and thick black hair. Quite long, it was. I remember your mother showing me how it was almost long enough to plait. About half an inch."

"Was Chris pretty then too?"

"I've never seen such a little horror. Bald, and her face sort of squashed up sideways."

"Did you mind?"

"After all that trouble? I wouldn't have changed her for the world."

"What did my mother say? About my father? Or anything?"

"Told me she hadn't seen him for months. That was when I asked if her husband was coming at visiting time. Silly question. I should have known better."

"He was her husband, then? I mean, was she married?"

"I told you, might have been. She called herself Mrs., but then they mostly do. The nurses like it better."

"She didn't say anything else about him? My father, I mean?"

"Said once you didn't look like him. Like her, you were. Dark hair like yours, she had. Lovely girl. I cried so much when she went, I almost couldn't feed Chrissie."

"When did you decide you'd take me too?"

"I wanted to as soon as I heard she'd gone. But of course I had to ask Dad. It was his business just as much as mine."

"What did he say when you told him about me?"

Mrs. Stanford unexpectedly laughed. "You know Dad. First thing he asked was, what class did your mother come from."

"And what did you say?"

"I told him your mother was a nice girl. Well spoken. Might have been a secretary or something like that. But she was a working girl. Working class like us. Then he wanted to know about her family, and I told him your mother said she hadn't any."

"What did he say then?"

"Said he supposed I meant to have you and he wouldn't stand in my way. It wasn't as if I could have any more of my own, you see."

"Did you mean to? I mean, if you hadn't had to have all that done after Chris was born, would you have had another?"

"Always meant to have six. Well, four at any rate."

"Did Dad want six?"

"I don't think I ever got as far as asking. I think he's quite happy with just two of you."

"If my father did know about me, I suppose he could have found me? If he wanted to, I mean?"

"If your mother changed her name, I don't see it would be easy for him."

"But if he really wanted to, he could have?"

"I don't see how."

"So he might have tried and never found me?"

"You shouldn't go on worrying about it, Vicky. You know Dad and I think just as much of you as of Chris. You're just the same as if you were our own."

"It's not that. It's just not knowing."

"What do you want to know then?"

"I don't know. What he's like, I suppose. I mean if I knew what sort of person he was, I'd know more about me, wouldn't I?"

"I don't see that. The way I look at it, it's the people who've brought you up, who've had everything to do with you since you were a baby, that make most difference to what you're like. Not a man you've never even seen."

"I might have seen him. He might live around here. He may be someone I see every day and don't know about."

"You'll only make yourself unhappy if you . . ." Mrs. Stanford began, but was interrupted by Chris's voice from upstairs.

"Mum! Mum! I'm ready for the rinse."

"Coming!" To Vicky, Mrs. Stanford said, "Just make up your mind you're our Vicky, and don't bother your head about anyone else."

Vicky still sat on at the table when she'd gone. She knew that what her Mum had said was sense, but it didn't stop her wondering about her real parents. Not so much about her mother, that lovely girl who had proudly plaited her half-inch of dark hair and who had loved her enough to "want to eat her." More about the father who hadn't known, or if he had known hadn't cared. Or perhaps had cared, but couldn't find his daughter. She wished she knew who he was, what he did, what he looked like. Without knowing anything about him, she felt somehow incomplete. She would like to be like Chris who could count back in a family rich with grandparents and aunts and uncles and cousins and see exactly where she fitted in. Vicky hadn't had a frame like that to explain her to herself, she had only Mum and Dad, who, however much they loved her and pretended she was their own, couldn't give her the confidence of an unbroken tradition. It was silly, as her Mum had said, to go on and on about it, but she did just wish she *knew*.

Her eye fell on the piece of the wooden egg on the table. It reminded her of the morning's incident. Uncomfortable. She didn't want to have to think about it. It must have just been a coincidence, like Chris had said. You couldn't really see the future, things that hadn't happened yet, unless you were a fortune-teller, one of those who looked into crystal balls, or could read the stars. If the egg that boy made such a fuss about had been a crystal ball, she might have thought there was something in it, perhaps. Or perhaps not. There was nothing mysterious about just a wooden egg. But the dark shapes around the bright picture—and she knew she had seen it, whatever anyone told her—had looked like this bit of wood. She held it up as she had over the table in the café so that it half-framed the kitchen doorway. Bright sunlight from the passage outside made the shape very dark.

"If it was magic, I could see anything I wanted. I could see my father," Vicky said to herself.

A man stepped into the frame. With a start of fright, relief and disappointment, Vicky saw Mr. Stanford, her Dad, back from the tube-train depot at the end of his Saturday morning shift.

The term ended. Suddenly released from the pressure of work and from regular hours, Chris and Vicky had an orgy of self-indulgence. They stayed up watching the late-night shows on television, fell into bed after midnight, and didn't get up next morning till lunch time. They went up to Oxford Street and window-shopped for hours, coming back exhausted and almost as much pleased with themselves as if they'd bought any of the stupendous clothes they'd seen. They spent whole lazy mornings sitting in cafés, making one cup of coffee and a packet of biscuits last for an hour. Fired by Mrs. Stanford's success with the dress for Vicky, Chris bought a length of white material and a pattern and made herself a skirt for the first time ever. She bought a pale pink, skinny cotton top to wear with it and looked like a delicious ice cream. Vicky was half-envious, half-proud to be seen with her. Boys swarmed round her, pressing her with invitations, eager to please, and Chris dealt with them all sweetly and firmly and politely and went out with those she liked, her head totally unturned, choosing, in spite of the flattery of these male attentions, to spend most of her time with Vicky as she had for the last fifteen years.

"You don't have to turn anyone down because of me. I wouldn't mind if you wanted to go out with a fellow," Vicky said one day that first week of freedom. They were sitting over their coffees in the café near the pedestrian crossing. Vicky would have liked to avoid it, but it was the only one nearby that supplied proper coffee and where the biscuits were not infinitely old.

"I don't not go out with anyone because I think you'd mind. I didn't want to go with Joe . . . he's not my type."

"What is your type?"

"Don't know, really. Suggest someone."

"Timmy?"

"I like what he looks like, but he's terribly conceited."

"Nick?"

"Not really. I mean I like Nick all right, he's sweet, but I wouldn't want to go out with him. I mean be going out with him properly, if you see what I mean."

"What about Alistair?" Vicky asked. She had rather a thing about Alistair herself, though he'd never taken any notice of her.

"He looks great, but he's terribly dull. When we went out the other evening he hardly said anything at all."

"Perhaps he's shy."

"He may be, but it's not much fun for whoever he's with. Go on."

"Can't think of anyone else," Vicky said lazily.

"I'll tell you who I do like. I like Paul."

"*Paul?* But he's—what do you like about him?"

"Don't know. I just do, that's all."

"I like him. He's nice. But I wouldn't have thought you'd want to go out with him. Properly, like you said," Vicky replied.

"Because he's lame? That's what you were going to say, isn't it?"

"I know it really doesn't matter. I just wouldn't have thought you'd fancy him."

"You talk about him like he was some kind of leper," Chris said, for once unusually disturbed.

"I didn't mean to."

"He's clever. He's about the cleverest boy they've ever had in the school. Molly told me. He's in her father's class."

"Has he ever asked you to go steady?" Vicky asked.

"No."

How surprising it was, Vicky thought, when you thought you knew someone, when you'd lived with them all the years she and Chris had lived together, done the same things, worn the same clothes, shared friends and lessons and confidences, to find that the other person had feelings and ideas you'd never guessed at. Chris had never let on that she'd even looked at Paul twice. He'd been to the house occasionally, but so had all Chris's other admirers. But, thinking about this secret life that presumably everyone had going on inside them, Vicky realized that she didn't say everything to Chris any more than Chris did to her. For instance she hadn't said anything like as much as she'd thought about the experience with the accident nearly a week ago. Chris might well imagine that she'd forgotten about it, or at least written it off as unimportant.

As if on cue, Chris said suddenly, "There's that boy again."

"What boy? Where?"

"Outside on the pavement. Look, going back past the pedestrian light."

"I can't see," Vicky said, craning.

"Well, it was him, I'm sure of it. That's not the first time, either."

"What d'you mean? Did he go past before?"

"Not just now. But I've seen him around before."

"Where? How d'you mean?"

"I'm sure I saw him yesterday when we went to swim. And then afterwards in the library, while I was waiting for you, I thought I saw him sitting at the table where the papers are. He had one up in front of his face, but I'd seen it was him before."

"What d'you think he's doing it for?" Vicky asked unhappily.

"I don't know."

"P'raps he wants to take you out."

"He could ask, couldn't he? I mean, it's stupid just hanging about like that."

"I suppose so."

"What did you do with *Honey?*" Chris wanted to know.

"It's here. What do you want?"

"Want to see my stars."

"They're never any good."

"I like reading what they say."

"Tell me what mine is then."

"Wait a minute. Look, someone's left a *Standard* at that table. You look in that and then we'll see if they're the same."

Vicky retrieved the paper from the next table and searched for the forecast as predicted by the stars and Madam Katina.

"I don't think he's come after me. I think he wants that bit of his egg thing you've got," Chris said, busily riffling through the pages of *Honey*.

"I don't see why I should give it to him."

"It is his."

"You can't be sure of that."

"You could let him try and see if it fits."

"I found it. Findings Keepings."

"You are funny. What do you want to keep it for? It's no good to you," Chris said.

"I just don't see why I shouldn't. Here we are. What are we? Libra. Says, 'Venus in conjunction with Mars indicates difficulties and promises in your emotional life which may be hard to deal with. . . .'"

"He's there again!" Chris said.

"Where?"

"He was standing by that woman with the little girl."

"I can't see."

"I swear it was him."

"I think you're imagining things."

"I'm not! You're the one who sees things that aren't there."

Vicky didn't listen. She'd begun to read the story on the

opposite page. "Chris, why do people steal babies? It seems such a crazy thing to do."

"I don't know. Who has?"

"Says here, 'BABY STOLEN FROM PRAM WHILE MOTHER SHOPPED IN HIGH STREET.'"

"Which High Street? There's High Streets everywhere."

Vicky didn't answer. Chris, looking up, saw that she'd gone very pale.

"What's the matter? Vicky!"

Vicky handed the paper across the table with a shaky hand.

"Read what it says. On that page, not the one with the stars."

Chris read the top headline. "Angry householders protest about new airport plans."

"Not that. Farther down. Isn't there anything about someone stealing a baby?"

"Not a thing. Must have been on another page."

"It wasn't. It was opposite the stars."

"You must have turned over without knowing."

"You look, then."

Chris went through the paper, page by page. It was the midday edition, more than half was racing forecasts, there weren't many sheets of newsprint. She handed it back to Vicky.

"Nothing there."

"I saw it."

"You didn't. You just thought you did."

"I did. Chris. . . ."

"What?"

"It was like the other time. It had those sort of black things around it."

She didn't have to explain. They looked at each other across the table.

"You mean, you think it might be going to happen? Like the accident?"

"I don't know. I just don't like it, that's all."

"Which High Street, Vicky? Vicky! Which High Street?"

"It didn't say. I didn't see, anyhow."

"Perhaps you could see it again. Try."

Unwillingly, Vicky took the newspaper and spread it out on the table, the page with the forecasts of the stars on the left, the page of news about the angry householders, a baby who needed a kidney, and the advertisements on the right.

"It's not there."

"Have you got that bit of wood? Try with that."

Vicky put the odd-shaped fragment down on the newsprint. "Well?"

"It doesn't make any difference. I only saw it for a moment, then it changed back into like it is now."

"You mean, you saw it here, on this page, and then it disappeared."

"Mm."

"You didn't see the name of the baby? Or its mother? Or anything?"

"Just what I told you. I saw the headline, and I said to you, 'Why do people take babies?' or something like that, and you said, 'Who?' and I read the headline again, and then you said, 'Where?' and it all disappeared."

"Tell you what. Did you notice the date?"

"Of course not. I just thought it was today's paper."

After a pause, Chris said, "If it's like the other time, it hasn't happened yet. Perhaps we could stop it happening."

"How? It could be anywhere."

"It could be here. We'd better see if there are any babies in prams in the street. Then we could warn their mothers."

"They'd think we were crazy."

"That wouldn't be as bad as having their babies stolen."

Vicky reluctantly saw Chris's point.

"You go and start walking down the street while I pay."

Outside in the gray street, Vicky saw several prams and made toward them. But none of them was unattended. Three together were being guarded by an alert small girl. Four prams were being packed or briskly pushed by the occupants' mothers. Toward the southern end, prams petered out; these were not the shops for everyday buying, they were estate agents, tool-makers, betting shops. Vicky turned back and met Chris.

"Only one. I went into the shop and found the mother, but she wasn't nice about it . Not at all."

"I didn't see any," Vicky said.

"But one could come along any minute."

"I don't believe it's going to happen."

"The accident did," Chris reminded her.

"Well, I don't think it was anything to do with what I saw."

"That wasn't what you said."

"I don't care. I think it's all stupid. I'm going home."

"But Vicky! Think if someone really stole a poor little baby. . .!"

"We don't know if it's going to happen. And even if we did, we don't know where. Or when. We can't stay here all day just waiting for something that probably won't ever happen."

On their silent walk home, Chris asked only one question.

"You going to tell Mum?"

"No. And you don't, Chris. Please."

Chris agreed, and not another word was said.

Vicky's guess had been the right one. Stephen had, to his own
immense surprise, and rather to his disgust, "happened" to find
himself in Chris's neighborhood more than once, not so much
because he had the conscious intention of approaching her as
from an unexpressed, submerged feeling that to be near her, to
see her going about her ordinary life, somehow conferred an
extra dimension on his own. He had spent a long time examining television sets in a shop near the café where he and the two
girls had sat on that day when he'd seen—what had he seen?
When he'd been so sure that the screech of brakes he'd heard,
and the flashed picture of someone falling, had meant an
accident, that he'd called out. Like when you see a dog run out
into the road and your heart jumps and you cry out as your eyes
involuntarily close, and then when you open them again the car
has barely slowed and the dog, unconcerned, is trotting down
the opposite pavement, unaware of having caused any anguish.
He'd felt a fool for opening his mouth, and even more of a fool
when the dark girl, who'd fainted, had seemed to know why. In
spite of his disinclination to think about the incident, Stephen
continued to think about Chris. And to spend more time than
usual in the High Street and near the end of the rather ordinary
little road where she lived. In the same vague, unformulated

way he had supposed that if he ever got to know Chris, he would be in a better position to persuade her friend—he still supposed them to be friends rather than sisters—to give him back the missing piece of his Chinese Egg which she'd so inexplicably found.

He saw them that morning, sitting in the window table of the café, drinking apparently innumerable cups of coffee. Or was it only one cup that took them forever to drink? And talking. What on earth did girls always talk about so much? The boys he knew didn't go on and on like that, they said something and someone answered, and that was that. Girls chattered; like his mother, who could ask the same question twenty times, not appearing to notice that you'd answered it the first time.

He dodged about a bit among the shopping crowds, and strolled down the street to admire the patterned window of tools in the universal suppliers. When he came back, the two girls were still there. They weren't talking, however, they were reading. The pretty one had a magazine, the plain one was looking through an evening paper.

Suddenly, just as it had happened before, the scene quivered, was shot with an intense and painful light, trembled into fragments and re-formed itself. He was looking not at two girls at a coffee table the other side of plate glass, but at a totally different picture. A shop front, people gathering around, and at the center of the crowd a perambulator. It was empty, the shawls thrown aside as if the baby had been lifted out in a hurry. At the same time he heard sobbing, a voice saying, "It wasn't more than a minute," and he saw a desperate, shocked face, a chalky face like a clown's, a cascade of long brown hair. The next instant the picture had gone, switched off like a light, and he was standing staring at the café's big open window. But it wasn't all just as it had been before. The two girls weren't just sitting there reading, they were leaving their table in a hurry, arguing as they left, one—the plain one—making for the door, the other, Chris, the pretty one, taking out her purse and going toward the cash desk. Stephen ducked out of the way and saw the plain girl go weaving down the High Street as if she was searching for something. She didn't see him. He had a horrible sort of premonition that he knew what she was looking for. When he saw her hesitate by a group of three prams, in the charge of a little girl who couldn't have been more than ten, he said, almost out loud, "Oh *no*," and set off for home. It was more than he could take, this was.

He found his mother in the kitchen, dithering between four cookery books and several newspaper cuttings. He felt the need for the reassurance of the bread-and-butter side of living and said, "What's it for, Mummy? Lunch or dinner?"

It was painful to see how pleased she was by his unusual interest. "Dinner, darling. Daddy's got one of those people from Vienna coming, and I want to make it specially nice."

"What, for instance?"

"I can't make up my mind whether to give them veal escalope—that's veal with egg and breadcrumbs, you know—with green peas, or chicken marengo. I've never done veal escalope, of course, but it doesn't look too difficult."

"Why try it out when we've got someone coming to dinner? You ought to practice on us first," Stephen said.

"It's Viennese, you see, that's why I thought it would be nice."

Stephen felt the well-known surge of irritation.

"But Mummy, if the bloke who's coming lives in Vienna, what on earth's the point of giving him exactly what he gets at home? It'd be far more interesting for him to have something different." He didn't add that it would also be a mistake to provide a poor version of a national dish.

"Yes, of course, you're right, darling. How silly of me not to have thought of that."

"If I were you, I'd do something you know you can bring off."

"What?" his mother asked hopefully.

"I don't know. There must be something."

She turned the leaves of a cookery book, then picked up one of the newspaper cuttings.

"This looks terribly easy. A sort of casserole with wine."

"Let's have a look." Stephen glanced through the recipe. "You have to leave the meat doing something or other in the wine and everything for three days."

"Oh dear, I didn't see." She bent over her books again.

"Why not roast beef and Yorkshire pudding?"

"You don't think that's a bit—well, too simple? Daddy says he's something very important in the society over there. The psychological society, I mean."

"That doesn't mean you can't give him roast beef for dinner. Not as long as it's properly cooked."

"I wish I could make up my mind," Mrs. Rawlinson said hopelessly.

"Well, don't be too elaborate. I'm sure you think that the longer something takes to cook, the better it is."

"But darling, it is! I mean it ought to be. I mean, if it comes out right it ought to be better the more trouble you've taken," Mrs. Rawlinson said.

Stephen left it. He had had enough of the subject. His mother continued to look through all the possible delicious recipes, wondering which would be most appropriate for a distinguished Viennese psychoanalyst guest. He had reached the door and was almost out of it, when his mother said, "Stephen! There was something I wanted to ask you."

He said, on an exasperated sigh, "Oh all *right*," and came back.

"Not if you're in a hurry."

"I'm not in a hurry."

"You sounded as if you wanted to go."

"It wasn't that."

"But there was something?"

"It's just that you always wait to begin talking to me till I'm practically out of the door, and then you call me back."

"Do I? Oh, I am so sorry. I didn't know I did that. I'll try to watch it. Yes, I see it must be very irritating."

"Well anyhow. What did you want to say?"

"It really doesn't matter, darling. Any time will do."

"Now you've got me here again you may as well get on with it." Stephen knew he was being unnecessarily tough, but there were times when his mother's indecision and fear of doing the wrong thing exasperated him almost as much as it did his father.

"It was something Daddy wanted you to know. I mean, Roderick."

"I know who you mean. Well?"

"He thinks perhaps you're getting a bit old to go on calling us Mummy and Daddy. He says he thinks perhaps you'd feel better about it if you used our names instead."

"You mean call him Roderick?" Stephen asked, astonished.

"He thought Roddy," his mother said, apologizing to the outrage in his voice.

"Why? What's wrong with Dad? I don't call him Daddy anyway, it's you that does that."

"Well, I think he thinks you're getting a bit too old."

"You mean he doesn't want someone my age calling him Dad, so that everyone knows how old he is."

"Daddy—Roderick—thought you might like it better."

"Well, I don't. You can tell him that. And anyway, why can't he tell me himself? Why did you have to do it?"

"Perhaps he thought it would be easier for you to tell me what you think about it," Stephen's mother said deprecatingly.

"I think it's a lousy idea. I think it stinks. And you can tell him so," Stephen was saying emphatically when the door opened and his father walked in.

"You sound fairly roused, Stephen. What's up?" He asked. Then, without waiting for an answer, said to his wife, "Can we have something to eat quickly, dear? I've got to be out at Roehampton by two o'clock. Not one of your elaborate cookery-class dishes. A simple omelette will do for me perfectly well."

Mrs. Rawlinson disappeared into the kitchen in a flurry of

haste and alarm. Stephen, left with his father, and already angry, said, "Mummy says you want me to call you Roddy."

"Oh, she's spoken to you about it, has she? Good, good, good."

"I don't think so. I think it's a silly idea."

"You don't want to?" For a moment Dr. Rawlinson was taken aback, but he recovered quickly enough to say, in the best analytical tradition, "You prefer to go on saying 'Dad'? I see that as clinging to a rather infantile form of relationship. After all, Stephen, you are—what is it—seventeen? At your age I certainly didn't any longer regard my father as omnipotent, as the supreme authority."

"I don't see that going on calling you Dad means that I think you can boss me around," Stephen said.

"Dad. Daddy. You must admit, the word belongs to the vocabulary of a very young child," Dr. Rawlinson said.

"I suppose so. Only it's what everyone says."

"Just because it has become common usage doesn't detract from the profound significance of the perpetuation of an infantile form of address."

"Look! I don't mind if you want me to call you something else. Only just don't think it means anything to me. Because it doesn't," Stephen said desperately.

"This is a very normal defense," his father said.

"What do I have to defend myself against, for Christ's sake?"

"Your normal aggression. Don't worry Stephen. What you are feeling about me now is the perfectly normal aggressive, competitive instinct that every healthy young male has against his father."

Stephen glared. Then speaking very slowly, as if to a half-wit, he said, "Look! *Daddy!* What you haven't got into your head is that we're not cases. We're not examples in any of your beastly books about how people behave. We're us. That's all. We're just us. Mummy makes mistakes with her cooking because she's so dead frightened of what you're going to say when she dishes it up, she can't even read a recipe properly. And I'm not being special and aggressive and infantile or any of that lot when I say I don't want to call you Roddy. I'm just being me. I don't want to call you Roddy because I don't feel like it. That's all. I've always called you Daddy or Dad, and I'm going on doing it. I'm not going to change all that now just to please you. If you'd asked me because it was what you wanted, I might have said, Yes. I don't know. But I don't like the way you made Mummy ask me, and I don't like the way you pretend it's because you think I want to. I don't."

There was an awkward pause, after which he added, feebly, "That's all."

His father made a good recovery. "I suppose all that was an example of your lack of aggression against me?"

"Why do you have to call it aggression? If you mean I'm bloody angry, all right, I am."

"You can admit your feelings of anger at the moment, but not the underlying hostility which always exists between an adolescent son and his father."

"Must you use that sort of language all the time? Why can't you use ordinary words like anyone else?"

"It's so interesting that you tend to attack me as a form of defense against insight. Do you notice that whenever I ask you something, you turn it back into an accusation? It's a very typical defense mechanism."

Stephen's extremely impolite answer to this was fortunately cut short by his mother, who at that moment opened the door to say, "Would you like a cheese omelette, dear, or just with herbs? The cheese is a tiny bit mouldy, but I can cut that off and I don't think it will taste."

"If you put it like that, it seems to me that the cheese is contra-indicated. A herb omelette will do for me very well."

"Is anything the matter?" Mrs. Rawlinson asked, hesitating at the door.

"I'm going," Stephen said hastily.

"What happened?" his mother asked his father when he'd gone.

"Just a perfectly normal adolescent exhibition of the Oedipus complex. Nothing to worry about," Dr. Rawlinson said airily. But he ate his omelette—leathery and burned at the edges—in a silence which his wife perfectly understood.

It took Stephen a week to make up his mind to go around to Chris's house to ask her to go to the pictures, and when he at last did it, he was disconcerted to find Vicky there too. It hadn't occurred to him that they belonged to the same family. He'd never seen sisters less alike. It wasn't as difficult as he'd thought, though, to invite only one of them to go out with him. Vicky, after looking at him in what he felt was a hostile silence for a short time, left the room, and it became easy to ask Chris if she'd come to the spy film at the Gaumont. He was pleased when she accepted at once. She didn't pretend not to be able to decide or fuss about what she was going to wear, like some girls he'd met. Perhaps, he thought, she knew she'd be the prettiest girl anywhere they went, so she didn't have to worry. He liked her more and more.

Vicky had retreated upstairs to the bedroom she shared with Chris, partly because she knew quite well that it wasn't her that Stephen had come to find, partly because she herself didn't want to see him. She didn't want to be reminded of the two incidents in which he and she seemed to be involved together. It was bad enough having queer turns without the embarrassment of sharing them with a stranger. She felt as if the boy brought her bad luck, as if it was his fault she'd seen things that weren't there and that she didn't want to know about. She was glad it was Chris he wanted to take out and not her. She stayed upstairs until Chris called out to her that she was going to the pictures, would she tell Mum that she wouldn't be back till ten, or just after? Vicky heard the front door shut and saw Stephen and Chris go up the road together. Then she came down and had just begun getting supper ready when her Mum came back from visiting Carol, her eldest niece, in the hospital where she'd had her first baby.

"Where's Chris?" Mrs. Stanford asked.

"Gone to the pictures."

"Alistair take her?" Mrs. Stanford asked.

"No."

"Who then?"

"That boy who brought us back that Saturday when I didn't feel so good."

"Oh, him! Seen him again since, has she?"

"Not really. Not to speak to."

"He speaks nicely," Mrs. Stanford said.

"Mm."

"You don't like him?" Vicky's Mum said.

"Not much."

"Something wrong with him?"

"No. I expect he's all right. I just don't like him, that's all. He's . . . posh," Vicky said.

"Well off, you mean? Why's that against him? You're talking like Dad."

"I dunno. I don't feel comfortable when he's there. That's all."

"You want any help with the supper?" Mrs. Stanford asked.

"It's all right, I can manage. You keep sitting down."

"I shan't say No. It's a long drag up to St. Monica's and the bus only goes every half hour."

Vicky went on slicing onions and crying into them, while Mrs. Stanford sat in front of the telly, only half-attending to the end of an old film. Vicky heard its closing, syrupy music and saw the screen, out of the corner of her eye, flicker to a different sort of picture. She wasn't listening to the newscaster's voice and only heard her Mum's exclamation. "I don't know how anyone can!"

"Anyone can what, Mum?"

"Take away a baby."

Vicky just had time to say, "No!" when she heard the front door open and Chris came in followed by Stephen.

"I thought you'd gone to the pictures," Mrs. Stanford said.

"So did I." Chris, for once, was angry.

"What's up, then?"

"Ask Stephen."

Stephen, horribly embarrassed, said, "I'm really sorry. I just had to come back."

"Feeling bad?" Mrs. Stanford asked, ready to sympathize if there was really something wrong.

"Not like that. It was something I read in the paper." He had an *Evening Standard* in his hand. He glanced at Vicky, but she wouldn't meet his eyes.

"Why were you reading the paper at the pictures?"

"We were in the lobby. It looked as if we were going to have to wait to get in, so I bought a paper."

"Something about someone you know?" Mrs. Stanford asked.

"Not exactly. Only something I ought to do something about, so I asked Chris if she'd mind skipping the film. I had to get back, you see." It was clear to Mrs. Stanford that Stephen was appealing to Chris as much as to herself. She waited for him to excuse himself and go, but he didn't. Instead he said to Vicky, "Could I talk to you for a minute?" Mrs. Stanford couldn't understand this at all. Nor could she understand why Vicky looked so much disturbed by the suggestion and glanced at Chris. But Chris did seem to know what was going on. She said to Vicky, "Was it . . .?" and when Vicky nodded, Chris said to Stephen, "You ought to have told me what it was about. I wouldn't have minded if I'd known."

"What's this all about?" Mrs. Stanford demanded.

Stephen said carefully. "I'm sorry. It must sound crazy. It's just that there's a story in the paper that might be something to do with something that happened to us."

"Let's go around to the coffee bar," Chris said.

"You'll come?" Stephen said directly to Vicky.

"I was just getting supper ready."

"That'll wait. You aren't in a hurry, are you, Mum?" Chris said.

"Anyway I can be getting on with it," Mrs. Stanford said.

"You said you were tired," Vicky said.

"I'll do whatever it is when we get back. You've got to come Vicky. It's to do with you," Chris said. Mrs. Stanford found the whole situation more and more puzzling. Vicky had as good as said she didn't like this boy much, and yet here she was, clearly not wanting to, agreeing with Chris that she'd had to go. She washed her hands slowly under the cold tap of the sink and went to get her coat. Chris and Stephen stood around silent, waiting for her. When she reappeared they all three went out, Chris saying, "Don't do anything about supper, Mum, we shan't be more than half an hour. I'll help Vicky with it when we get back." Vicky said nothing, and the boy said, "Good-bye. I'm sorry to upset everything like this." Polite. In spite of what Vicky had said, her Mum rather liked the looks of the boy.

Sitting in the coffee bar, Stephen, Vicky and Chris looked at each other. Then Chris said, "Well?"

Stephen said to Vicky, "You saw about the baby?"

Vicky, very pale, nodded.

Chris said, "What about a baby?"

Vicky said, "You know when I thought I saw in the paper a baby being stolen? And we went looking down the High Street and there wasn't anything?"

"I'm not likely to forget. It was me told a woman her baby wasn't safe, and boy, was she furious!" Chris said with feeling.

"It's happened. It's happened, Chris," Vicky said.

"It hasn't! It can't have! Who said?" Chris demanded.

"On the news on the telly. I saw it," Vicky said.

"And it was in the paper I had this evening."

"But how d'you know it's the same? It could have happened anywhere," Chris said.

"No. It's the same. I know it is," Vicky said.

"You said it was only your imagination. . . ."

"That's what I wanted to think."

"I think she's right, Chris. The thing is, I saw it too," Stephen said.

"When?"

"Last week. When you and she were in the café."

"So it was you outside the window?" Chris said, momentarily distracted.

"You saw it?" Vicky asked.

"Sort of. And then you came out and wandered down the High Street."

"I was looking to see if there were any prams with no one looking after them."

"So I didn't like it. I went away."

"But you really did see it. A baby being stolen?" Vicky asked.

"I saw a girl looking into an empty pram and saying, 'It was only a minute.' Terribly upset," Stephen said.

"Where?" Chris asked.

"I don't know. Nowhere I knew. Outside a supermarket. But that's no help, there are hundreds."

"What I don't understand is how you and Vicky see the same things. You both saw the accident," Chris said.

"I saw a car come up behind a blue van and I thought it was going to hit the old lady. Then it wasn't there, there wasn't anyone on the crossing."

"And then it happened. Just like you'd both seen it. Right?"

"I suppose so."

"And now it's happened again. Well, you say it has. How d'you know it's the one you saw? How do you know?"

Stephen said slowly, "I don't know about Vicky, but both times I've seen what happened like in a picture. With . . ."

Vicky cut in. "Like in a frame? Funny-shaped pieces round it, dark?"

"Yes. Dark. Like—like battlements."

"That's right. Like the top of a castle. And the picture's very bright in the middle."

They looked at each other with the relief of shared experience. But the relief didn't last. Stephen said, "I don't understand. Why do we see something that hasn't happened yet? I can't see how we can."

"Mum says people think they can. In crystal balls and that. Or the stars," Chris said.

"The stars! They're always wrong," Vicky said.

"Did you see it too?" Stephen asked Chris.

"Me? No. Thank goodness. I'd be scared out of my wits," Chris said.

"It's horrible," Vicky said.

"I wish I understood," Stephen said.

"Should we tell the police? Or something?"

"Who'd believe us?"

"Suppose it happens again? Suppose you and Vicky see something else? How will you prevent it happening?" Chris asked.

"I don't know. It's all so vague. If we don't know where it's happening or when, what can we do?"

"Perhaps you could see some more about the baby. Why couldn't you and Vicky see where it is? Then we could tell someone. Rescue it. Why don't you do that?" Chris said enthusiastically. She was disappointed that neither Stephen nor Vicky seemed eager to agree.

"I wish we understood how it works. What's so maddening is that we're wasting it. We know, but we don't do anything," Stephen said.

"Let's try everything we can think of to get you and Vicky seeing a picture again."

Stephen said, "Wait a minute. I've got an idea."

The girls waited.

"It was something you said. An idea sort of began to come into my head and then went away again."

"I said let's try everything."

"Not that bit. I know! You said—don't you see? Vicky and I have always seen the things at the same time."

"That's right! And when you've been together."

"Not that time in the café, when I saw it in the paper. Stephen wasn't there then," Vicky said.

"No more he was."

"But I was quite close. I was just outside the café," Stephen said.

"And we were all of us there the first time, the time with the blue van."

"Perhaps it's only here it works," Chris said.

"Seems a funny place," Vicky objected.

"Funny? Why funny?"

"Not mysterious enough. You know. Daytime, and lots of people about."

"It's worth trying, though, isn't it? Isn't it?" Chris said to Stephen.

"I suppose so. Though I agree with Vicky. I don't think it's only that."

"What d'you mean? That there's something else we don't know about?"

"I just think there must be. If that's all, why doesn't it happen to other people too? Why Vicky and me?"

"I dunno. P'raps it's like dog whistles," Vicky said.

"What about dog whistles?"

"You know. You can buy whistles that only dogs can hear, humans can't. The note's too high or something. Perhaps we're hearing something other people can't. Seeing, I mean. It just could be something like that."

"Vicky! You're brilliant! Isn't she, Steve?"

Although he wished he'd thought of it himself, Stephen looked at Vicky with a new respect. He had to admit it was a good idea, and it immediately made him feel better about the whole thing. He hated the thought that they'd got mixed up in something spooky; and as for magic, the whole idea was ridiculously babyish. But Vicky had suggested something with a perfectly good scientific background. He could even imagine his father saying, "Yes, not beyond the bounds of possibility." Only then his father would go on and start analyzing dogs. Or whistles. In spite of himself Stephen half-smiled.

"What is it?"

"Nothing. Only, Vicky," it was the first time he'd called her by her name, "why do you think it might happen in one special place?"

"No idea."

"Anyway, let's try it out. Let's come back here tomorrow and see if you do see anything," Chris urged.

"All right. When?"

"Not too early. It's bad enough having to get up at quarter-past eight every day for school."

"Ten too early for you?" Stephen asked.

"Make it eleven."

"I'll order the coffees if I get here first."

"Fine."

Stephen said directly to Vicky, "You'll come, won't you?" He knew Chris would, Vicky was more unpredictable.

"Of course she's coming," Chris said.

"Yes, I'll come," Vicky said.

8

But the next day in the café, nothing happened that couldn't be explained in the most ordinary ways. Stephen, Vicky and Chris drank coffee and shared an enormous number of packets of biscuits. To the amazement of the sloppy girl behind the counter, they tried the experiment of being all together inside, two in and one outside, two out and one in, all three outside. No one saw anything that wasn't there, and there all the time. There were no accidents on the dangerous crossing, and every pram that passed them was capably filled by a baby. Chris was simply disappointed, Vicky's and Stephen's disappointment was tinged by relief. If they couldn't see anything then they also needn't do anything.

"We'll have to be getting back. It's nearly dinner time," Chris said.

"Dinner? It's not lunch time yet," Stephen said.

"Goodness! What time do you have lunch then?"

"About one o'clock. Sometimes later. It depends whether my father's there or not."

"Of course! I forgot. Posh people call dinner lunch, don't they?" Chris said, unembarrassed.

"I'm not posh," Stephen said, red with shame.

"Yes, you are. Compared to us, anyway. You needn't worry

about it, we don't mind, do we, Vicky? It's only Dad who goes on and on about how awful it is to be one of the upper classes. I wonder sometimes what he'd do if he won a lot of money on the pools or something, so that he was rich for a change."

"I know. He'd give it all to his blinking Party," Vicky said.

"That's right, so he would. To give everyone guns so they could kill off the aristocrats when the revolution begins."

"Is he a Communist?" Stephen asked.

"Not like that. Just very keen on workers' rights and Unions and that sort of thing. He'll certainly think you're up to no good when he knows you have lunch instead of dinner," Chris said, teasing.

"Anyway, Chris is right, we'd better go," Vicky said.

"Wait a minute. I've just thought of something. When you were in here before, you saw about the baby in a newspaper, didn't you?" Stephen asked.

"Yes. *Evening Standard*, it was. Same as you saw last night."

"I'll get one of today's. It might be something to do with the paper," Stephen said, and was off before they could answer. He was back in a minute with the midday *Standard* in his hand.

"Vicky. You look at the middle bit and I'll look at the outside."

Chris craned over Vicky's shoulder to read. Vicky turned the page slowly and unwillingly and breathed a deep sigh as she finished. "Nothing there. What about you?"

"No flashes like the others. But there's a lot about the baby."

There certainly was. Almost the whole of the front page was given up to an account of the snatching. It was the nurse's half-day off—"There, I thought they were posh," Chris said— and Mrs. Wilmington had taken the baby out in its pram to do a little shopping in the supermarket in Kensington High Street. She'd spent about ten minutes in the shop and thought she could see the pram all the time—"What, when she was getting fish sticks out of the deep freeze? Tell me another," Chris said— but when she came out, the pram was empty. Other shoppers hadn't noticed anything unusual. There was a picture of the Wilmingtons' wedding, all grinning faces and ridiculous hats, another of the baby when aged two months, a picture of the house where the Wilmingtons lived in Kensington, and a fourth photograph of Mrs. Wilmington, her faced screwed up with crying, her hair all over the place, quite different from the pretty girl in white satin and roses who smiled out of the wedding picture, leaning on her bridegroom's arm.

"She's really nice," Chris said.

"Not when she's crying."

"No one is when they cry. Let's see the house. Golly, it's enormous. Wonder how many servants they have to keep all that clean."

"He looks all right too," Vicky said.

"Mm. Terribly good-looking. Only I don't like those little moustaches."

There was a pause.

"What are we going to do then?" Vicky said.

They looked at each other.

"Absolutely nothing," Stephen said, half-angrily.

"It seems so feeble, somehow," Vicky said.

"You don't think the police . . .? It says here, the police are asking anyone who might have seen anything suspicious to come forward," Chris said.

"They'd never believe us. Anyway, what have we got to tell them? Nothing they don't know already."

"If you got another flash, it might help."

"And it might not."

"Come on. We'd better get back," Vicky said. They left the café. In the street outside, Stephen said to Vicky, "If anything happens, you'll let me know, won't you?"

"Yes. Wait a minute. I don't know where you live."

"Fourteen, Partlett Crescent. And the telephone number's 132-2735. Shall I write that down?"

"No, I'll remember it till I get home. Only if I get a flash and you don't, it'll mean we don't need to be anywhere near each other. Partlett Crescent's quite a way from us."

"I suppose it would prove something though."

"Come on. Dinner'll be cold. Hope you enjoy your *lunch*," Chris called out to Stephen as they separated.

The Wilmington house was full of policemen. They suddenly appeared in unexpected places, so that Paolo, one of the Spanish couple who did the cooking and the housekeeping and most of the cleaning, found men in blue uniforms on the stairs, in the hall, coming out of bedrooms, even in his own, sacred, pantry. His wife, Maria, who was quite as suspicious of the police as they could possibly be of her, retreated to their bedroom in tears, and announced that she was not coming down again until everybody had gone. Nora Hunter, the beautifully trained young nurse whose business it was to look after Caroline Ann for five and a half days a week, was red-eyed and very much less trim and confident than she usually appeared.

Mrs. Wilmington, in spite of the tranquilizers prescribed by her doctor, wandered around the house. Sometimes she was down in the library, sometimes in the hall. Sometimes she was up in Caroline Ann's nursery. Sometimes she was in her bedroom. But wherever she was, she couldn't keep still. If she sat down, it wasn't for more than a moment; she would be up again. It was as if it was only by walking that she could bear to be awake and conscious of what was happening. And while she walked, she touched. Her hand went out to books in the library, to the carved ends of the oak bookshelves; from them to the lamp on the little table, then to the curtains over the window. Moving toward the door, she touched the telephone on the desk; hesitated, then moved on again. Opened the door, and moved down the hall toward the sitting-room, but didn't go in, went, instead, upstairs. Her hand turned the handle of the nursery door, slid over the flowers on the nursery table, over the back of a rocking-chair. The hand went on to the smooth china knob of the room next door, the night nursery, where the baby and her nurse slept. Opened the door and touched the mantelpiece with two cottage china dogs, one each end, tongues lolling, looking sentimentally out of their china eyes at the small pink and white room. Stroked the dogs' heads, then went up to Mrs. Wilmington's eyes as if to discover whether there were tears there. She had remembered taking one of the two china dogs off the mantelpiece only yesterday and holding it in front of the baby's eyes, making it jump up and down while she barked for it, "Woof! Woof!" Caroline Ann had chuckled. She had clutched at the china dog, and her mother had gently disengaged her fat baby fingers and put the dog back on the mantelpiece. They had been laughing, she and Nora and Caroline Ann. Now the dog sat smirking on the mantelpiece, Nora was crying downstairs, she was here, in this empty room, and Caroline Ann? Where was she? Was she laughing now? Who was looking after her? Was she frightened? Lonely? Missing the people, the only people she knew and trusted? The hand gripped the side of the wooden cot to which Caroline Ann had just been promoted, and the steel supports of the dropside bit into the soft palm. Sally Wilmington held on. She wanted to be hurt. It was her fault that Caroline Ann was lost. It hadn't happened to Nora, it had happened to her, to Sally Wilmington, Caroline Ann's mother. If any pain she felt could bring Caroline Ann back, she would welcome that pain. And no pain could be worse than what she was already feeling. Presently the hand relaxed its grip and Sally Wilmington moved on. Out of the night nursery, down the stairs, back to the library, out into the hall, into the sitting-room, into the passage, the dining-room, back again to the hall. There is no rest for this sort of torment.

Everyone in the house had been interviewed, but there was nothing in anyone's statement to help. It had been such an ordinary day. Nora always had Thursday afternoon off; it was usual for Mrs. Wilmington to take the baby out. Mr. Wilmington was away on a business trip. No one had seen anything suspicious. Had any strangers been seen loitering outside the house in the past week or so? No. Had there been any unidentified telephone calls? None. Had Nora, on her walks out with the baby, ever been approached by strangers and asked questions about her employers? Never. Had she ever had the notion that she might have been followed on these walks? No. She and the two Spaniards had impeccable references, there was no reason to suspect any of them; yet it was Nora who most interested Chief Superintendent Price. Not because she gave in any way the impression of guilt, but simply because as a young, reasonably attractive woman in a position of trust, she was, he considered, the most open to persuasion or threat. He meant to keep a very sharp eye on Miss Hunter.

The most difficult job, he'd found, was with Mrs. Wilmington herself. When he'd first seen her, on the day of the snatch, she'd been in a state of shock. Today, the morning after, she was more under control. He could see from her shadow-ringed eyes that she hadn't slept much, if at all. She was shaky, could hardly hold the coffee cup without spilling the contents, and her voice was tuned high like a fiddle string, ready to break, but she tried to sit still and to tell him what he wanted to know. She reminded him of a child who is under a strain almost too great to bear, but who is trying to be good. Yes, she said, anyone could have discovered from watching the house that Nora had a regular day off on Thursdays and that she took the baby out in the afternoon if it was fine. She often did a little shopping on the way back from the Gardens. Her husband was away a fair amount, often had to go on business trips abroad. Anyone could have known this. No, she hadn't been able to speak to her husband yet. He was in the States, should have gotten back to the East Coast last night. She'd booked a call to the New York office, but hadn't heard anything yet. "We've wired him the news, he'll know by now what's happened," Price said, thinking that the poor girl wouldn't be very intelligible on a transatlantic call.

"Just one more thing, Mrs. Wilmington, and then I hope you'll try to get a little rest. Your nurse, Nora Hunter. I know she's got good references and all that sort of thing, but I want you to tell me, if you can, what you feel about her personally. One's own personal impressions are sometimes more valuable than any number of references. Do you like her? Get on well with her?"

"Yes, very well. She's a very nice girl."

"Nothing you feel you don't quite understand about her? Nothing that has ever made you say to yourself that perhaps she's not exactly what she seems?"

"No. Oh no. Nothing like that."

"You'd trust her absolutely? As you'd trust yourself to look after the baby?"

He realized directly he'd said it that the question was unfortunately put. She flushed, put her poor trembling hands to her face and tears began to run down her cheeks again, as she said, "It wasn't Nora who wasn't to be trusted with Caroline Ann. It was me." Price could only hope that the violent storm of sobbing that followed would exhaust her so much that in spite of herself she might fall asleep when she'd gone upstairs to lie down. He had no more questions at present to ask her.

That afternoon, Stephen went to the library. He'd got two books overdue for return, and wanted another. He also surreptitiously looked through the catalogue to see if he could find anything that might enlighten him about the extraordinary thing that was happening to him. But the catalogue was unhelpful. He looked under "Occult" and found books about witches—he hadn't realized that there were still people who believed in witches—and about magic, about rites and religions of primitive tribes in remote islands, and several books on conjuring. In despair, he asked the librarian whether there were any books about seeing future events before they happened. The librarian looked at him sharply and said, "What's this? A joke?"

"No, I just want to read about it."

"This isn't the time or the place for fooling about," the librarian said.

"I don't know what you mean."

"Didn't you know that you're the second person to ask for the same thing all in ten minutes?"

"I tell you, no. Is there a book then?"

The librarian said something that sounded like "Extra sensi-

tive-preception" and pointed to a table in one of the distant
bays. "There. Girl's reading it. You'll have to wait."

It did not need any uncanny flash of knowledge to tell Stephen who the girl would be. Vicky looked up from the book as
he sat down opposite her, and almost broke the strict library
rule of silence. Her surprise came out in a suppressed squeak.

Since they couldn't talk, they had to communicate in sign
language. Stephen pointed to the book and raised inquiring
eyebrows. Vicky shook her head, hunching her shoulders. Stephen took the book from her and read a sentence or two. It
seemed to be about people who could tell in one room which
playing card was being held in front of a screen in another. Or
couldn't tell. There were tables of figures and statistics. It was
very boring. He pushed the book back across the table, and
Vicky shut it and stood up. They went together to the counter,
where Vicky formally borrowed the book. Then they went out.

"Are you really going to read it?" Stephen asked when they
were free to talk out loud.

"I might. I could try anyway. There must be some bits I
could understand."

"Does it say anything about what makes people able to see
those cards?"

"Dunno. I'd hardly read any of it when you came in."

"I mean, like you said about hearing dog whistles."

"I said, I've only read about a page."

"Can I have a look for a minute?"

She handed him the book, and he looked at it as they walked
along the pavement. Once he tripped, by stepping off the curb,
once an annoyed woman found him wrapped in the lead con-
necting her with a small, furiously yapping dog. Vicky wished
she'd got Chris's confidence. Chris would have firmly held him
by the elbow and guided him in safety while he read. Vicky
thought of it, decided it would be too familiar, decided that she
really could and ought to, decided that after all this thinking
about it she couldn't do it easily, it would somehow come out

wrong. She left him to make his blundering way. She was relieved when he handed the book back.

"Did you find anything?" she asked.

"Not really, I just wanted to see what sort of a book it was."

"What d'you mean, what sort of book?"

"Whether it's serious. I mean, scientific. Or whether it's written by cranks. You know, the sort of people who see little green men coming off flying saucers and saving the world."

"Do they really?"

"I've never seen any."

"I didn't mean the little men. I meant, do people really believe in them?"

"Yes. And write books about them. But it's all right. This is serious. It's scientists that did the experiments. With the cards and that."

"I don't see how it matters," Vicky said.

"Because I don't want to be mixed up with something stupid. It's bad enough it happening. It isn't quite so bad if there's a proper scientific explanation. Don't you see that?" Stephen asked, annoyed.

Vicky said, "Yes, I suppose I do," rather doubtfully. Then she said, "I suppose it's because your father's a—what you said—a psychologist, makes you feel it's got to be scientific."

"No it isn't. It's nothing to do with my father."

"All right. You needn't jump down my throat."

Stephen said, "Sorry," and they walked on in silence.

"Where's your sister?" Stephen asked, after a pause.

"Gone shopping."

"Would you like some coffee?" Stephen asked to show that he'd got over being angry and that he wasn't only interested in Chris.

"I can't! Mum's out this afternoon and I've got the door key and I said I'd be back by four o'clock to let Chris in."

"That's a pity."

Without giving herself time to think about it too much and

get self-conscious, Vicky said, "If you'd like to come back I could make tea."

"Thanks. I'd like that."

Vicky felt better. Then she remembered that her Dad was on a late shift and would be getting up from a day-time sleep to go out to work in the early evening. He was never at his best directly after he was woken up, and she hoped Stephen would be gone before he came down. Otherwise she could foresee trouble.

He wasn't around when she and Stephen went into the kitchen, which was a relief. She made tea, opened a packet of biscuits, and then, greatly daring, brought out a tin that had the remains of one of last Christmas' cakes. Mrs. Stanford always made two or three big cakes of incredible richness each Christmas, and they were brought out for special occasions during the following year. Vicky wasn't sure if this counted as special enough, but she wanted to impress Stephen and show off her Mum's cooking.

"Gosh. It's fabulous! You don't have this every day?" Stephen said, his mouth full of delicious sticky fruit and only just enough spicy dough to keep it from falling apart.

"Mum makes them every year. But we don't eat them every day. Just when we have visitors."

"Your mother must be a marvelous cook."

"She makes good cakes. Mostly for dinner she does ordinary things. Sausages. Fish sticks. Baked beans. Fried potatoes. You know," Vicky said.

Stephen was just beginning to say, "I wish my mother did ordinary things," when the flash hit him. It wasn't as bright, as dark around the edges and as bright in the middle as the former two, and it was very quick. He saw Chris in her white skirt and pink top, coming toward him. Just behind her was a boy. A boy he'd never seen before. He had time to get the impression of dark hair, an expression on the face which he knew he ought to recognize but didn't, and of there being something unusual about the boy's way of holding himself. He heard, quite distinctly, Chris's voice say, "Paul's got a place at York!" and then it was over. He was in the kitchen with Vicky, looking stupidly toward the door as if the real Chris had come in at that moment.

He wanted to cover up. He looked at Vicky and saw her looking intently and frightened at him.

"Did you have it too?" she asked.

He said, "Who's Paul?"

"Oh! You did. He's . . ." the doorbell rang. She went out and Stephen heard her open the door and other voices in the hall. The next moment Chris appeared in the doorway. She wore the white skirt and pink top. She was speaking to Vicky over her shoulder and over the shoulder of the boy immediately behind her. She said, "Paul's got a place at York! Isn't it astronomic? Hullo, Stephen! This is Paul."

Paul was dark. He had a clever face, with lines of humor around his eyes and mouth. The expression, Stephen saw now, was one he'd often noticed on the faces of people whose childhood had been affected by illness; people with deformed hips, people partly paralyzed, people who have been kept much in bed; a look of being older than their contemporaries, of having learned to live with pain. Paul's shoulders were not quite straight, and he walked into the kitchen with a slight but definite limp.

Vicky and Stephen did not look at each other. Chris, finding chairs for herself and Paul, and talking, made it unnecessary for them to do anything but sit.

"Isn't it super? I knew he would. I always said they'd take him once they'd seen him. It's his first choice too, that's what's so fabulous. None of the other boys got their first choice straight off like that."

"It isn't all that certain. Depends on my 'A' levels," Paul said. He had an attractive, quiet voice and very bright dark eyes.

"We all know you're going to get nothing but A's."

"For goodness sake, touch wood when you say things like that," Paul urged.

Chris touched the kitchen table. "But I don't need to. I just know. You're not the only ones to know what's going to happen," she said teasing, to Vicky. It was an unfortunate remark. She saw Vicky's face change, and Stephen was looking cross, which meant embarrassed. She said quickly, "Any tea in the pot, Vicky? I'll get the cups if there is."

Vicky said gratefully, "I'll fill it up," and went back to the kettle.

"Only it ought to be champagne," Chris said, clattering the china and spoons more than usual to mask the awkwardness. She put plates in front of Paul and herself and said, "Mum's Christmas cake! You are showing off!"

"She won't mind. We often have it when people come in," Vicky said.

"If you hadn't got it out for Steve, I'd have for Paul," Chris said comfortably, cutting generously.

"If that's for me I'll only have half," Paul said.

"Mm. It's come out bigger than I meant. Never mind. Let's share it," Chris said, giving him rather more than half.

"It's the best cake I've ever had," Stephen said.

"Paul knows. He's had it before," Chris said.

Stephen, feeling suddenly out of place, a stranger among people who knew each other better than he knew any of them, coming from a different background, without the signals which they could pick up from each other to tell them what was going on, said to Paul, in what he heard miserably was what Chris would call his "posh" voice, "Sorry, I haven't congratulated you yet."

Paul looked at him without answering for a moment and then said, "Thanks. But I'm not there yet. I'll wait for the champagne till I've finished with my 'A's.'" He didn't sound unfriendly, but Stephen thought he remained on his guard.

"Isn't it a good sign they've offered you a place even if it's provisional?"

"Better than if they'd said they wouldn't have me at any price," Paul agreed.

"What subjects are you taking?" Stephen asked. He didn't want Vicky to start talking about what had just happened. At the same moment Chris said to Vicky, "Where did you get to this afternoon? You went off without saying."

"Library. I had to take a book back." She didn't add that she'd wanted to take one out as well, Stephen noticed with relief, only half-attending to Paul's answer to his own question. "Two lots of maths and French."

Stephen was just saying in astonishment, "What a fantastic combination!" when Chris said quickly, "There's Dad! Isn't it, Vicky? He hasn't gone out yet?"

"Not yet." Gosh, she thought miserably, it only needed this on top of everything else, to have Dad coming down and asking questions. She just hoped he'd be in a hurry and go almost straight off. But she was unlucky and it was worse than she'd expected. Mr. Stanford came heavily down the stairs, still not more than half-awake after an afternoon sleep which never really quite made up for being up most of the night. He came into the kitchen and was not best pleased to find his daughters entertaining. He was even less pleased when he saw that one of the visitors was Stephen.

"Hullo, Paul. Got any tea for me, Chris? Hullo!" He said this last hullo in Stephen's direction but not actually to him. He sat down on the opposite side of the table and looked at Stephen suspiciously.

"Paul's got a place at York. All right, a provisional place. Isn't it super?" Chris said into the silence.

"Don't know what good you think college is going to do him," her father said, stirring his tea.

"Well, if he wants to do math . . . ?"

"What'll he do with it then?"

Paul said, "I'd be interested working with computers. Programming them and that. Or I might teach."

"You want a white-collar job?" Mr. Stanford said, making it

quite clear from his voice what he thought of white-collar jobs.

"Now, Dad! You can't say anything against computer programming. I'm sure they have Trades Unions too, don't they, Paul?" Chris said.

"It's not just a question of Unions, girl. It's this trying to live a bourgeois way of life, that's what I'm against. Always looking for a safe middle-class job so you can buy a car and a dishwasher and color telly, and no real sense of direction. No responsibility to society. That's what I can't take."

"But there's got to be teachers. S'pose he gets to be a teacher?" Chris said.

"If he's a good teacher and stays in State schools . . ." Mr. Stanford allowed. He fixed Stephen with a challenging stare and asked him, "What about you? What sort of job are you going for?"

"I don't know," Stephen said inadequately.

"Don't need to, I suppose. Your Dad's got enough money so you can afford to wait and see?" He made it sound like an accusation rather than a question.

"He's not all that well off," Stephen said.

"He's a psychologist, isn't he?"

"Sort of."

"Sees someone every day for five years and tells them what they were thinking about before they were born? Or what their dreams are about? Takes money for it?"

"Something like that."

"What's he want to do that for when there are plenty of people with proper illnesses and not enough doctors to look after them? Rich people, I suppose his patients are?"

"Some of them. He works in a hospital too," Stephen said, surprised that he should be the one to be defending his father.

"I reckon he sees it as charity, his hospital work. Thinks his patients there ought to be grateful for him seeing them."

"Some of them get better," Stephen said uncomfortably.

"They're paying for it, aren't they? Every week they're paying out for their stamps. They're entitled to the best doctors going. That's what the Health Service is all about, isn't it? Does your father ever think of that?"

Stephen looked ostentatiously at his watch and said, "I'm terribly sorry, I'll have to rush. I said I'd be home by half-past five." It was quite untrue, but the only way he could think of to stop this horrible conversation. He said good-bye hurriedly around the table and made for the door. Paul gave him a polite smile, Chris hardly looked at him. Vicky came out into the passage with him and half-whispered, "Sorry about that," overcome with shame. He felt for her, as much as he could feel for anyone but himself at that moment. He knew what it was to have to blush for a father. He said, "Bye. See you," and left.

Back in the kitchen Mr. Stanford was orating. Vicky recognized a familiar piece about the aristocracy and the complacent middle class, the wrongs of the consumer society, the fight that was still necessary before the workers could claim their rights. Paul seemed to be listening, Chris was busy washing up the tea things at the sink. Vicky went over to dry and would have let her Dad run himself down as she usually did if she hadn't heard, " . . . take this boy that's just gone out. What use is he going to be to society? Brought up with all his father's money behind him, doesn't even know what he's going to do and doesn't care so long as he's doing nicely, thank you. Going to be another like his Dad, I'll be bound, getting money out of a lot of rich women who want to talk about themselves and are willing to pay for it. . . ."

To her own surprise, Vicky interrupted. "He's not like that!" She came back to the table and saw her father's astonished face. She said passionately, "You're not being fair! You don't know anything about him! How do you know what he's going to do?"

Mr. Stanford was taken aback, as he often was when someone he knew and was fond of got between him and his ideas. He said, "Look here, whose friend is he, this boy?"

Chris, you could always rely on her, said, "He's both of ours friend." It wasn't grammar but it carried weight.

"He's all *right*," Vicky said.

"He's middle-class bourgeois," Mr. Stanford said with distaste.

"If he is it isn't his fault," Vicky said at the same moment that Chris said, "Dad, don't be silly. If Steve's bourgeois and all that he can't help it. He's ever so funny about his father too. He doesn't hold with what he does anymore than you do."

Mr. Stanford looked from his pretty Chris to his angry foster-daughter Vicky, and said, "Here, what's going on? Whose boyfriend is he, anyway?"

No one answered.

"You went out with him yesterday," he accused Chris.

"Dad! I went out for ten minutes. Then we came back home. You're talking as if I'd been going out with him for years."

"All I want to know is, are you or aren't you?"

"He's just a friend. Vicky and I met him one day. We're neither of us stuck on him. He's just a boy we got to know."

"What's all the fuss about, then?"

Vicky repeated, stupidly, "You weren't being fair."

"Don't you tell me I'm not being fair! What's there to be fair about when it's a boy with money and opportunity and everything he wants?"

"You're still unfair. You're saying he's no good because his father's got more money than we have. You don't *know*."

Mr. Stanford wasn't stupid. He stopped now and thought and then said, "You're right, Vicky."

She was so much surprised that she didn't understand. She repeated after him, "I'm right? What about?"

"I'm showing class prejudice. I don't know about this boy. All the same I don't want you to go about with him."

"Why?" Vicky burst out.

"Because you'll get hurt, that's why. Anyway if he's not your boyfriend, nor Chris's, what's the fuss about? Why can't you go about with a boy from your own background? Isn't that good enough for you? It is for Chris, isn't it?"

Chris said, "Dad, you do go on. Neither of us is going out with Steve the way you mean." She looked at Paul again, as if she were telling him something as well as her father. And Vicky knew from Chris's voice that she knew that underneath this discussion about Stephen, Vicky and Mr. Stanford were both thinking of the same thing, that Vicky wasn't his own daughter as Chris was; that he was, in a way, telling her that if pretty Chris was satisfied with a working-class boy so ought she to be who hadn't any claim to be any class at all. And Vicky, feeling all this and wanting to reassure him that she wasn't any different from him, was at the same time wondering just where she did come from. And on top of all this wanted quite straightforwardly to defend Stephen on grounds of justice, not because she was gone on him—Chris didn't think she was—but because she couldn't bear for things to be unfair, even to people she didn't like.

Mr. Stanford said, "Hm," and drank his tea. Vicky recognized gratefully that the worst of the row was over; as long as neither she nor Chris did something to stir it up again, he'd let it ride for the moment. She'd meant, at the beginning, to say defiantly that she and Stephen had to go on seeing each other because they were mixed up in what might turn out to be a crime, but now she decided to keep quiet about it. She was going to see Stephen again, but she needn't tell Dad. For the moment she'd have to keep their companionship a secret.

Andrew Wilmington got back to his home early on Friday afternoon after a delayed flight during which the sympathetic crew of the Pan American jet kept him up to date on the news coming in over the radio. It was no news as far as he was concerned. He had slept briefly and deeply for an hour and woken up ashamed of having allowed himself to slip into unconsciousness. Not that keeping awake helped anyone, and he'd had no sleep the night before after receiving that first appalling message. When he let himself into his house at a quarter-past two Paolo was waiting for him in the hall and it didn't need words for Andrew Wilmington to see that there was still no news.

"Where's Mrs. Wilmington? Upstairs?" he asked, but before he'd finished the question Sally was out on the landing and running down the stairs into his arms. He was disturbed by the frantic way she clung to him, by her shaking, and when he saw her face even more by the disfigurement caused by a day of misery and fear. Her eyes seemed to have sunk into her head, there were lines from nose to mouth and the skin around her eye sockets was puffed and reddened. Seeing her like this gave the horrible story an immediate reality it hadn't quite had before. He took her into the dining-room and made her sit at the breakfast table, pretending to be more anxious for his coffee than he really felt in order to give her something to do, in the hope that when she was going through the ordinary routine motions of looking after him, she'd calm down. After that first demonstration she tried to put a firm guard on herself, tried not to cry—she knew it annoyed him and upset him when she cried—tried to answer his questions, to tell him just the facts and no more. She couldn't control the shaking of her hands, or the lump in her throat that sometimes prevented her from speaking. He persuaded her to drink some coffee too, but she couldn't eat. They sat at the oval polished table with the sunlight coming in through the elegant French windows and making patterns of light and shade over the pretty room, while she told him the story as well as she could.

"What are the police doing?" he asked.

"They've been very good."

"They haven't found anything at all? No clues?"

"They say they have ways of finding out things like this. I don't know what."

"Didn't anyone see it happening? There must have been plenty of people about at that time in the afternoon."

"They couldn't find anyone. People might not have noticed. . . ."

"Don't upset yourself, Sally darling."

"I was just thinking. . . ."

"What?"

"If you see someone lifting a baby out of a pram, you don't think of her stealing it. You think she's just going to take it with her into the shop. That's what. . . ."

"That's what . . . ?"

Sally Wilmington was crying now so that he could hardly hear her when she said, "That's what I ought to have done."

The telephone bell had rung all morning and it didn't stop now. Sally's mother to ask how she was, should she come to London to be with her? The police to ask when Superintendent

Price could come around to see Mr. Wilmington. No, they had nothing to report. Sorry, sir. One of Sally's friends, just disembarked from a cruise holiday, having heard nothing and wanting a cozy chat. The chief cashier of Grey, Teake and Whipple to ask if Mr. Wilmington would be coming into the office today, and to offer his condolences. Sally's best friend Alison, asking if there was anything she could do to help. It went on and on. And each time the bell rang, Sally was at the phone before anyone else could reach it, waiting in the hope that there might be news. She imagined it so intensely, she could almost hear Price's kindly voice telling her, "We've found your baby, Mrs. Wilmington. She's alive and well." Each time another sickening drop of the heart, despair gradually creeping in where she'd allowed hope to well up in spite of everything. After a time Andrew left her, to drop into the office for half an hour. First, he found Nora, occupying herself at a pretense of tidying a cupboard in the nursery, and sent her to sit with Sally. Though afterwards he wasn't sure that they'd be good for each other. It was just that he didn't like the idea of leaving Sally on her own.

There wasn't much for them to say to each other, but Sally did find it comforting to have Nora there. From time to time they talked a little, about ordinary subjects; about Maria's mother who might come to England on a visit next year, about Paolo's new and wonderfully colored shirt. About Nora's holiday in Yugoslavia last year, about Sally's mother's dog. It was important to avoid the subject both of them were thinking about in case they couldn't keep up the pretense of being ordinary. Each time the telephone rang and Sally rushed to answer, Nora saw and ached for her. When Price rang again she saw Sally's face quiver, heard the hope in her voice as she said, "Superintendent, there's news?" and felt the misery when she heard that it was only to confirm that he'd be coming to the house that afternoon. When he'd rung off, Sally sat there still, the receiver still clutched in her hand, tears running down her face. She looked, Nora thought, like someone who had heard a death sentence. She forgot about Sally's age, she forgot that this was her employer, she saw only a girl like herself in deep trouble, and she went over to her and put her arms around her. Sally turned and put her head on Nora's kind shoulder and allowed herself to cry. What was the point of pretending that everything was ordinary and sane and bearable, when she'd lost Caroline Ann and the world was black around her?

It was at this moment that the telephone rang again. Sally's hand went out automatically. Nora drew a little away, she didn't want to seem to intrude.

Sally looked puzzled. She said, "I'm sorry I can't hear you."

Nora heard the voice at the other end speaking louder, "Who is that speaking?"

Sally said, "Sally Wilmington. Who do you want to speak to?"

There was a click as the connection was broken. Sally said, "Funny! I wonder who it was?"

"You didn't recognize his voice?" Nora asked.

"No. It was a callbox call too."

"Could have been a wrong number," Nora said.

"I suppose so. I thought perhaps it would be. . . ."

"I expect he'll ring back if it was important."

Sally said, "I can't think of anything else that's important now." But she seemed to have recovered from the last outburst of tears, and she allowed Nora to get coffee and even drank a little while they resumed the only occupation possible: waiting.

When Superintendent Price arrived in the early evening, Andrew took him straight into his study and shut the door, hoping that Sally hadn't heard the doorbell.

"No news, I'm afraid, sir," Price said, sitting in one of the big leather-covered armchairs.

"Absolutely nothing? You haven't any evidence to go on? There must have been people around. Someone must have seen something."

"Trouble is, sir, there were too many people. And seeing a woman take a baby out of a pram isn't suspicious in itself. Mothers are doing it all the time. No reason why anyone should take any notice. Of course, because of all the publicity we've had the usual number of crackpots writing in and telephoning to say they know something. . . ."

"One of them might really have something useful to tell you."

"We shall follow them all up, don't worry about that, sir. But at present there's nothing, I'm sorry to say."

"What can you do, then? You must be able to do something," Andrew said.

"We're interviewing some of the assistants in the shop. The exit from the supermarket is near the front, of course. It's just possible that if one of the girls who do the checking out wasn't too busy she might have glanced out into the street and seen something. We're asking them all. Then there are the neighboring shops and the shops opposite. Only the High Street's too wide to see across easily, especially with the amount of traffic there is on it. I'm not very hopeful about that." Superintendent Price sighed.

"What else?"

"Well, of course, we've broadcast an appeal to the public for anyone who might be able to come forward. And we've got our people all over the country keeping a lookout for a girl with a baby she can't account for. And hospitals, in case she had to take the baby in for anything. But it's early days yet. Barely twenty-four hours."

"Twenty-four hours is a long time in a baby's life," Andrew said drily.

"Of course, I do appreciate that, sir. We're doing everything we can. By the way, how is Mrs. Wilmington this afternoon?" Price asked.

"She looks dreadful. I don't know how much longer she can keep going if there's nothing. . . ."

"Has her doctor seen her?"

"I think he was here yesterday. If she isn't better this evening I'll ring him and get him to come back to see her again."

"I would, sir. I don't want to seem gloomy, but things like this sometimes do take several days before one gets to the bottom of them. Especially when this amount of time has elapsed after the taking of the baby. There are some women who snatch a baby, and within a few hours they've brought it back, or taken it to a hospital,or brought it to us. They get frightened, you see. Start thinking over what they've done and want to cry off. But after twenty-four hours you can't count on that sort of reaction. By now it looks as if whoever has the baby must have gone off with it somewhere and means to keep out of harm's way for the present. That doesn't mean that the baby's in danger, it just means that much longer anxiety for you and Mrs. Wilmington. Which is bad enough."

"And if that's the pattern, what happens next?"

Superintendent Price hesitated. "Difficult to say without knowing the motive. When it's a woman who's done it on impulse, as you might say, she doesn't generally want anything, only the child. In the ordinary run of baby-snatching it's something like that. But in this case it could be different."

"How do you mean, different?"

"There's a question of money," Price said, almost apologetically.

"You mean a ransom demand?"

"That's it. You haven't had one, I suppose? Or Mrs. Wilmington?"

"No. How would it be made, do you think?"

"Letter or telephone. There haven't been any anonymous calls, have there?"

"Not as far as I know. What do we do if we get one?"

"Try to keep him talking. I'm having all calls to the house monitored, if there's anything suspicious we should be able to find out where it's coming from."

"If they ask for money, what do we do?"

"Stall. Haggle a bit if you can. Don't give in too easily or they might become suspicious. Don't turn them down flat; when they warn you against letting us know, try to sound doubtful, as if they might be able to persuade you. More convincing that way."

"You really think all this is possible? Likely?"

"It's impossible to say at this stage, sir. I just don't want you to get taken by surprise and wish afterwards you'd said something else."

"Thank you," Andrew Wilmington said. Price might know his job inside out, but he was not the sort of person from whom Andrew was accustomed to taking orders.

"And there's another thing. If you don't mind my mentioning it, sir. Your good lady. She's likely to see it differently. She'll be all for agreeing to whatever they say as long as she gets the child back. Don't let her, if you can help it. Some of these people haven't any scruples. You can't tell, just because you give them the money without telling us, that they're going to hand over the child. Don't say that to her. Just warn her to be careful."

He saw the sick look on Andrew's face and said quickly, "Once they've made contact and asked for the money it's much easier to track them down. Don't give up hope, sir. I haven't, not by a long chalk."

Andrew Wilmington groaned.

In the Stanford kitchen an argument was in process. Chris, Vicky and Stephen sat around the table getting warmer and warmer and more and more convinced, each, that he or she was right and that the others were wrong. So far everyone had been fairly polite, but the moment was approaching when that would no longer be true.

"I don't know what you want us to do. We haven't got anything to go on," Stephen said for perhaps the fifth time.

"You could go and tell the police . . ." Chris said.

"What? What on earth could we tell them that they'd take any notice of?"

"That you see things that haven't happened yet."

"A lot of help that would be."

"You sound as if you didn't want to be able to see what's going to happen."

"I don't," Stephen said.

"Why not?"

"You wouldn't if it was you," Vicky said.

"Yes, I would. If it was going to be useful. . . ."

"We've been very useful to date, haven't we? Seen an old lady knocked down and a baby stolen and helped to prevent both of them," Stephen said with heavy irony.

"I know if it was me I'd do something!" Chris said hotly.

"I ruddy well wish it was you and not me, then."

They glared at each other. Stephen was astonished to hear himself speaking like this to someone he hardly knew. Especially a girl and such a pretty one.

There was a pause, then Vicky said, "It isn't like you think, Chris. You're talking as if it was something like watching telly. Getting news, only early, before anyone else does."

"Well? What is it like, then?"

Vicky hesitated. "You feel sort of funny. Nothing's quite real. Only it's not like dreaming. In a way it's more real than real things. More important. A bit like fainting. There's just a minute before you go right off when you feel, 'That's it!' and then you've gone. It's like that."

"If that's all, I don't see why you're making such a fuss about not wanting it."

"That's like fainting too. Coming 'round afterwards is horrible. You're cold and you shake and you can't remember anything for a minute."

"Is it like that for you?" Chris asked Stephen.

"A bit. I've never fainted so I don't know about that."

"I still think it's a lot of fuss about nothing."

"It isn't just what it feels like. It's. . . ."

"Go on."

"I don't like being mixed up with something I don't understand. I like knowing what's happening."

"That's partly it," Vicky said.

"What else?"

"Not knowing what to do. Like now. I partly agree with you, there ought to be something we can do. Only I agree with Stephen too, I don't see what. No one's going to believe us."

"I'd come too and say that you'd told me about the baby before it happened."

"They wouldn't believe either of you. No one ever does when it's people our age," Stephen said.

"Suppose you got another flash and you saw something that really would help?"

"That'd be different," Stephen said. He glanced across at Vicky sitting silent at the opposite side of the table, and saw her eyes suddenly widen. He saw her go very still just before the flash hit him too and he felt himself go rigid as she'd been. From miles away he heard Chris saying something, but the words didn't make sense and he couldn't absorb them. He was totally bound up in what was going on in front of his eyes. Inside the dark, irregular frame was the very bright picture. He saw first a dark, roundish object which moved from side to side and blocked out everything else, until it jerked suddenly to one side and he saw that he'd been looking at the back of someone's head, which had been moving while the someone was talking. A man's voice, but the words were already lost. When the head was out of the way he found he was staring straight into a face. A girl's face, frightened. Fuzzy fair hair and too much make-up. The girl was holding something in her arms and was turning away from the owner of the head, as if she wanted to hide something from him. He heard her say in a sort of whisper, "You said you wouldn't hurt her . . ." and then he saw the girl wince as if someone had hit her. Then the blackness closed in and he was sitting at the Stanford's kitchen table again, shaking, and Chris was saying, " . . . heard a word I've been saying."

He couldn't speak. He saw Vicky, at the other side of the table, give a shiver and come back to the present as he had. He didn't need to speak to her, they simply looked at each other and understood. It was Chris who was saying, "What's the matter?" And then, quickly perceiving, "Oh! Another flash?"

"Yes."

"What?"

Stephen said, "I saw the girl."

"What's she like then?"

Why did he feel this intolerable disinclination to talk about it? He said, "Sort of fuzzy."

"*Fuzzy?*"

Vicky said, "It's her hair. It's crinkly."

"Oh, that. What else?"

Neither Vicky nor Stephen answered. Chris looked from one to the other, impatient.

"Why don't you say? There must have been something."

Stephen said to Vicky, ignoring Chris, "You saw her too?"

"I only saw the back of her head."

"I saw the back of *his* head. Did you see him properly? What's he like?"

"Not clearly I didn't. Her head got in the way. I think he's got. . . . Wait a minute. There was something funny about him."

Stephen waited.

"He's got funny hair."

"How d'you mean, funny? You mean fuzzy, like hers?"

"No."

"What then?"

"I don't know. I can't remember properly. All I know is when I saw him I thought his hair looked funny."

Chris cut in. "It was about the baby, wasn't it?"

Stephen and Vicky looked at each other again, as if each needed confirmation from the other.

"I suppose so," Stephen said.

"Was it, Vicky?"

"Yes."

"Well, then!" Chris said triumphantly.

"What?"

"*Now* you'll go to the police."

Vicky looked at Stephen and Stephen looked at Vicky.

"Well? Why not? You said. If you got another flash."

Stephen glared at Chris and Chris glared back.

"Why not?"

Stephen said, "It's having to go and tell people something so stupid."

"You mean you're going to let whoever it is get away with

stealing a baby, because you're frightened what people'll say about you if you tell them?"

"It's not only that. . . ."

"Vicky! You'll do something?" Chris said urgently.

Vicky understood Stephen's feeling of not wanting to tell people. Who wanted to make themselves look like some sort of freak? But she saw, too, that he minded the idea much more than she did. Was it something to do with his being a boy, she wondered. Or the difference of class? As she thought this, Chris burst out again. "I never saw what Dad meant before, when he talks about being middle class. You're too frightened of looking silly to mind about what happens to a baby! A little baby!" Her face was red and there were tears in her voice.

"I do mind. If only I was sure."

"Vicky!" Chris appealed.

"I think we'll have to tell someone. Try, anyhow. Even if they don't take any notice. We can't not, Stephen. Think what you'd feel like if they did hurt the baby and we'd just kept quiet," Vicky said.

"Are they going to hurt it?" Chris demanded.

"She said something about how they'd said they wouldn't. Only the way she said it, I think they might. Did you hear that?" she asked Stephen.

"Yes."

"Anything else?"

"I didn't hear anything else."

"Let's go now. They may be doing something terrible," Chris said, standing up and looking as if she were going to rush out of the room immediately.

"Wait a tick. We've got to decide who to try to tell."

"But think what's happening. . . ."

"You've forgotten, Chris. It hasn't happened yet. I mean, if it's like the other times we've seen what's going to happen."

"But it could happen any minute now!"

"Who d'you think we ought to go and see?" Vicky asked Stephen.

"If we went to the police they'd think we were crazy."

"What shall we do, then?"

Stephen said, slowly, "I think we'd better go to see the parents. They might listen, I should think."

Chris said fervently, "I know I'd listen to anyone, if it was me."

"Where do they live?"

"It said in the paper. Did you keep it, Vicky?"

Vicky said, "It's upstairs. I'll fetch it," and left the room.

When she'd gone the hostility between Stephen and Chris was somehow more apparent. She said, "I just don't see how you can be like that!"

"It's not just finding it embarrassing. . . ."

" . . . as if it mattered whether you're embarrassed . . ."

" . . . it's *knowing* no one's going to believe us."

"I do! Why shouldn't other people?"

"It's different for you. You know Vicky. . . . You know she isn't the sort of person who'd make up a story like this. . . ."

" . . . so bloody careful! When it's something like this . . . a *baby*. . . . If it was me I wouldn't care what anyone thought, I'd go ahead and anyhow *try* to do something."

Chris roused was even prettier than Chris composed. Stephen, even at what was a very uncomfortable minute, saw this. He saw also the enormous gap that existed between people like Chris and her mother, and the sort of person he was, and he suspected Vicky was too. Chris, when she saw a wrong that should be righted, would wade in and do her best to do something about it, without stopping to wonder whether she had the weapons or the right. She lived in direct contact with events. He, Stephen, would never be able to act straight off the cuff like that. For him there would always be other considerations holding him back, making any choice of action infinitely complicated. He admired Chris's singleness of view and wished he had it; at the same time he found it irritating that she couldn't understand his hesitations.

He was grateful when Vicky returned.

"It's twelve, Kensington Walk."

"Where's that?"

"Somewhere in Kensington," Stephen said stupidly.

"Great brain! How big is Kensington?"

"Dunno. We've got a Directory at home—no. It's in the car, and Dad's out in it somewhere."

"How shall we find it, then?"

"We could go to somewhere like the High Street station and ask. It's on the Circle Line."

"Might be South Kensington, that's on the Piccadilly."

"Look them up in the telephone book," Stephen said.

"While we're at the Post Office we might as well ask where Kensington Walk is."

"Haven't you got . . . ?" Stephen asked without thinking, and then could have kicked himself.

"You've forgotten. People like us don't have telephones," Chris said.

"Paul has," Vicky said at once.

"Well. That's because his father runs his own business."

"Anyway, let's go to the Post Office. It's only just 'round the corner."

"What are we going to say when we get to the house?" Stephen asked.

"For goodness' sake! Don't start all that over again! Come on! We can think what to say while we're getting there. It'll take hours," Chris said. She picked up her coat and marched out of the kitchen. Stephen and Vicky followed. They knew they had to do as she said.

13

They arrived at number twelve Kensington Walk, after a certain amount of misdirection, at about three o'clock that Saturday afternoon.

"Gosh, it's huge!" Chris exclaimed. It wasn't a terrace house, it stood discretely separated from its neighbors by high brick walls, and from the road by a closely planted line of dark evergreens.

"They must have pots of money," Vicky said.

"That's probably why their baby was stolen. Ransom," Stephen said.

"Come *on*," Chris said, stimulated by this thought. She led the way up to the front door and rang the elegant worked-iron hanging bell. Stephen and Vicky had just about reached the doorstep when Paolo opened the door. Chris was taken aback by his darkness. She hadn't expected posh Mr. Wilmington to look like this.

Paolo stood there unsmiling. It seemed to him that he'd answered the door five hundred times already in the last two days and the news was always bad, never anything good. He was frightened for the Wilmingtons and for Caroline Ann and he was also frightened for himself. In Spain the police didn't necessarily wait till they could prove you guilty they sometimes took you away on suspicion and kept you shut up and then you were lucky or had very good friends indeed if you ever got out again. Mrs. Wilmington had tried to explain that that was not going to happen to him in England, but Paolo was wary and every new person who came to the house might well be a threat. In the ordinary way he would have smiled at Chris because she was a girl and because she was very pretty, but now he simply stared at her and wondered if the police had sent her to trap him.

"Are you Mr. Wilmington?" Chris asked, sounding a good deal braver than she felt.

"Mr. Wilmington won't see anyone," Paolo said, according to his instructions.

"Oh, then you're not. . . . Could we see Mrs. Wilmington, then, please?"

"Mrs. Wilmington, she doesn't see anyone too."

"Please! Please! It's very important."

By this time Vicky and Stephen were standing beside Chris.

"No. Sorry. They don't see anyone." He started to shut the door.

"Oh, don't! Don't go away. It's about the baby. . . ."

"So is everyone coming about the bébé." He went on shutting the door. Stephen pushed forward suddenly and got his foot in the remaining crack. Paolo stepped smartly on the foot. Stephen yelped, but kept it there. Paolo promptly put on the chain inside the door, which meant that it couldn't be opened any further, but at the same time he couldn't shut it owing to the foot.

"You go away. I don't let you in," Paolo said, still trying to kick the foot out of the crack.

"We're not going. Not until we've told someone in authority what we've come for," Stephen said, surprising himself by the way he seemed to have taken charge. He was also surprised when Paolo stopped attacking the foot and said in a much more reasonable voice, "Mr. Wilmington say not to let anyone in."

"All right; don't let us in. Just go and tell someone that we're here because we think we might be able to help."

"Mr. Wilmington won't like. He get very angry," Paolo said.

"I should think he'd be even angrier if he finds us sitting outside his front door all night," Stephen said. Vicky took the hint and immediately sat down. Chris, a moment later, did the same.

"You can't stay," Paolo said.

"We're not going. Not until you've told someone we're here."

Paolo said, "Okay. You take your foot back, I tell Mr. Wilmington."

"Oh no. You can perfectly well go and tell Mr. Wilmington while I keep my foot there."

Silence from inside the house.

Suddenly Paolo said urgently, "Look! Someone with a bébé just there behind you. . . ." Stephen wasn't quick enough. He'd turned to look, and at that moment a well-directed kick on his ankle made him withdraw his foot. Instantly the door shut with a heavy bang. The letter-box flap lifted and Paolo's voice from inside said, "Now you goes away, all of you."

"No we don't, we're staying," Vicky called back.

Stephen sat down beside her rubbing his ankle. "I was an idiot. I ought to have known."

"How could you? I don't think he meant to tell them or let us in or anything even if you'd kept your foot in the door all night."

"Anyway, if we sit here long enough someone's sure to notice," Chris said.

They sat in a row on the top step but one, leaning back against the top step, with their feet on the one below. Kensington Walk was a very secluded, very select little backwater. So far there were no passers-by.

"I do feel a fool," Chris said. She had recovered her usual good humor during the journey from her home.

"You really think someone will see us here? From the house?" Vicky asked Stephen.

"They've only got to look out of one of those windows and they can't help it."

"But people don't much, do they? Go right up to the window and look out, I mean. Mostly when you're in a room you just go on doing whatever there is to do, and when you look out you see things opposite. Or sky."

"Someone might look out if we made a noise," Chris said.

"What sort of noise?"

"Well, if we were singing or something. I know we can't. Not sing."

Vicky absolutely saw this. You can't sit and sing outside a house that has lost a baby.

"We could talk," Stephen said.

"Loudly enough? Go on, then. You start," Chris said.

Silence.

"You can't just talk when there's nothing to say," Vicky said.

"You could say rhubarb, rhubarb, rhubarb, like we did when we were in the crowd in *Julius Caesar*."

No one said anything. Presently Stephen said, "We can't really stay here all night."

"We could stay for another two hours, though," Vicky said.

"One of us'd have to let Mum know we're going to be late if it takes longer than that," Chris said.

There was a sound of footsteps on the pavement. A young woman came along the street; she must, Stephen noticed, have been quite pretty in the ordinary way, with light, curling hair and a neat-featured face, but just now any pretense to good looks the girl might have had were ruined by her distress. She had obviously been crying and, from the look of her red-rimmed eyes, crying for quite a long time. She walked quickly but uncertainly, stumbling a little on the smooth paved surface. She turned in at the entrance to the house, then hesitated when she saw Stephen and the two girls sitting on the steps.

"Are you Mrs. Wilmington?" Chris asked.

"What are you doing here?" the young woman said, and her voice, too, indicated how recently she'd been in tears; it came out choked and rough. She swallowed, and said, "You ought to go away."

"We've got something we want to tell them, but the man, the foreign one, won't let us in. He won't even tell them we're here."

"You ought to go away. They're in terrible trouble, they aren't seeing anyone."

"We might be able to help," Stephen said.

The young woman shook her head and went up the last steps to the front door, taking out a latchkey from her handbag.

"Won't you please tell them we're here? *Please*," Chris said.

She said, "I'm sorry" . . . and choked. She let herself into the house and shut the door after her quickly. Perhaps she was afraid they might try to rush in behind her. Stephen did think of it, but dismissed the idea as impossible, a bad beginning to any meeting they might have with the Wilmingtons.

"If she isn't Mrs. Wilmington, who is she?" Chris said.

"She isn't. I saw Mrs. Wilmington when I had the first flash about the baby. She's quite different."

"Who then? She looked really upset."

"Perhaps she's the nurse," Vicky said.

"She looked awful. As if she'd been crying all day."

"Do you think she will tell them about us?" Chris asked.

"No, I don't."

There was another longish pause. Although it was mid-April and the sun was still well up in the sky, it was chilly. Vicky shivered. Stephen said, "I think this is silly. Vicky's right, we might never be noticed." He got up.

"What are you going to do?"

"I'm going to keep on ringing that bell until one of the Wilmingtons comes out." He gave the bell a violent pull which made the bell clatter wildly. He heard steps inside and the letter-box opened again and Paolo's dark eyes looked through it.

"Is no good. No open the door."

"I'm going to go on ringing until you do. Or tell them about us."

He pulled the bell again.

"Don't do that."

"Tell Mr. Wilmington then. . . ."

"He say no tell . . . ."

Stephen rang the bell again, if anything harder.

He could hear a new voice behind the letter-box. Steps in the hall. A voice said, "Paolo? What the hell are you doing there? What's the matter with the bell? Who's there?"

Stephen bent down to the letter-box level and shouted. "Mr. Wilmington! Please. It's important. I've got something to tell you."

There was a confused noise inside the house, then the door was quickly opened, and Stephen saw a youngish man, obviously very angry.

"Get out or I'll call the police!"

"Please listen . . ." Stephen began desperately.

"I have nothing to say, and there's nothing I want to hear from you. Now, will you go or do I have to use force?"

"I'm not going," Stephen said, again surprising himself.

"Haven't you any decent feelings at all? What can you possibly hope to get out of this . . . this battening on other people's misery?"

"I'm not . . ." Stephen began, when Vicky called out from the step, "We're not. We know something."

Mr. Wilmington took a step backward and looked at the two girls and then again at Stephen. Suddenly, instead of looking furious, he looked immensely tired. He said, "What's all this about? What do you know?"

It was Stephen who now stammered, and Chris who said, "They've seen the people who took your baby."

Mr. Wilmington took this calmly. "How on earth do you know?"

"They see things. Vicky and Steve. They see what's going to happen. They saw. . . ."

Mr. Wilmington said, "Oh God, no, not that!" To Stephen and Chris he said, not angrily, but with a frightening coldness,

"Now you two, stop play-acting and get out. At once. There's a policeman at the corner. If you aren't out in one minute from now, I shall call him and give you in charge. Understand?"

"We're not acting. It's serious. They saw your baby being stolen before it ever happened . . ." Chris said, angry again. Mr. Wilmington took no notice. He had his watch in his hand and he was counting. "Twenty-two, twenty-three, twenty-four, twenty-five. . . ." Stephen was standing undecided on the step below him, Chris next to him, Vicky was standing silent and trembling on the next step down. Mr. Wilmington continued to count out loud, the other three didn't move, when someone came quickly along the dark hall inside the house and said, "Andrew? Andrew? What is it? Did someone say they knew something?" Sally Wilmington came to the open door. She saw a boy and two girls, all distressed and anxious, and her husband counting down seconds. She caught the hand which held the watch and said, "Andrew? Who said they knew about Caroline Ann?"

Stephen and Vicky and Chris saw the girl of the photograph. Chris saw the mother of a little stolen baby and her warm heart swelled in sympathetic horror. Stephen recognized the brown hair and the face that had been so chalky white and the lips, red then, pale now, that had whispered, "It wasn't more than a minute," and he knew, with a sinking heart, that he was inextricably mixed up in this affair, however much he didn't want to be. And Vicky? Vicky saw a mother who had lost a baby. A girl not very much older than she was. And at that moment she saw that the loss of someone you'd known, for whom you were totally responsible, whose thoughts you had thought, whose feelings you had felt, who was contained within your grown-up conscious self, was even worse than to lose an unknown mother whose place was so completely and lovingly taken by another mother who'd happened to be in the next hospital bed. But seeing this didn't make Vicky less strong, it rather gave her more courage. So, to Chris's astonishment, it was Vicky who spoke to Sally Wilmington. She said, "Stephen and me, we've seen things we can't explain. We saw about your baby being stolen before it happened. And this afternoon . . ."

"Will you please ask your two girl friends to shut up and go away?" Mr. Wilmington said in a dangerously quiet voice to Stephen.

"We're not!" Chris burst out, at the same time as Sally Wilmington had caught her husband's arm and was saying, "Don't, Andrew. Let me hear what they're saying."

He took her hand in both of his and said, "Sally, darling, don't. They're just cashing in on our misery. It's horrible, especially with . . . ," he hesitated, " . . . children. But I'm afraid. . . . In a moment they'll be asking how much we'll pay for their 'news.' Or selling the story to the gutter press. Come back into the house, dearest. . . ."

He was interrupted by a furious Stephen. "We're not asking for money. We've nothing to do with newspapers. We've come in case what we've seen might be useful. I wish to God we hadn't. I didn't want to, I said you'd never believe us. I wouldn't if it were me." He was shaking with anger, and this seemed to have some effect on Mr. Wilmington, who looked at him more carefully.

"Andrew. Please let them tell us. Nora's been questioned by the police ever since lunch. She's sure they think she's had something to do with it. Perhaps they really do know something that would find. . . ." Sally Wilmington didn't finish the sentence. And at that moment a uniformed policeman strolling with elaborate casualness past the end of the front garden, hesitated and called out to Mr. Wilmington, "Anything I can do, sir? Any trouble there?"

Stephen and Vicky and Chris held their breath. Then Mr. Wilmington called back, "No thanks, Officer. No trouble," and the policeman moved on and Andrew Wilmington said, unwillingly, "I suppose you'd better come into the house."

Inside a room with more books on its walls than a library, and looking somehow cluttered, but richly, with little dark pictures and dark shiny chairs and tables, and carpets patterned with soft dark colors, and heavy, deep red curtains, the two Wilmingtons sat side by side on a velvet-covered couch and faced Stephen and the two girls, who perched nervously on the edge of cane-backed chairs with oak knobs and twists on their arms and legs. They felt as if they were in a witness box, being interrogated by a hostile lawyer for the prosecution. Stephen looked, and felt, hideously nervous, but still angry enough to be defiant. Chris was interested, observant, confident that in the end they'd be able to prove their case. Vicky felt. . . . There isn't room to say all that Vicky felt.

"Come on then. Let's hear your story," Andrew Wilmington said.

Chris looked at the other two. Vicky said, "You start," to Stephen. He took a deep breath.

Once he'd started it wasn't so bad. He didn't attempt to explain, he simply told how he'd thought he'd seen an accident in the High Street near his home and how it had actually happened a quarter of an hour later. How he'd tried to dismiss it as impossible. How two weeks later he'd had a flash picture of the empty pram and Sally's face. Then, a week afterwards, he'd read about the kidnapping in the paper. He paused.

"I saw it too. Not exactly the same. But nearly," Vicky said.

"Come on. Aren't we going to have your version?" Mr. Wilmington said to Chris. She could see he wasn't believing a word.

"It doesn't happen to me."

"I see. Only to the others. You've just come along for the ride," he said.

"Andrew!" Sally Wilmington said.

"It's no good, darling. There's not a shred of evidence that they haven't made up the whole thing in the last twenty-four hours. There's been enough publicity. . . ."

"We didn't make it up. It happened. . . ."

"And even if they're young enough to believe in this sort of crystal-ball, fortune-telling racket, which I'm not convinced of, how is any of this rigmarole going to help us? Everything they've seen is very conveniently in the past tense anyhow."

"You don't listen. We had another flash today."

"We saw a man and a girl. . . ."

"They had the baby. . . ."

"They said. . . ." Vicky stopped abruptly.

"Go on."

"She was looking after it. She didn't seem so . . . bad," Vicky said. She couldn't possibly tell the baby's mother the words the girl had said.

"How do you know it was our baby?"

Stephen knew this was the weak part of their story. "We don't. Only why should we see anything about a baby if it isn't yours?"

"You saw her properly? And the man?"

"Vicky saw him."

"Could you describe him?"

Vicky said, miserably, "Not really."

"And what do you suggest I should do, now you've given me this valuable piece of information?"

"I don't know."

Stephen said, "Don't you see, if we're really somehow tuned in. Like on a radio, wavelengths. If we're on the right frequency for the people who've taken your baby, we might get more flashes. They might tell us something useful, something the police could work on. Like where they are. . . ."

"If your descriptions of places are as accurate and detailed as your descriptions of the people you say you've seen, I think you can spare yourselves the trouble of communicating with the police," Andrew Wilmington said, very coldly indeed.

Sally Wilmington said to Vicky, "Did you see the baby?"

"I saw she was holding it. That's all. I'm sorry."

"But you said. . . . You said the girl was looking after it."

"Yes. And she seemed. . . ."

At this moment the telephone bell rang. Sally had flung

herself at the instrument and was holding the receiver to her ear before anyone else had moved. The others heard her say, "Yes. Yes. Yes, I'm listening," and saw her troubled eyes go to her husband's face in a sort of desperate appeal. He whispered, "Keep them talking," and ran out of the room.

"Yes. Yes, I'm here," Sally said again. "You have?" in a sort of gasp. ". . . how is . . . ? No." There was a little pause and then she said, "How much? No, I won't. But just tell. . . ." They could all hear the vicious little click with which the receiver the other end was jammed down.

Sally was still standing there with the receiver in her hand when Andrew came back into the room. "Rang off before I got there. What did they say?"

"They've got Caroline Ann."

"I suppose they're demanding money?"

"So she's not dead. . . ." She began to sob.

"Darling. Try to tell me. How much?"

"Two hundred . . . thousand. . . ."

"Who was it? Did they say? Did they tell you how they wanted to collect it?"

"No, nothing. Just how much. . . . And. . . ."

"And what?"

"They said . . . he . . . said. . . ."

"Try to tell me, darling."

"He said . . . if you want . . . if you want . . . her safe back. . . ."

Andrew Wilmington said, "Bloody swine."

"Andrew, we will, won't we? You won't say no? You wouldn't let them hurt Caroline Ann?"

"Darling, you don't know these chaps. Paying over the money's no guarantee she'll be safe."

"But if we don't pay . . . if we say no, then they'll. . . ."

"Darling, I know it's difficult, but you've got to try to be reasonable about this. It's blackmail. It's impossible to give in to blackmail. They don't stop at the first demand. If we paid this amount now, they'd only ask for more."

Chris, Stephen and Vicky were listening, astonished. Two hundred thousand pounds! It was incredible that anyone should demand that much, even more incredible that Mr. Wilmington shouldn't even comment on the amount, but should talk about paying that and then being asked for more. To the girls it was an unreal sum. No one they knew had even one thousand pounds. Two hundred thousand was the sort of astronomical money other people occasionally won on the pools. When they said to each other, "What would you do if you had . . . ?" it was generally a hundred pounds, sometimes a thousand. Even then they didn't know where to begin to make a hole in something so enormous. Stephen appreciated more what this meant. He realized that young Mr. Wilmington, whom he didn't much like, must be really immensely rich. Perhaps a millionaire. He felt sorry for Mrs. Wilmington. He wasn't sure that her husband really cared about the baby, but she quite obviously couldn't think of anything else.

"But Andrew! We can't risk them doing something terrible . . ." she said now.

"Sally darling, they're not going to give up this damnable game until they've got every penny they can out of us. We simply mustn't let them feel they've got the upper hand of us. It's a matter of principle. . . ."

Sally Wilmington cried out, "It's a matter of my baby!" and at the same moment Vicky said, loudly, "I can't think how you can!"

Mr. Wilmington's cold blue eyes came around to her. She went on, "It's a baby! A person! You don't know what they're doing, you don't know where she is. I don't see how you can talk about principles. That's just thinking. If it was me, and I had that much money, I wouldn't bother about anything like that, I'd go straight off and get her. I wouldn't mind how much it cost!"

There was a really horrible silence, during which Vicky, red with anger and shame, wished she were anywhere else. Then

Chris—blessed Chris—said, "I think Vicky's right. If it was my baby, that's what I'd do too."

Mr. Wilmington said, even more coldly than before, "I don't think anyone asked for your opinion." Stephen stood up.

"Come on. Let's go," he said to the two girls.

"But we haven't told them . . ." Chris said.

"It's no good. He's never going to believe us. Don't you see? We've got to have some sort of proof."

"Don't let them go, Andrew," Mrs. Wilmington said.

Stephen spoke to her, "I'm sorry. We honestly did come because we thought we might be able to help. But it isn't any good unless someone believes what we're saying. I see it's difficult."

"I don't want you to go."

"Let them go, Sally. As if we hadn't enough, without a gang of kids playing at second sight," Mr. Wilmington said.

Stephen ignored him. "If there's anything at all, we'll tell you. Come on, Vicky, come on, Chris. There's no point in staying."

He opened the door and went out, followed by Chris. Vicky took a last look back before she joined them. She stepped back for an instant to say softly and urgently to Sally Wilmington, who was sitting by the telephone, the tears running down and splashing on the smooth leather of the table, unchecked, "We shall find your baby. I know we will." Then she too left the room and they let themselves silently out of the big house which was full of misery.

In the train going back, Stephen said to the girls, "Why don't you come back to my place?" Chris and Vicky looked at each other. Chris said, "We mustn't be home later than seven. About. If we're not, one of us'll have to go around and tell Mum, or she'll worry."

"It's only six now. You could come in and have coffee or something."

"That'd be nice, wouldn't it, Vicky?"

"Mm. I mean, thanks, yes, fine."

"You won't get any cake like the one you gave me. My mother doesn't make cakes."

"Coffee'd do for me. Anyway we don't eat that cake every day."

Mostly, however, the journey passed in silence. The afternoon had been so beyond expectation awful and upsetting, none of them wanted to talk. Only after they'd left the underground station and were going up the hill to Stephen's house, Chris said, "Thanks for not rubbing it in."

"Not rubbing what in?"

"You said it wouldn't be any use going there. That they wouldn't believe us."

Stephen said, "The funny thing is, now I feel as if they ought to have."

"He was horrible. If it was just him I wouldn't mind whether he got the baby back or not."

"I think he wouldn't have been like that if he hadn't been so worried. And I'm sure it's true, they must have had all sorts of people bothering them."

"Well, I thought he was rotten. I liked her, though. Didn't you, Vicky?"

"Mm."

"I was pleased you went for him like you did."

Vicky said nothing.

"What's the matter? You still upset?"

"Mm."

Chris looked at her face, and said no more.

The girls didn't know, but it had been a great act of courage on Stephen's part to ask them home. It was a Saturday, and his father would almost certainly be there. At first Stephen had decided against inviting them for this reason. Then he suddenly felt sick with himself for being such a coward. What sort of life was he going to have if he didn't do something perfectly reasonable—and in this case an almost necessary courtesy, considering how often he'd sat in the comfortable Stanford kitchen without any return of hospitality? So, without giving himself too much time to think, he'd asked them back. He opened the front door and followed them into the hall, then steered them into the kitchen-dining room. As he'd expected, his mother was standing by the stove, looking preoccupied.

Stephen said, "Hi, Mum!" and introduced Vicky and Chris. He could see from his mother's face that she was pleased he'd brought friends home, but couldn't place these two girls, and that she was worried as well as pleased. Inevitably she at once began apologizing.

"Oh dear! If only I'd known. . . . Stephen didn't say he was bringing anyone back. . . . I could have made some biscuits . . . there was a recipe yesterday in the *Guardian*. . . ."

"We don't want biscuits, thanks. Just coffee."

"Oh but. . . . They sounded rather good. . . ."

Stephen said, "Don't worry, Mum. Chris and Vicky really only want coffee. Shall I get out the mugs?"

With a little pressure and reassurance, his mother was able to get around to making coffee. Vicky still looked a bit dazed. She obediently ladled sugar out of a packet into a china bowl, but it was Chris who competently found where the Rawlinson spoons were kept, who prevented Mrs. Rawlinson from starting the coffee grinder without screwing the lid on so that all the coffee beans went all over the floor, an accident which was so common in that house that Stephen unconsciously associated the smell of coffee with grovelling about with a dustpan and brush, sweeping up a horrid mixture of grounds, beans and dusty crumbs. When the coffee was finally being poured out of the filter jug, Mrs. Rawlinson's cheeks were pink with the pleasure of being helped by Chris and with her admiration of the coffee machine. "It's super coffee too," Chris said appreciatively, sipping it out of her blue-and-green mug.

"I'm sure it's not better than your mother makes," Stephen's mother said.

"It is though. Mum makes instant most of the time. Mind you, I like that too. Only this is really good. Like you get in that posh place up the High Street where they charge you 20 pence a cup."

"It is good, Mum," Stephen said.

"I'm so glad. It does taste different. Perhaps it's because I don't generally put in quite so much coffee. . . ." She glanced guiltily at Stephen.

"But didn't the instructions tell you how much to put in?"

"I suppose. . . ."

"Mum! I bet you've never even read the instructions!"

"Well, it seemed such a simple thing. Just making coffee."

"How long have you had the . . . thing? The coffee machine?" Chris asked.

"About six months, I think. Perhaps not quite that long."

"It's nearly a year. And this is the first time you've looked at the instructions. Isn't it?" Stephen asked.

"It was me who read them," Chris said. She sounded delighted. "That's exactly like our Mum. Isn't it, Vicky? She never looks at how it tells you to do things till she's halfway through. Dad always teases her, says she thinks she knows better than anyone. He says if she had to drive a bus, she'd tell the instructor not to bother telling her how, she'd rather work it out for herself."

Stephen had rarely seen his mother so relaxed. She looked almost as if she were enjoying having visitors. She produced a wholemeal loaf, not very stale, out of the refrigerator and they toasted it and ate it with butter and honey. "It's luscious. Must tell Mum to get brown bread next time, it's got more taste than that white sliced stuff," Chris said, her mouth bulging. Mrs. Rawlinson beamed. Not one of her carefully prepared continental dishes had had such appreciation.

The door of Dr. Rawlinson's study clicked shut, and he appeared in the doorway saying, before he saw Chris and Vicky, "Margaret, why didn't you tell me . . . ?" He stopped at the sight of the two girls.

"Dad, this is Chris and this is Vicky. My father," Stephen said.

Dr. Rawlinson shook hands with each of them, rather over-politely, and sat down at the table next to Chris.

"Any coffee for me?" he said to his wife.

"Of course, darling. I'll just get a cup. . . ."

"Sit still, Mum, I'll get it." Stephen didn't want the chance that his mother might show her nervousness by some piece of clumsiness. As it was she managed to pour the coffee awkwardly, spilling a little.

"Are you just off somewhere?" Dr. Rawlinson said pleasantly to Chris and Vicky and Stephen together.

"No, back from somewhere. Vicky and I are on our way home."

"Where from, may I ask? Or perhaps that's a question you'd all prefer not to answer?"

"I don't mind. Kensington," Chris said.

"Kensington! The Royal Borough of. Several quite good museums. The Palace is worth a visit," Dr. Rawlinson said.

"I don't go much for museums," Chris said.

"Perhaps it's as a shopping center that you find Kensington amusing?"

"Never been there to shop."

"Perhaps you saw that there's been one of those interesting baby-snatching cases there. I always find these cases present a very stimulating problem. In most instances there seems to be no financial motive. . . ."

His voice ran on, but no one was listening, until the words "evening paper" caught Vicky's ear, and she said abruptly, "Is there something about it in the paper today?"

"About what? In which paper?" Dr. Rawlinson asked her politely.

"About the baby that was stolen."

"I believe the police are questioning some girl. The *Standard* has quite a long. . . ."

"Where is the *Standard?*" Stephen said.

"In my study. What . . . ?"

"Excuse me a minute," Stephen said to his mother and disappeared.

"You must forgive my son's abrupt manners," Dr. Rawlinson said to the two girls, but addressing himself particularly to Chris.

"I don't see what's wrong with them," she said.

Stephen came back with the paper folded to show the headline "KENSINGTON BABY-SNATCH CASE." He showed it silently to the girls and then sat down to read it.

"Why this sudden interest in crime, Stephen?" his father asked.

Stephen got out of that one by answering, "Wait a tick, I'm reading."

"What does it say, Steve?" Chris asked.

"They're interviewing some girl. They say she's been helping them with their inquiries. Doesn't that generally mean they're suspicious of her?"

"You three seem very much occupied with this case," Dr. Rawlinson said.

"We've met the parents," Stephen said briefly.

Dr. Rawlinson said, "Oh really," but no more. Chris saw him look from one to the other of them. He obviously couldn't make it out at all. Good for Stephen, she thought. He's really got his Dad guessing this time.

Stephen said, "It says, 'A woman spent several hours today at the police station helping the police with their inquiries.'"

"Let's see," Chris said, reaching across the table for the paper.

It was maddening not to be able to talk. Stephen wondered what his parents would say if he invited Vicky and Chris up to his room, but decided he couldn't risk it. He handed the paper over to Chris and looked at Vicky. Vicky looked back at him. He could see she was still upset.

His mother was fussing around again with the coffee. His father was sitting, legs crossed, in an elaborately casual manner, studying the two girls. Vicky caught his eye and immediately looked away. She got up and spoke to Mrs. Rawlinson.

"I'm afraid we'll have to go now."

Chris took the hint and got up too.

"Thanks for the super coffee and the bread and things."

Dr. Rawlinson got up.

"It's been most interesting to meet you."

"It's interesting for us too," Chris said politely.

"I hope you'll come again," Mrs. Rawlinson said.

"Love to."

"I'll see you out," Stephen said. He had to talk to Vicky alone—or rather with only Chris as audience. But his father came out into the hall and accompanied them to the front door. Vicky gave Stephen an imploring look. He let his father say the final politenesses on the doorstep and then, just as he was shutting the door, said, "Wait a minute. I forgot something. I'll start you on the way."

As he thought, his father had committed himself too far now in his farewells to offer to come too. He merely said, "A very sudden change of plan, Stephen! I wonder why?"

Chris giggled. This was what she'd been told to expect. Stephen simply said, "I shan't be long," and shut the door firmly behind him. He ran down the steps and fell into step beside the two girls. He said, "Did you hear what Mrs. Wilmington said about someone being questioned by the police this afternoon? She said, 'Nora.'"

"Who is Nora?" Chris asked.

"Don't you remember? Nora Hunter. She's the nurse," Vicky said.

"But don't you see? If the police really think she's the one who took the baby. . . ."

"She isn't the girl I saw with it. She's quite different," Vicky said.

"Will they arrest her?" Chris asked.

"She could have arranged the kidnap, but got someone else to look after the baby. In fact she'd have had to, or she'd have been suspected at once," Stephen said.

"That crying girl? I'm sure she didn't . . ." Chris began.

"Whoever did, and however much we know, I don't see what we do next," Stephen said.

"Tell the police they've got the wrong person. Now. We could go on our way home."

Vicky said, "Chris, don't. It'd be like this afternoon. No one . . ." and Stephen finished with her, "No one's ever going to believe us."

"Can't you stop that bloody kid?" Skinner said, after the baby had cried for what seemed like hours in the early morning.

Maureen, aching for sleep, feeling him rigid with anger beside her, tried not answering. What she really wanted was just to let go and know nothing, but better than waking up properly and having to talk was the sort of half-naps she seemed to be able to snatch between the baby's wails.

"Go on. Do something," Skinner said. He pinched her arm suddenly and hard so that she cried out.

"That hurt!"

"You'll get hurt more than that if you don't make that bloody kid shut up."

"I've done everything I know."

"I don't care what you do, only stop it. Take it out somewhere. I got to get my sleep."

"It's dark outside," Maureen said.

"Don't talk." He gave her a shove which nearly threw her out of the lumpy double bed.

She found her coat and put it on. The nights were still cold. She could see well enough by the street light coming through the curtains to pick her way around the room and to avoid the heavy furniture. She picked the baby out of the carry-cot put across two chairs and wondered what to do. The baby's cries stopped for a moment, then began again, but louder. It wasn't going to be enough just to hold her, she'd have to take her out of the room somewhere. But where? The baby howled and struggled. She was cold, her feet were like ice and she was wet again. She'd have to be changed; that meant putting on the light. But if she put on the light here Skinner'd just about murder her.

She pulled the blankets out of the cot and wrapped them around the baby. Good thing they seemed fairly dry. Perhaps if the baby got warm she'd stop crying. But until she did they'd have to get out of the room. The other lodgers in the house might complain, but nothing they could do to her would be as bad as what Skinner might do. She carried the baby out into the passage. It was dark here, so she turned on the light. It went on, and then off again after what was supposed to be a minute, but it was never enough to get up or down the stairs by. She got halfway down when it went out, but that was all right because the toilet was on the half-landing and she reckoned she'd be all right in there with the baby for a bit at this time of night. She went in and balanced herself on the edge of the seat.

It wasn't a very nice place to have to sit holding a baby. It was uncomfortable too. But at any rate the light stayed on, and that made her feel better. She was frightened of the dark, always had been. She wondered if the baby had been frightened of the dark in the bedroom. She couldn't remember being a baby like this. She didn't know if babies did get frightened of the dark and that sort of thing, or if they had to be older, knowing about what could happen to you, before they got properly frightened. Or perhaps it was the cold that had made the baby cry. She did seem to be quieting down a bit now. Maureen had got her poor cold feet under her own coat against her side to try to get them warm quickly. The baby was still half-crying but she wasn't bawling any longer. She was hiccupping a lot with sobs and her face was all red and swollen. No wonder. She must've been crying for two hours or more.

Maureen wondered what the time was. Last night when she went to bed she'd taken off her watch, the posh one Skinner had given her soon after they'd met—it seemed much more than a couple of months now. Skinner had taken her around to what he called the Club to meet Jakey and Ted and Bus. They'd gone into a huddle together, talking quiet and secret, and she'd been left with Sharon, Jakey's girl friend. Sharon was older than Maureen and thought she knew a lot more about everything. She was very thin and looked good in the expensive clothes Jakey gave her, and Maureen knew that Sharon despised her for being younger and fat and for not knowing her way around. Sharon couldn't be bothered with Maureen and let Maureen see it. When she spoke to Maureen she did it out of the side of her mouth, sort of, and so quiet it was difficult to hear, so that Maureen found herself saying "What?" and "Pardon" all the time. Maureen hated Sharon. She'd said once to Skinner that she thought Sharon was awful the way she let Bus mess her about when she was supposed to be Jakey's girl, and how she'd come to the club one evening wearing a see-through blouse and nothing underneath, and Skinner had said, "She hasn't anything on her chest to hide like you have, but she's got more of everything else that counts." It had been Sharon who'd taken the baby; they'd decided it wouldn't be safe to let Maureen as she was going to be the one to look after it. "If anyone sees Sharon going off with the kid, it won't matter, see? She'll have an alibi, a good one. What no one'll look for is Fatty," Skinner said. He called Maureen Fatty, sometimes she thought because he knew she didn't like it.

Sharon had taken the baby the day before yesterday. No. By now it must be Sunday morning, so it had happened the day before that. Maureen had been waiting in Skinner's lodgings all afternoon, and it was getting on, it was nearly evening when Jakey and Sharon had come in a car, with Bus driving. Skinner'd been on the lookout, he'd gone down and brought Sharon up to his room. Sharon had the baby with her and she'd put it down on the bed and said, "Over to you, and am I thankful," to

Maureen, and then she'd gone straight out. Never looked back. Then Skinner had made Maureen change the baby's clothes into the ones she'd bought at Marks. He was in a hurry to be gone, kept telling her to get on with it. He wouldn't listen when Maureen had told him she'd never dressed a baby before and she couldn't do it any faster. And the baby, who'd not been crying when Sharon brought her in, started to yell and she struggled and Maureen felt her fingers getting stupid and she was slower than ever, and Skinner standing there all the time swearing at her for not being quicker.

Then they'd gone out, Maureen with the baby and Skinner with the new blue suitcase he'd bought, and they'd got a taxi to one place, and then they'd changed into another and gone somewhere else, and then Bus had picked them up, but in a different car this time, and he'd brought them here, to Edmonton, to this house where the landlady was called Mrs. Plum and where Skinner said they'd got to stop for a bit. He'd told Mrs. Plum he and Maureen were married and that this was their first baby. Maureen had to wear a ring and remember that she was now Mrs. Deptford and that Skinner was to be called Johnny. The baby was Linda.

It was all very difficult; she kept on forgetting when Mrs. Plum called her Mrs. Deptford and looking around for someone else. She hoped Skinner hadn't noticed. If he did he'd be angry again and she didn't like him being angry with her. He seemed angry a lot of the time now, not like when he'd first taken her out, when he'd been nice and given her some smashing presents and she'd been so proud that at last she'd got a proper boy friend, older than her, with loads of money. Well, on and off he had loads, sometimes he didn't seem to have so much. But if she'd known what it was going to be like having the baby to look after, with it crying such a lot and her feeling frightened, she wouldn't know the right things to do for it, and being frightened of Skinner too, she'd never have said she'd come. Only she hadn't said she'd come really, Skinner had made her. After he'd helped her to lift the handbag she'd wanted from the shop, he'd told her where the watch he'd given her had come from, and then he'd told her that if she didn't do what he said he'd get her copped or worse. Sometimes he was nasty like that, and she'd think she'd run off somewhere he couldn't find her, perhaps to her auntie in the country. Then when she'd nearly made up her mind to this, he'd be nice again and love her and say she was his girl. When he was like that Maureen thought she'd do anything for him. Especially when all he wanted was for her to look after a baby for a week. It hadn't sounded hard, and she knew she'd be nicer to the baby than Sharon. When he was nice Maureen wanted to please Skinner because she wanted to be loved. It seemed a long time since she'd been loved by anyone.

Maureen's bottom ached where the seat of the toilet cut into it. Skinner would have said it was because her bottom was so fat. But she didn't like to shift her weight so as to get more comfortable, because the baby had quieted down. She was still giving an occasional hiccup, but she wasn't crying any more. Her head was against Maureen's arm and she just couldn't see whether the baby was asleep or not. She thought from the even breathing and the way the baby's head lolled, that she must be. She felt the small feet. They were really warm. If only she dared to creep back into the bedroom, she could pop the baby back into the cot and get in beside Skinner. She yawned as she thought of this, and felt her eyelids begin to drop. She so terribly wanted to get back to sleep. She wondered if the baby would wake up again if she was carried back. If she dared she'd take her into bed with her. But she thought she wouldn't dare because when she'd tried that the first night when the baby yelled, Skinner had been really nasty. He didn't want the kid pissing in his bed, he said. Maureen had thought he was going to hit her; she'd taken the baby out quick.

But she couldn't sit there all night. If only there was another room she could go where she could lie down with the baby. Her mind pictured a big room with one of those beds with curtains around the top end like rich people had on the telly. With frilly pillows and big soft blankets and fur rugs on the floor and a white dressing-table covered with bottles and bottles of perfume. In the split second before she jerked her head back and her eyelids up, Maureen dreamed that she was sitting on the top bar of the gate at the end of the lane near her auntie's cottage. The bar bit into her behind and she clutched the bundle in her arms as she woke. The baby stirred, hiccupped and whimpered. Maureen held her breath. Then she heard the regular breathing begin again. Her own head began to drop forwards, she could feel herself sliding down toward sleep. But she mustn't go to sleep here, sitting on the edge of the toilet seat. She might drop the baby if she went right off. It struck Maureen that if she'd got to spend the rest of the night here, she could be more comfortable. Very carefully she eased herself up from the seat and sat down on the floor. One thing about Mrs. Plum, she did keep the place clean. She found she could wedge herself up against the wall between the pipe at the back of the toilet fixture and the side wall. She had to be careful she didn't bang the baby's head either side, that was all. The relief of sitting solidly on the floor, instead of half-balancing on that ruddy seat, was so great that for a minute the floor seemed almost soft. Her head went back against the wall behind her, then she let it go sideways against the seat. The baby didn't wake. Waves of sleep broke over Maureen's head and thankfully she let herself fall into them. She felt herself go and this time didn't have to fight against going.

She didn't wake until two hours later, when Mr. Bodman, who rented the front ground floor, came up early to the toilet and was astonished and aghast at finding her there. She'd never thought to lock the door.

16

Maureen managed to get back into the bedroom without waking either the baby or Skinner. She eased the baby back into its cot and got into the bed, where she slept until after eleven o'clock.

It was the baby who woke them again. Skinner just said a bad word and went off to the bathroom. At least it was light and Maureen felt better for the sleep she'd had. Before Skinner got back she'd dressed herself and changed the baby. Then she went out on the landing where the stove stood, to warm up the baby's feed.

Mrs. Plum came up the stairs, stout and jolly in a quilted nylon housecoat, very brightly colored. She must have heard the baby crying and had come to see if she could help. She was kind, Mrs. Plum, only she was nosy too, and Skinner had warned Maureen not to talk to her.

"If she starts talking to me, I can't just not say anything," Maureen had said.

"'Course you've got to answer. Only don't tell her anything, see? About us and the kid."

"She asks. She asked me where I had the baby."

"What did you say?"

"Said I'd had it in the hospital."

"That's all right. Only don't tell her anything like how bad it was having it or that sort of stuff. You'd get it wrong and she's the sort of old bag who'd know. She ask any more?"

Maureen lied. She'd learned to lie much better since she'd known Skinner. "No." She wouldn't tell him about the wedding she'd made up for Mrs. Plum. The sort of wedding she'd have liked, in a church with flowers and her all in white with a big bouquet sort of drooping on one arm and everyone dressed in their best, clapping and hoping she'd be happy. If she told Skinner that, he'd look at her with his eyes half-shut the way he did when he was going to be angry, and he'd say, "You're useless." Useless was what he called her when she'd done something wrong.

"Morning, Mrs. Deptford!" Mrs. Plum said now, panting slightly from climbing the stairs.

"Morning," Maureen said politely.

"I'm afraid you and your hubby can't have had much of a night. I heard Linda crying ever such a lot," Mrs. Plum said. She had to raise her voice to get across the wails of the hungry baby.

"I'm sorry."

"That's all right, dear. We've all been through it in our time. I know. My Stuart, he was ever such a difficult baby, I used to think I'd never get a good night's sleep again in the first months. I really did."

"How long was it before he got better?" Maureen asked. Perhaps the baby would stop crying half the night soon and she'd be able to sleep and Skinner wouldn't be so cross.

"I can't remember that, dear. Seemed like years, but I daresay it wasn't more than a few months. By the time he was a year I know he was ever such a good baby, you'd hardly know he was in the house. I daresay your Linda'll settle down in time. Let's see. You said she was three months, didn't you?"

"Yes."

"She's in a real tantrum now, isn't she? When did she have

her last feed, then?" Mrs. Plum shouted above the baby's cries of rage.

"Last night before we went to bed."

"You mean you didn't feed her this morning? When I heard her stop crying, I thought, There now. That poor Mrs. Deptford's got up and made a feed and put the little girlie back to bed all warm and full up and comfy. You mean you didn't give her anything this morning till now?"

"No. I didn't. . . ."

"Not even a drop of water in case she was thirsty, the poor little mite?"

"No. I didn't. . . ."

"Didn't they teach you that at the hospital?"

"Not water. Just to make up the stuff and warm the bottles and to give it to her at the times . . . you know."

"What I say is, it seems funny all these hospitals and clinics and everything saying different things from each other. What I say is, there must be a right and a wrong way, mustn't there? They can't all be right. So why don't they make up their minds and have it said the same, once and for all. At the Royal Free, now, they were all for the mothers feeding the babies themselves. No bottles. You know what I mean . . . ?" She paused delicately. Maureen stared at her, then said in a hurry, "I know."

"Didn't the hospital say anything about you putting the baby on bottles? Or perhaps you did feed her yourself at the beginning? You look as if you should have been able to. . . ." Her eyes sized up Maureen's shapes and Maureen felt herself going red. "Didn't they tell you you ought to?"

Maureen said quickly, "No. They didn't mind. They said bottles would be all right."

"There! You see? Can't make up their minds between themselves. No wonder half the girls come out of hospital without knowing one end of their baby from the other. Did they show you how to bathe her before you left?"

It seemed easiest to say, "No."

"I never! That's a shame. But I expect you had your Mum or someone to help you out when you got back home with her, didn't you?"

Maureen hated being asked about her Mum, it always made her cry. Silly. Because it was four years ago, and you'd think she'd have got over it by now. And it wasn't as if they'd got on all that well, especially that last year, they'd had ever such rows. Boys and clothes and make-up and smoking and school and everything. But she still couldn't answer. She found a handkerchief in the pocket of her coat and blew her nose.

"Have you caught a cold, dear? Perhaps your little Linda, she's caught it off of you and that's what makes her cry such a lot. Hadn't you better take her along to the clinic next week and see if the doctor can't give you something to help clear her little chest? Which clinic was you attending before you moved here?"

"I can't remember its name."

"Well, where were you and your hubby before you came to me, then? I think you did say, only I didn't quite catch. Your hubby speaks very quiet sometimes."

Maureen was thankful she'd been told the answer to this. "We come here from Birmingham. Sk . . . Johnny got offered a job."

"I've got a sister living there in one of those new council flats. Where did you say you lived? It might have been near my sister's place, then I might know it."

Pushed, and unable to invent, Maureen said the name of the street she'd lived in all her life in London. "Brady Drive."

"Brady Drive. No, I don't know that at all. Which side of the town is it then?"

Maureen could hear the bathroom door slam. Skinner would be coming up the stairs, he mustn't find her and Mrs. Plum talking, he'd be sure to ask how much she'd said. She said, "I think the water's hot enough now, I'll give the baby her feed." She heard Skinner's feet coming up the stairs.

"You'd best cool it down a bit before you let her have the bottle. If you give it to her that hot she'll burn her little tongue," Mrs. Plum said. She pulled her bright housecoat together across her front and turned to greet Skinner. "I was just saying to Mrs. Deptford, Mr. Deptford, that I'm afraid you can't have had a very good night what with your little Linda taking on so this morning."

Skinner could smile when he wanted to so that he looked really nice, really as if he liked you. He'd done that to Maureen when they'd first gone out together. He smiled like that at Mrs. Plum now and said that no, he wasn't feeling too bad now he'd had a wash and brush up, but he was sorry if Linda had disturbed Mrs. Plum or anyone else in the house. Then he cut short what Mrs. Plum was going to say, which would have been the same all over again that she'd said before, and he said to Maureen, very polite, that she'd better get on and feed Linda, hadn't she, to stop her crying any more. So Maureen took the pan with the hot water and the bottle into the bedroom. She heard Skinner outside telling Mrs. Plum that they were going out to see some friends and that, yes, it was cold for the time of year. Then he came in and shut the door behind him. Maureen was sitting on the side of the bed with the baby on one arm and the bottle in her other hand. The baby was screaming. Of course.

"Go on. Give the bloody kid its feed and get it to stop that row," Skinner said, speaking quite differently from how he had in front of Mrs. Plum. He was almost whispering too, and somehow it made it sound worse. More frightening.

"I don't want to give it to her too hot," Maureen whispered back.

"For Christ's sake! Why'd you hot it up so much then?"

They couldn't carry on a conversation in whispers against the noise the baby was making. When at last the bottle had cooled down and the baby was making greedy sucking noises, Skinner asked, "What did the old cow want to know this time?"

"Only about the baby. How old she was and that."

"You didn't say anything out of step?"

Lies again. "No, Skinner. Honest I didn't. I said we'd come from Birmingham like you told me."

He frowned. "Why did you have to say anything about where we come from?"

"She asked. She was going on about clinics. Wanted to know where I took the baby to. I didn't know about clinics. You didn't tell me about them, only about the hospital."

"Jesus! Don't you know anything? Baby clinics. You're supposed to take the kid there to be weighed and that. It said in the book. I read it to you. Don't you remember?"

She didn't, but to distract his attention she said, "What does it say in the book about water? She wanted to know why I didn't give her water in the night."

Skinner said, "I'll see." All the instructions that Maureen had had about infant care had come out of the book and had been given her by Skinner. He had shown her how to mix the feeds with water in a measured jug and how to pour the mixture into bottles which you then warmed up in a pan of water. He'd told Maureen what to buy in the way of diapers and rubber pants. He hadn't shown her how to change the baby because he wouldn't touch it himself. He was funny like that. He wouldn't even pick it up, it always had to be her. He'd shown her the picture in the book of the right way to put on the diaper and he'd shown her too the picture of the way to hold a baby in its bath, but Maureen was frightened. She hadn't bathed the baby yet once. She'd given it a wash where it most needed it, but she was hoping that before the baby really had to be bathed, they'd have got rid of it.

Thinking hopefully how soon this might be, she said, "Are we taking her back today?"

"Back where?"

"Back to her Mum and Dad."

He looked up from the book and said, "You're crazy. Without the money? What'd be the point?"

"I thought someone was going to ask for the money yesterday."

"That's right."

"Wouldn't they give it to us, then?"

"Not yet."

"Some time they will?"

"'Course they will. Takes time, though. They got to get anxious."

Maureen thought about this. "Aren't they anxious?"

"Not anxious enough. Just now they'd cheat. Bring the law in. We got to have the cash clear, without any strings. See? For that we got to wait a bit. So they don't know what's going on, so they'd do anything to know the kid's all right."

"How long do you think that'll be?"

Skinner's mouth turned up at the corners, only it wasn't really a smile with his eyes like that. He said, "Might be a day or two, might be a week. Don't know yet how quickly they'll soften up."

"We going to stay here, then?"

"For a bit. If nothing goes wrong."

"Like what?"

Skinner didn't answer.

"If what goes wrong, Skinner?"

"If the old bag gets too nosy. Or you say something out of turn. Or Smithy says to move on."

"Who's Smithy?"

"Smithy's the boss."

"What's he the boss of, Skinner?" Maureen asked, not really much bothered to know, but wanting to keep him there talking while the baby got the last drops out of the bottle, her eyelids already dropping as if in another minute she'd be asleep. Skinner stubbed out his cigarette. He was a chain smoker, he'd already got the next one in the corner of his mouth. He said, "Smithy works our lot. Bus and Ted and Jakey and me."

"You mean he tells you what to do?"

She ought to have known that was the wrong thing to say to

Skinner. He scowled. "Not like that. He's got the contacts, see? We work for him in a way. He looks after us, see? He sees we're all right. See?"

Maureen didn't. She said, "I always thought you were the boss."

"Don't let Jakey hear you say that."

"I don't like Jakey," Maureen said.

"Anything special?"

"He's cruel. I saw him kicking that dog the other night. He went on and on. He went on as if he liked doing it. There wasn't any need. . . ."

Skinner said, "Jakey's quite a boy."

"Did *he*—Smithy—say to take the baby?"

"That's right. He got it all worked out. When it'd be best to do it and that. How much to ask for. All that sort of thing, he knows. He's sharp. If he wasn't, he wouldn't be where he is now."

Maureen put the empty bottle on the bed. The baby seemed to be asleep.

"Skinner!"

"What?"

"How'll you know when it's safe to take her back? I mean, how'll you know her Mum and Dad will pay the money and not tell the police or anything?"

"We'll know, don't worry. Smithy reckons she'll break first. The kid's Mum. She'll be the one to say yes, she'll pay up and no business with the cops or marked notes or anything. He'll pull it off, old Smithy will. He knows just when to start being tough. He'll say when we ought to begin saying pay up or else. . . ."

"Or else what?"

"I don't suppose Mrs. Bloody Wilmington would like to think her precious little baby might just possibly never come back. She'd do a lot to be sure she got her back in one piece, I reckon. That's when we get the money and she gets her rotten howling kid back."

"What d'you mean, in one piece?"

"Look, Fatty, I know you're dim, but you can't be that useless. What d'you think's going to happen if they won't pay up? They will, mind you. But just suppose they don't, you don't really think they're going to get away with it, do you?"

"What'll you do with her . . . ?" Maureen whispered.

"Don't ask questions and you won't get told nothing you don't want to hear."

Maureen clutched the baby closer to her and saw Skinner through different, panicky eyes. "You said you wouldn't hurt her!"

"I haven't said anyone's going to hurt her. And you keep quiet or someone'll hurt you for a change," Skinner hissed. But it wasn't much good telling Maureen to keep quiet. The baby, so rashly squeezed by Maureen in her fright, woke up and began to bellow again.

17

Maureen was frightened. When she'd first met Skinner she'd found him a bit scary. He didn't talk much, often only answered Yes or No when you asked him something, sometimes didn't answer at all. She discovered after a time that this wasn't because he hadn't heard, but because he didn't mean to answer. He'd never told her his other name, for instance. She didn't know whether Skinner was his first or last name. Now that he'd said to call him Johnny, she wondered if that was really what he was called. She'd asked but he hadn't said. She didn't know where he came from, whether he had a Mum and a Dad or brothers and sisters. She didn't know what jobs he'd done, didn't know what sort of job he was doing now. She'd been scared by Jakey when she'd met him and seen what he did to the poor little dog. He wouldn't mind if he had to do something bad to anyone, even a baby. She wouldn't let herself really think what Skinner had meant when he'd said that about the baby going back in one piece to her Mum and Dad. Just remembering the way Skinner had said that made her feel a bit sick. Because though she was a nuisance, crying all the time, it wasn't really the baby's fault. And she, Maureen, was looking after her all right. It had been nice when she found she was right about that last bottle, that the baby was crying because she was hungry. If she had the baby a bit longer she'd probably get really good at knowing what she wanted and at keeping her quiet and that, and then Skinner'd be pleased with her and say, "Not bad," when she asked him how she'd done. All the same Maureen did hope the baby's Mum would get anxious quickly and say she'd pay over the money quite soon so that the whole thing could be over and done with and she could go back to being just Skinner's girl friend again.

They went around to the pub on the corner for lunch, leaving the baby in the stroller outside the door where they could keep an eye on her. Maureen thought how queer it would be if someone else stole the baby again.

Mrs. Plum bounced out of her kitchen door as they came back through the door.

"There's a young fellow been 'round here to see you. Said he was a friend of yours. I told him I didn't know where you'd gone and I couldn't say when you'd be back, so he said he'd wait around. He's only been gone just a few minutes," she said to Skinner.

"I'll go and see if I can see him anywhere," he said. He looked at Maureen. "Don't do anything I wouldn't do while I'm gone," he said. When other people said it, it was a joke, you laughed, but when Skinner said it, it was more like a threat. Maureen shivered.

Mrs. Plum said, "Why don't you come into the kitchen and keep me company for a bit? I've got the telly in there, you could watch that if you wanted. You wouldn't be in my way if you wanted to stop there for half an hour or so."

It was warm in Mrs. Plum's kitchen and tidy and clean. Maureen hadn't been in a kitchen like this since . . . for years. Maureen wheeled the baby into it and she never stirred. Mrs. Plum turned on the telly and then she bustled round making cups of tea. The telly flickered, the kettle whistled, there was a comforting smell of roasted meat and stewed apple, and soap. Maureen sat in an old padded basket-chair that creaked every

time she moved. Mrs. Plum was asking her questions. What sort
of business was Mr. Deptford in? How long had she known him
before they married? Did she know the boy who'd come 'round
to see her husband? What sort of work had she done before
she'd had the baby? Maureen tried to answer politely and
carefully but it became more and more difficult. She knew she
wouldn't answer right if Mrs. Plum went on and she got more
and more sleepy, and sure enough, when Mrs. Plum said
suddenly, "Brady Drive! That was where you lived, wasn't it?"
Maureen said quickly, "No!"

"I'm sure that's what you told me," Mrs. Plum said, surprised.

"I never. I never did," Maureen said.

"What was it then, dear? Funny! I could have sworn you said
Brady . . ."

"Wilmington," Maureen said. The moment she'd said it, she
knew she'd made an even worse mistake. Mrs. Plum was looking at her properly now, she'd stopped fussing with the tea and
the cups, and she was staring. But then all she said was, "That's
funny," and didn't go on about it, so Maureen hoped she hadn't
really taken that much notice. When she thought of what
Skinner would say if he knew about it, Maureen felt sick. But
even that thought couldn't keep her eyelids from dropping or
her mind from going all swimmy. When the cups of tea were
ready and Mrs. Plum came over to sit in the other chair, she saw
that Maureen's head had slipped sideways and, like the baby,
she was fast asleep. Mrs. Plum didn't mind. Having a bit of a
sleep in front of the telly was, she thought, the proper thing to
do on a Sunday afternoon.

Upstairs things were not so peaceful. Skinner had found
Jakey and brought him straight up to the bedroom. He didn't
want Maureen in on this conversation.

"How's it going?" Jakey asked, lounging on the unmade bed.

"Bloody kid yells all the time."

"Can't Fatty keep her quiet?"

"Only sometimes."

"Told you she wasn't any good. Hasn't as much brain as a louse. I suppose you picked her for her looks," Jakey said grinning.

"Shut up, will you?"

"Told you you should've got a girl who'd had one herself," Jakey said.

"Like your Sharon?" Skinner said with false sweetness.

"You lay off Sharon," Jakey said.

"More to the point if you did," Skinner said.

"What about the old lady?"

"What old lady?"

"That one that was in the hall when we came in."

"She's the landlady."

"She's all right? Swallowed the story?"

"Why shouldn't she? There's lots of couples moving around with kids. Nothing funny about that."

"Only as long as Fatty doesn't go and say something she shouldn't."

"She won't." Skinner said grimly.

"How can you be sure?"

"She's frightened, that's why. She wouldn't dare."

"You better keep her away from people she can talk to," Jakey told Skinner.

"Yes? That would look like normal, wouldn't it? What am I supposed to do, take my wife and kid to work with me every day so she doesn't get the chance to say anything?"

"I could get Sharon to come around and take her out for the day."

"That's crazy. You know what he said. One girl to take the kid, a different one to look after it. I'd like to see you, after Smithy heard, if you let Sharon come 'round here."

"She says no one saw her take it."

"Where is Sharon?"

"Keeping out of the way just for the moment."

"What about the money?"

"He phoned yesterday."

"So what?"

"He told them two hundred thou. And left them to think it over."

"When'll he phone again?"

"A day or two. You'll stay here?"

"As long as it seems all right."

"You mean as long as your loony bird doesn't open her mouth."

"She won't," Skinner said again.

"Well, keep in touch."

"How? He said. . . ."

"Callbox if you must. If everything's O.K. just stay put and act normal. He'll tell you when you have to do anything." Jakey got up from the bed.

"You coming around tomorrow?" Skinner said.

"Might do. He doesn't want more'n one of us to come to the same place. So if anyone comes it'll have to be me. He says keep off the Club for a bit."

"How're the others doing?"

"Ted's having a fit of the sulks. Don't ask me why."

"Bus?"

"After a new bird. To hear him talk she must be something quite special. Don't you wish you was him?" Jakey said, grinning. He opened the door. "Don't worry about seeing me out. I can find my way," he said. He ran down the stairs and slammed the front door behind him. Mrs. Plum felt the house quiver with the impact and woke, clucking her tongue in disapproval. Poor tired Maureen never heard a thing.

18

Stephen and Vicky and Chris were engaged, that Sunday, in heated argument. It was the same old story, Chris urging action, Stephen and Vicky agreeing that something ought to be done, but unwilling to commit themselves to doing it.

"You'll have to tell the police. Suppose they arrest that girl!" Chris said.

"You tell me why they should believe us any more than Mr. Wilmington did," Stephen said.

"Because . . . you could say you'd seen the girl with the baby. You could tell them what you heard her say."

"And then they say, 'Well where is she then?' What do we say next?"

"He's right, Chris," Vicky said.

"You could give them a description."

"We've got no evidence. We can't prove anything."

"*Oh!*" Chris said, exasperated.

"If only we had some sort of lead. I wouldn't mind trying if we could say where we'd seen those two with the baby. What I hate is going along with a daft story and nothing to back it up."

"But we will have to do something," Vicky said for the tenth time.

"I know we will. Trouble is, what?"

The conversation went round and round in circles. Chris became more and more impatient. Presently she got up from the table in the coffee bar where they'd been sitting half the morning, and said abruptly, "I know what I'd do if it was me, but it isn't, and listening to you just makes me cross. I'm going." She left.

Vicky and Stephen stared at each other across the table.

"Is she really upset?" he asked.

"She won't stay like it. Chris never stays cross for long."

"I'm sorry, though."

"She can't see why we don't rush off and do something at once. She would, you see. She wouldn't stop to think about how people might think she was silly, she'd just know she was right and she'd go and do it. Sometimes I wish I was like that."

To her surprise, Stephen said, "I know. You mean you get the feeling that the more you think about a thing, the more difficult it is to do it." He added, "You sort of see all the things that might happen and you can't make up your mind to start."

"That's it! I didn't know anyone felt like that. Except me."

"Hamlet did."

"Hamlet?" She wondered if he was laughing at her.

"Whether it be
Bestial oblivion, or some craven scruple
Of thinking too precisely on the event
A thought which, quartered, hath but one part wisdom
And ever, three parts coward, I do not know
Why yet I live to say, This thing's to do,"

Stephen said.

"Is that Hamlet?"

"He's wondering why he still hasn't killed his uncle."

"Mm. Say it again."

Stephen repeated it.

"You must know it fantastically well."

"I had to last year. It was the set play for my exams."

"Did you learn it all off by heart?"

"Of course not. Just bits. That wasn't one of the bits we were told to learn, I just liked it because it said how I feel. About not doing things because of thinking about them too much."

Vicky considered this. Then she said, "Funny how he knew all that."

"Who? Hamlet?"

"Not really, Shakespeare, I meant."

"Don't say it!"

"Don't say what?"

"I thought you were going to say what the psychologists always say. How wonderful that Shakespeare knew so much about human behavior when he hadn't had a chance to study modern psychology."

"Is that what your Dad says?"

"It's one of the things he says."

Vicky said, "It must be more difficult to write like that now. I mean because there's such a lot of people knowing things and telling you. Sometimes you get told when you'd rather have found out for yourself."

"Perhaps I shouldn't have told you that piece out of *Hamlet*, then you could have found it out for yourself," Stephen said, teasing her gently.

"Not that sort of thing. I mean, when someone says just what you've been feeling. It's nice to know someone else feels the same."

"There's you and me and Hamlet. That makes three of us."

"It's much easier to be the other sort of person. Like Chris."

"Much. And what's so unfair is that often they're right. They go off and get the thing done, whatever it is, and just because they're that sort of person who hasn't any doubts, they bring it off."

"That's right. Chrissie does. Mum does too. She doesn't take ages trying to work out what'll happen next."

"What about your father?"

He was surprised by the way in which Vicky pounced on this. "What about him? What do you want to know?"

"I only wondered if he was like you. Thinking too much instead of doing whatever it is."

"No he isn't," Vicky said shortly.

"I'm sorry. I didn't mean. . . ."

There was an uncomfortable pause.

"I'm sorry," Stephen said again.

"It's all *right*," Vicky said.

"I honestly didn't mean. . . ."

"I said, it's all *right*."

There was a pause. Then Vicky said, "He isn't my father really."

Stephen stared.

"I'm adopted," Vicky said, with a tremendous effort.

"You mean . . . you're not really Chris's sister?"

"Not by rights." Vicky hated to have to say it.

"But I thought. . . . You said you weren't like your father. . . ."

Vicky said, "How do I know who I'm like?"

Stephen felt Vicky's need to stick to the facts. He realized it wasn't any good trying to get by with only good feeling and sympathy. He said, "Do you know anything about your real parents?"

"My Mum died. Two days after she'd had me." She said it as if it had been a betrayal.

"What happened to you then?"

"Mum—this Mum, that belongs to me and Chris—she was in the bed next to my own Mum and she knew there wasn't anyone else wanted me. And the doctors had told her she couldn't have any more babies. She didn't want to have just the one, so when she went back home from the hospital, she took me too."

Stephen looked at her, sitting aslant him at the table, hunched against the world. "Why do you mind so much?"

"Wouldn't you?"

He thought. Difficult to imagine. He had a longing fancy of how wonderful it would be to be free. Not to feel he must do credit to his analytical father, all intelligence, or become like his frightened mother, browbeaten by that intelligence. But at least he knew what he had to cope with. This girl didn't. He said, "I suppose it could be difficult."

"You don't know who you really are."

"Why can't you just be yourself? That's what's important. Not what your parents were like."

Vicky said impatiently, "That's what everyone says. It's all right for them. They know what sort of family they've come from and what their fathers did and all that. It's all very well to say it doesn't matter. It does when you haven't got it, what other people have. That's all."

Stephen saw what she meant. He found he wanted to say something that wouldn't hurt, that might even help. He said, "I see that. When you do know who your parents are, you sometimes wish you didn't. You feel you'd be freer to be whatever you really wanted instead of having it all mapped out for you beforehand."

"But you do know where you are. And you could be different from what people expect."

"It probably looks easy to you because that's not your problem. For instance, I've got an uncle called Lou."

Vicky suddenly dissolved into giggles. "Loo, he can't be! That's what some people call the toilet!"

"His proper name is Louis, you see."

"Never heard of it."

"Yes, you have. All the French kings were called Louis. Well, a lot of them were."

"Oh! French! Go on anyway."

"The family wasn't French. I don't know why he was called that. What I was going to tell you was that I was always supposed to look exactly like him. When he'd been young, I mean. When I knew him he was bald and a bit fat. He was a great-uncle, you see. And he was really a horrible old man. He was the youngest of a lot of sisters, and they all adored him and sort of hung around saying wasn't he marvelous, and then they used to do the same to me, only not saying I was marvelous, but how like Lou I was, and wasn't it wonderful. And I didn't want to be like Lou. He'd been quite successful in business or something and he'd made a lot of money, but he was the meanest man I've ever met. He never allowed his wife enough money for the housekeeping or her clothes, and when he had to give anyone a present for Christmas or birthdays, he used to look out for something he'd had for ages and pretend he'd got it specially for them. Once he gave my mother an old teapot that hadn't got a spout or a handle and he told her it would look pretty in the garden with a climbing plant growing out of it. When he died it turned out he'd got masses of money. He was just fantastically mean."

Vicky sat and looked at him. She didn't speak.

"So you see. When everyone said I was just like Lou, I felt sort of doomed to be like that. Not just mean, but bald and fat too."

"You aren't yet," Vicky said.

"I'm not bald, but how do you know I'm not mean?"

"Are you?"

Stephen couldn't answer this. He said, "I do see it could be hellish not knowing about your family, too."

"It's not exactly family. It's not knowing about my father," Vicky said.

"Didn't he come to see your mother while she was in the hospital?"

"Mum reckons he probably didn't know anything about me being born."

Stephen wasn't quick enough to conceal the surprise he felt, and Vicky said, "They probably weren't married, Mum thinks."

"Do you mind that too?"

Vicky said, "Not that much. I might have if my real Mum had had me without being married and had given me away. I'd have felt bad about it, then. I used to think only girls who didn't like their babies let them go for adoption, but now. . . . There was this girl in our class last year, had a baby, and everyone told her she ought to have it adopted. . . ."

She stopped.

"What happened?" Stephen asked.

"She did what they said. But she cried. She went on crying. I. . . . I didn't know it was like that. I wouldn't have wanted my own Mum. . . ."

"But your mother . . . I mean . . . well, your and Chris's Mum. She's terribly nice, I thought."

"She's fabulous," Vicky said.

"And you get on with Chris. Don't you?"

Vicky couldn't imagine life without Chris. She nodded.

"You don't know how lucky you are having a sister. I wish to God I'd got brothers or sisters. Or someone."

Vicky, faintly interested, asked, "Why?"

"If you're an only, you're sort of a target. Everything your parents think or feel has to be worked out on you."

"Why does that matter?"

"My mother worries, for instance. If I'm five minutes late home, she's sure I've had an accident. When I was a kid and had the usual sort of illnesses, she always thought I was going to die. And now I'm older, she worries about my exams and about smoking and drugs and sex. All the usual things. If there were more of us, we'd only get a share. As it is, I get the lot."

"I don't think Mum worries like that about anything. I don't think she would even if she had only got the one," Vicky said.

"I still wish there'd been more of us," Stephen said.

Vicky was used, by now, to having boys tell her how lucky she was to have pretty Chris as a sister. She was waiting for Stephen to say, "Chris is really pretty, isn't she?" Instead of which, Stephen said, "I suppose that's why you're so different from Chris."

"You mean why she's pretty and I'm not?" Vicky said, sharply.

"No, I didn't. I meant, you've got different sorts of minds."

"We get the same sort of marks at school."

"I wasn't thinking about that sort of mind. I meant what we were saying before. About thinking about things too much before you do them."

"That's just being stupid," Vicky said.

"No, it isn't. It means you see things Chris wouldn't. No. I didn't mean *that*—not like we see things in flashes. I meant— damn! I don't know how to say it. You're more considering. That's more like it."

Vicky was pleased but not sure what he meant. "I don't see how that helps."

"It's more interesting."

He was embarrassed directly he'd said it. It seemed too personal. He guessed that Vicky was embarrassed too, from the speed with which she followed this remark by saying, "Anyhow, what are we going to do?"

Stephen said slowly, "I think we've got to go to the police."

"But you said all along. . . ."

"I know. And I still don't think they're going to take any notice."

"Then why . . . ?"

"Because it's the only thing we can do. We haven't a thing to go on, so we can't go looking all over the country by ourselves. And I don't want to go back to the parents."

"If only we'd seen where they were."

"I didn't see anything except those two who were talking."

"I didn't either. . . . Wait a minute!"

"What?"

" I did. I did see something. Only I can't remember what."

"That's not much help, then."

"Wait a tick, I almost got it then."

Stephen waited.

"It was behind his head. On the wall."

She shut her eyes.

"A picture. It's a place. Only I don't know it. It's colored. There's a sort of mountain. It's got a flat sort of top, with fire coming out of it."

"A volcano," Stephen said.

"That's right. And it's night. There's some country round the bottom, only I can't see that properly. The frame's black and gold."

She opened her eyes.

"That's all."

"Fantastic. How did you manage to remember that, when you said you couldn't?"

"It was like remembering a dream. You know. You say to yourself you've forgotten it completely, and then something reminds you, and you know you've sort of got a clue, and then suddenly you get it. Little bits at first and then the whole thing. You sort of see it and know that's it."

"I know."

"It's a bit like what we get. You know. The flashes. D'you think they could be like that? Only working backwards?"

"Sorry, I don't get it."

"Well. You know how you remember things. They sort of come into your mind when you're not expecting anything?"

"Mm."

"Why shouldn't it work the other way around? Sometimes. So you remember things that are going to happen, instead of what did?"

There was a silence.

"You think it's all stupid," Vicky said, disappointed.

"No I don't. I think it's brilliant."

"Do you really?"

"Because we don't really know about time. I mean, my father says we just think of it moving one way. You know. Forwards. But it could just as well go both ways. Backwards sometimes. It's something to do with causality."

"What's that?"

"I don't understand it really. Something like if you do something today, something different happens tomorrow, because of what you did. So if you don't believe in time moving the way we think it does, you don't really know whether there was a cause or not."

Vicky thought about this. "If time didn't work like we think, it wouldn't matter whether we went to the police or not. I mean, nothing we did would matter. Would it?"

She surprised Stephen again by her quickness. "I suppose not."

"Do you think that might be how we see things?"

"Could be. Gosh, I wish it was. If it was really just that, I wouldn't feel so—"

"So what?"

"So peculiar."

"You're not the only one," Vicky said.

They looked at each other.

Stephen said, "That picture of the volcano."

"I'm afraid it doesn't help much."

"At any rate it's something we could tell the police."

"We have got to tell them?" Vicky asked.

"We've got to, Vicky. Even if it isn't any good. We'd feel awful if we didn't. I would anyway."

"You said they wouldn't believe us."

"They won't."

"And you said we hadn't got anything . . . what was it?"

"Positive."

"Positive, then. To tell them."

"I've thought of one thing. They've probably got heaps of pictures of people who've been had up for something or other. If we could see them we might recognize one of those two."

"I wish I could remember what it is that's funny about his hair," Vicky said.

"It'll suddenly hit you when you see his photograph. You'll say, 'That's him, with the rabbit's ears sticking up through his hair.'"

"You're crazy!" Vicky said, laughing.

"Come on. For one thing, Chris is never going to let up till we've done it."

"We won't say anything about flashes. We just say we've seen a couple with a baby," Stephen said, meeting Vicky that same afternoon by pre-arrangement.

"How would we have known it was that baby? There's heaps of men and girls with babies."

"Didn't you hear the news this morning? They're asking anyone who's noticed anyone behaving peculiarly with a baby to tell them."

"What'll we have for this peculiar behavior?" Vicky asked.

"Suppose we said we'd been there when that girl took the baby?"

"Wouldn't they want to know why we didn't say so before? It's three days."

"It's going to be very complicated," Stephen said gloomily.

"We could tell them what we heard. About not hurting it. That's peculiar enough."

"That's right! We could."

"But it wouldn't have to be in that room, because we don't know where it is."

"It could have been in a café like the one you and Chris go to."

"Sitting at the next table and quarrelling."

"Only we'd have to make up which café it was."

"What about a park? We could make it Kensington Gardens the day it happened."

"But they wouldn't. Would they? Just go and sit on a park bench just near where they'd taken the baby from?"

"I know! A bus. Or a train. We could've been sitting in the seat in front of them. . . ."

"And heard them quarrelling and not thought much about it till now. . . ."

"Till we heard the appeal on the radio this morning."

"We'll have to make up our minds where the bus was going. We've got to have it all worked out. Or the train."

"Train," Vicky said.

"Why?"

"Because if it was a bus and we say which one, they could get hold of the conductor, and he could say there wasn't a baby on it then. But no one could say there wasn't a baby on a tube train."

"That's brilliant," Stephen said.

"Let's say the Victoria Line. That goes a long way, it could be anywhere."

"No, you can't."

"Why not?"

"The way the cars are built. You can't sit in front of anyone."

"Which line, then?"

"I think Northern. It's longer than the Victoria. Anyway it isn't much of a clue, because they might not have been going to a station on that line. Like us. We changed on to the Piccadilly at Leicester Square. They could've changed too."

It took time. As Stephen said, it was complicated working out a story that held together, that couldn't be faulted. But when it was ready it sounded a good deal more credible than the account of the flashes.

"How are we going to explain that we aren't absolutely sure of what they look like?" Stephen said finally.

"If they were sitting behind us, we'd only have sort of looked at them when we got out. You don't notice much, looking quick, like that," Vicky said.

They'd rung 999—"I've always wanted to," Vicky said, and Stephen said, "Go on, then. Have fun!"—they were put through to something called Information and asked questions which seemed to them to have very little to do with what they had to say. Their names, their addresses, the names of their parents. Their ages, their schools. "What about the maiden name of my grandmother?" Stephen said impatiently to the sound over the instrument of the scratching ballpoint taking down all particulars.

"Pardon?" said the voice at the other end, and Stephen said, "Sorry. Nothing. Sorry."

"Would you be able to go to the Kensington station?" the voice asked.

"Which station? High Street or . . ."

"The police station. Earl's Court Road. Thirty-one bus goes right past it. The Detective Chief Superintendent in charge of the case is working there. He might want to put a few questions to you."

"You mean go there now?" Stephen asked.

"Where are you speaking from?"

"Hampstead Heath. Well, Southend Green actually. . . ."

"Should take you about forty minutes. No, Sunday, a bit more. I'll ring Kensington and say you'll be over, shall I?"

"I suppose so," Stephen said, but the line was already dead.

In the Kensington police station they found a young, dark-haired sergeant at the counter expecting them. He asked the same questions and wrote down the answers, but very quickly, searching them with bright dark eyes, smiling occasionally at Vicky. From him they were passed on to a higher-up officer in a room with several desks, walls covered with maps and charts. "It's like cops and robbers!" Vicky whispered, and Stephen whispered back, "Of course. They do their homework." Here they sat silent while a big burly man with knobbly knuckles and curly brown hair, so exuberant and wiry it seemed trying to become airborne, read through the notes brought up by the dark-haired sergeant from the front counter. Behind them a woman police officer sat at one of the desks, relaxed but alert. Here, at last, they told their story, almost without interruption; the burly detective sergeant asked the fewest possible questions, never interrupted, listened intently. Stephen, who did most of the talking, felt that beneath the wiry hair, there was a critical mind, weighing up every statement, watching for inaccuracies and uncertainties. It was nerve-racking, as bad as an examination. Stephen could tell from the way she fidgeted that Vicky was nervous, though she was all right when she was actually answering a question. She answered straight and short, no hesitation. He was proud of her. After what seemed a long time, wiry-hair looked across at the woman officer and said, "Chief Superintendent Price'll want to hear this," and she nodded back, "Yes." So on to another room and another listener. This time he was in plain clothes, a tall lean man with graying hair and a lined face stamped with fatigue. More questions. Innumerable, endless questions about every detail of that train journey, every event that had led up to that key line, "You said you wouldn't hurt her!" Just as well they'd agreed on their story, Stephen thought, and just as well too they hadn't come with the unbelievable truth. At least now they were being taken seriously. But it was exhausting, keeping a watch on everything you said, trying to make sure you didn't contradict yourself. After more than half an hour of it, Stephen's brain felt woolly, he found he was taking longer over each answer, his thinking was confused. Price must have noticed. He stopped suddenly, in the middle of a sentence and asked one of the waiting sergeants to bring tea. It was hot and strong and sweet and did Stephen a lot of good. While he was drinking it, Price asked. "You'd recognize those two again, would you?"

"I'm not sure. We really only just glanced at them," Stephen said.

"Would you?" Price asked Vicky.

"I might."

"I'd like to take you along to the Yard and show you some pictures we keep there. It needn't take long."

"Right away?" Stephen asked, dismayed. He'd thought their ordeal must be nearly at an end.

"Yes. Is anyone going to worry if you don't get home for another hour or so? You could ring up if you like."

They were driven very fast through the empty Sunday streets to St. James's Park, signed in at the entrance of New Scotland Yard's imposing block, taken by Price to see the officer in charge of the "pictures." "Witness albums. That's what we call them. Rogues' Gallery's what you probably know them as," the competent, small, carroty-haired officer said, and then started asking his own questions. He wanted detailed descriptions of the man and the girl with the baby. Age? Color of eyes, hair, complexion; height. Stephen looked quickly at Vicky, hoping she'd remember they were supposed only to have seen the pair sitting down. Fat, thin, medium? Heavily or slightly built? Shape of eyebrows, nose, mouth? Outline of face? It was like feeding information into a computer, you could almost see the cogs turning and the counters falling under the carroty hair. And the result was amazing. The photographs Stephen and Vicky were shown were all of faces not unlike those two they'd seen. Muddling, to have to look at so many so much the same, and yet there were very few over which they hesitated. One or two Stephen looked at twice, girls with enormous dark rings around their eyes, Cupid's Bow mouths and long hair that was so curly it was almost frizzy, but not quite. There were plenty of them, but none of them dead right. He was examining one to try to define what it was that made her different from the girl he'd seen, when Vicky exclaimed, and the sergeant and Stephen moved over to her and looked at the picture she was pointing to.

"Is that him?" Stephen asked.

"I think so. It's like what I remember."

"You're right, he has got funny hair."

The face that looked up at them was narrow and bony. The

eyes were a little too close together, the nose was small and pointed above a tight, spiteful mouth. The hair, which was sparse, grew in tufts, as thin as a newborn baby's in some places on the scalp, thicker in others. It looked, Stephen thought, moth-eaten and rather nasty.

"That's the one you fancy?" the sergeant said. He looked up the name and read it out. "James Henry Purfitt. Armed robbery with violence, threatening behavior. Had an address in Walthamstow five years ago. Did a stretch of three years. Nothing definite since. Suspected of being in with a lot of boys who ran a protection racket, but it wasn't proved against him."

"Does it sound as if it could have been him?" Vicky asked.

"Can't tell. You'd have to talk to one of the officers who knows him. Doesn't look very pleasant to me, but you never know. You'd swear to the identification, would you, Miss?"

"I think it's him. Only I didn't look at him for long."

"Supposed identification, we'll call it. Well, thank you, Miss. We'll keep in touch. If there's anything new comes up, we'll let you know. If there should be a question on another identification, we can find you at this address, can we?"

They left the Yard convinced that they'd only been half-believed and that they wouldn't hear any more. It all seemed very flat and unsatisfactory. But at least Chris could no longer reproach them. Vicky told her as they went to bed, after an evening made uncomfortable by the necessity of inventing yet another story to explain how she'd come to be out most of the day without warning and without Chris. Mrs. Stanford was on edge, unusual in that comfortable woman, and Mr. Stanford was sharp. He told Vicky off for coming in late, which was fair enough. She took that in good part, but floundered when he wanted to know whom she'd been with. She told him, Stephen, and that they'd been for a walk round Parliament Square and hadn't noticed the time. She said she was sorry, but it didn't help. Mr. Stanford wanted to know why she couldn't go around with a boy of her own sort, like Chris did. Chris began to defend Stephen and there was the making of a row. Mrs. Stanford stopped it by saying she had a headache and was going to bed and that the girls had better go up too. They left Mr. Stanford sitting gloomily in front of the television. Vicky couldn't remember a more thundery evening.

Chris's reaction to the great news was disappointing too. She was pleased, but not as much pleased as Vicky had expected. She said, "Good. That's marvelous," but stopped there, not asking the questions Vicky wanted to answer, and without any of the warm sympathy and bounce that she generally showed. Vicky was forced to tell the whole story straight off without the interruption of eager questions. Like this it seemed short and bald and very inconclusive.

"Aren't you pleased we went like you said?" she asked at the end.

"'Course I am. You had to, didn't you?"

"Stephen said we had to."

Silence.

"Chris?"

"What?"

"You angry we didn't ask you to come too? Stephen thought if there was the three of us again, like when we went to that house, they wouldn't listen."

"No. I don't mind."

"But you're glad we went?"

"Told you I was."

They were in bed by this time. Chris lay with her back to Vicky. She picked up a book and made as if she were going to read.

"Chris. What's the matter?"

"Why should anything be the matter?"

"You sound different, that's why. *Are* you cross with me?"

"No, I'm not."

"I would have told you before we went, only there wasn't a chance. Dad was there all the time, and you know how he is about Stephen."

"It doesn't matter. I guessed anyway."

"What did you do while we were there?"

"I went out."

"With Paul?"

No answer.

"With Paul, Chrissie?"

Chris said, "Turn off the light, Vicky, will you? I think I've caught Mum's headache." Vicky turned off the light, but couldn't go to sleep at once. And she listened in the darkness to Chris's long deep breaths and couldn't make up her mind whether they were muffled sobs. Once she said, "Chris?" but there was no answer. She lay awake for what seemed like hours.

Mrs. Plum sometimes treated herself to a glass of port or half a pint of Guinness in the pub on the corner at the end of the day. She had cronies there with whom she gossiped about the weather and the local characters. Other middle-aged friends of hers exchanged their views on the Government and the shocking prices of everything in the shops and about their grown-up children and their precious grandchildren, and they swapped memories, often well-edited so that they became more impressive and more glamorous, or more terrible than the real facts would have been. Most of them were only semi-retired, like Mrs. Plum; they let lodgings, they had part-time jobs in the shops, one was a lollipop man and several were traffic wardens. They talked a great deal and they didn't listen very carefully to what the others had to say, but there was a general feeling of amiability and good will which prevented them from interrupting each other's stories too often or engrossing the general attention for too long. And by and large they absorbed, without listening, the trend of the information, so that everyone was always up to date with the condition of each other's ailments and children's marital status and number of offspring. Since most of Mrs. Plum's tenants were single ladies and gentlemen who went out to work all day, these meetings provided her with the company she loved. During the long day with no one to speak to, she looked forward to the evenings when she could find relief in the spate of words which had to be dammed up so many long working hours.

This Monday evening, Mrs. Hedges had a long story about her sister's husband's interesting operation in one of the big London hospitals. What the surgeon had said and what Mrs. Hedges' sister had told him to his face, and the appearance of whatever it was they'd taken out of his stomach, occupied the first half hour of pleasurable horror. Then Mrs. Morley wanted to tell them about the customer she'd served in the department store where she worked who had tried to get out of the store without paying. And Mr. Griggs, the elderly widower, who was supposed by the other ladies to have a soft spot for Mrs. Plum, wanted to talk about some bill that was just going to be put through Parliament and made law; he got very indignant about it, and Mrs. Morley joined in and there was quite a tussle between them. After which it was Mrs. Plum's turn to relate anything of interest in her life; but she felt that her tenants and even the happy married lives of her two daughters were rather small beer after shouting surgeons and dishonest shoppers, so she only just mentioned that she'd let her front double on the first floor to a young couple with a baby, and that the baby cried a lot and the girl didn't seem to know the first thing about looking after it, and then she was ready to move on to more general topics. But it was, surprisingly, Mr. Griggs who took her up, reminding her of her duty as a citizen to keep abreast of the news and to relate it to her own life.

"What about this young couple, then? You been listening to the news tonight?"

"Not tonight, I didn't. Tell you the truth I was upstairs seeing to the drains. The cistern of the toilet's been overflowing again and there I was standing on the seat, if you'll pardon the expression, trying to get the valve to close off when it should, like my son-in-law told me to."

"You didn't hear the six o'clock news then?"

"That's the radio, isn't it? No, I didn't. I watch the telly. I like seeing the chap who's telling it. Makes it seem more as if it mattered."

"But this was yesterday's."

"Sunday? No. Six o'clock I'd got over to my eldest daughter's place. They don't watch much. There's always kiddies about, see? Why, what'd it say?"

"About this baby that got snatched from its pram."

"Yes, I did hear about that. Dreadful thing, isn't it? And I was just saying to young Mrs. Deptford, that's the girl in my front double, I don't know how anyone could! What a dreadful thing to do, I said to her, suppose it was your little Linda, I said, whatever would you do?"

"Didn't you say this girl didn't seem to know how to look after her baby?"

"That's right. How the hospital ever come to let her . . ."

"You ought to tell the police," Mr. Griggs surprisingly said.

Mrs. Plum was shocked. "Go to the police for a thing like that?"

"Mr. Griggs means she may be treating it really badly. Battering, they call it," Mrs. Morley said.

"No, I don't. Though there's that to think of . . ." Mr. Griggs said.

"Then what do you mean about the police? I'd have thought it wasn't their job to see that a girl knows how to handle her own baby. . . ."

"Ah!" Mr. Griggs said with immense meaning.

"What's 'Ah!'?"

"How do you know it is her own baby? That's what 'Ah' is."

"But why ever . . .?" Mrs. Plum began, when Mrs. Hedges, always rather inclined to do everyone else's talking for them, cut in.

"What Fred's saying, Mary, is how do you know this isn't that baby everyone's looking for, that was taken from her pram in Kensington last week?"

"I suppose you haven't seen that baby's birth certificate, have you?" Mr. Griggs asked.

"No, of course I haven't. When a young couple come to take a room and they've got a baby with them that they say's theirs, I don't go asking for certificates."

"Did the girl say where she'd had the baby?"

"Said she'd had it in hospital in Birmingham."

"She tell you what sort of time she had with it?"

"No . . . Now I come to think of it she didn't say much. And whatever hospital it was, they ought to be ashamed of theirselves, letting her go out with a baby and not knowing the first thing about how to look after it."

"That's the point. She probably never did. What sort of a girl is she?" Mrs. Hedges asked.

"She's a poor soppy thing. Doesn't look to me like a girl who'd go and do a thing like that. Not enough guts, and not bad either. Tell you the truth, I'm sorry for her," Mrs. Plum said.

"She must be wicked if she took the baby," Mrs. Hedges said.

"She might have been made to. What's the husband like?" Mr. Griggs asked.

"Now there you may be right. I don't much take to him. He's quite polite. Speaks quite well. But I don't like his looks. He's what I'd call the ferretty type."

"Carroty?" Mrs. Hedges asked.

"I said, ferretty. I don't know what color hair he's got, he's always got a hat on when I see him."

"Not in the house?" Mrs. Morley said.

"In the house as well as out. I remember the first time I noticed it, I wondered if he was bald. Being a young man he mightn't want anyone to know."

"How long have they been with you, Mary?" Mr. Griggs asked.

"Moved in last Thursday evening. He—Mr. Deptford—he'd been along in the morning and said how his wife was coming down from Birmingham that evening with the baby. He took the room, said how much he liked it, and then went off to fetch her from the station, he said."

"Which day was it the baby was taken?" Mr. Griggs asked, and Mrs. Hedges answered at once, "It was last Thursday, that's right, because I was up in Oxford Street for the late night shopping, and when I come back and Julie told me I said, There now, I said, I might have been in Kensington myself, I did think of going on there if I couldn't get what I wanted in Oxford Street. I might have been right there and seen it happen, I said. I've never been so shocked in my life!"

"Anything else suspicious about them?" Mr. Griggs asked Mrs. Plum.

"I don't see that the girl's not knowing how to look after the baby's all that suspicious," Mrs. Morley objected.

"When she's arrived out of nowhere the very day the baby was lost?" Mrs. Hedges said.

"There's plenty of girls don't know how to look after babies and plenty of them probably moved one day last week."

"All right, there may be. What I'm saying is, Mary ought to go to the police. In the news tonight they sent out an appeal to anyone who's noticed anything funny going on with a baby."

"I shouldn't have thought they'd be very impressed by hearing there's a mother can't stop her baby crying," Mrs. Morley rather acidly said.

"Trouble with you, Marge, you've no imagination," Mrs. Hedges said.

"It's true I'm not always seeing things that aren't there, or thinking things mean something special when anyone with a bit of common sense can see they don't," Mrs. Morley replied.

"Wait a minute! There's one thing we don't know, and it could make all the difference. That baby that was snatched, was it a girl or a boy? Because if the kid in Mary's rooms is the other one, then we're getting all steamed up about nothing, aren't we?" Mr. Griggs said, happy to be able to interrupt.

"It's a girl," Mrs. Hedges said at once.

"And what's this one that cries all the time?" Mr. Griggs asked Mrs. Plum.

"She's a girl too. Linda. Pretty little thing."

"Like the picture in the papers? You've seen them? They've been in the papers every day since."

"I never thought. . . . Yes, I suppose it could be the same. Only Linda, she's got more hair."

"That picture they had of her was taken more than a month ago. She'd have changed quite a bit since then," Mrs. Hedges said.

"You really should go to the police, Mary," Mr. Griggs urged her.

"Suppose it was her and you didn't go! You'd never forgive yourself," Mrs. Hedges added.

"If it was me, I shouldn't do anything in a hurry. Why don't you ask them a few questions and see what they say?" Mrs. Morley said.

"If they're innocent, they'll have nothing to hide," Mrs. Hedges said.

"It wouldn't be very nice for them, though, would it? Being questioned by the police and that," Mrs. Plum said. She thought of that poor girl fretting over the baby that she didn't know a thing about. She didn't want to get the girl into trouble. She'd already reckoned it was a runaway match and that more than likely they weren't properly married. They hadn't done her any harm, she didn't want to make more difficulties for them.

"I'll come with you to the police station around the corner if you like," Mrs. Hedges said.

"What, tonight?"

"No time like the present," Mrs. Hedges said, ready to get up and go any moment. But her attempt at hurry had just the opposite effect to what she'd intended. Mrs. Plum settled herself more firmly in her seat and shook her head. "Not now, I'm not going. I'll have to think about it, first."

"I'll come 'round tomorrow morning and go with you, then."

"No thanks, Pat. If I decide I ought to go, I'm quite capable of going on my own. But I haven't made up my mind yet. I might do what Marge said, just have a few words with the girl and see how she takes it."

"Another Guinness while you're thinking it over?" Mr. Griggs suggested. But Mrs. Plum didn't want to be put under any more pressure, and she left the three of them discussing the rights and wrongs of the case and went home. As she let herself into the house, she heard the baby crying again. The sound pushed her a fraction nearer the decision she'd got to take.

The next morning, at twenty-five minutes past ten, Mrs. Plum was seated in her local police station, telling the superintendent her story. She was relieved that it was heard with dead serious-ness, and flattered, though also rather alarmed, at having it all taken down by a very young police officer with steel-rimmed glasses, who sat behind her and scribbled away as she talked. She told the superintendent about the Deptfords' arrival on the Thursday evening. She told how her friends the night before had reminded her about the missing baby and had told her she ought to go to the police. She told how she hadn't wanted to do anything in a hurry. She did hope if it was all a false alarm they wouldn't make trouble for the poor girl, who was so tired she couldn't hardly stand, and who didn't look like the sort of girl to go snatching other people's babies, and who certainly didn't mean to be unkind to Linda, seemed even quite fond of her, only clumsy! All thumbs! And not too bright with it.

"Were the couple in the house when you came out this morning?" the Superintendent asked her.

"I didn't hear him go out. Yesterday he went off to work about half-past eight, but I don't know about this morning."

"What time did you leave the house?"

"Let's see. I did my bit of washing-up because I like to leave the place tidy. Then I went out to do my shopping, nice and early. See? That'd have taken me half an hour. No, more. I had to wait at the vegetable shop. Then I went up and did the rooms of my two gentlemen who go out all day. Must have been around half-past nine when I come out of my front door."

"Was the girl there with the baby when you came out?"

"She was when I went to do my shopping. The stove for that room's out on the landing, see? And she was there heating up the baby's bottle."

"Did you speak to her?"

"Asked her how she'd slept. Because the baby was crying again last night, so I thought. . . ."

"Did you have any other conversation with her?"

"I may just have asked her if she was quite comfortable. Something like that," Mrs. Plum said.

"You didn't mention your suspicions about the baby?"

"Nothing like that," Mrs. Plum said, in rather too much of a hurry. She didn't want to tell them she'd asked Mrs. Deptford about that street name again, and she'd repeated "Wilmington."

The Superintendent sent for the police car, and he and Mrs. Plum rode through the streets in it back to Magfontein Road. There was a plainclothes man and woman with them, and the car stopped in Shelley Lane, around the corner, and Mrs. Plum had to go in first with the policewoman, with the others watching from the end of the street in the car to make sure that no one got away. Mrs. Plum opened the front door and she knew in a minute, as you do know with a house you've lived in for a time, that it was empty. She went up the stairs and saw the door of the front bedroom open and the mess inside. Just to make sure, she said, "Mrs. Deptford? Mrs. Deptford, dear?" But there was no answer as she'd known there wouldn't be, and she went downstairs and told the young policewoman waiting in the hall.

"Sure they're not just gone out?" she said, very neat and trim and not looking like what she was at all, wearing a red miniskirt and a tight white top that any girl might have liked to be seen in.

"All the cupboards are empty. And the baby's things aren't there."

"The stroller? Where did they keep that?"

"Upstairs in their room. It was a folding one. That's gone too."

It was, Mrs. Plum thought, a bit of a do. In a way she wished she'd never made up her mind to go to the police. If she'd known what they were going to do to her front double, turning everything inside out, testing for fingerprints, photographing, spending the whole day there, she might not have. And the questions were worse. She was taken to another police station, in Kensington, and spent the whole afternoon there with a new chap, quicker and more of a gentleman than the other, looking at photographs of boys and girls, hundreds and hundreds of them, till she got so tired she felt like picking any one of them and saying, "That's her," just so she could stop. She had to tell her story a dozen times, with different bits of it being picked on each time for her to be asked about. They gave her cups of tea and biscuits and they were quite polite, but she got tireder and tireder. The bit they always came back to, again and again, was what she'd said to young Mrs. Deptford that morning before she'd gone out for her shopping. She stuck to it for ever so long that all she'd said was to ask if everything was all right. What had the girl answered to that? She'd said she was all right, only tired because of the baby crying again. Hadn't Mrs. Plum said any more after that?

No, she didn't want to stand there gossiping, she wanted to get her shopping done.

She hadn't asked the girl any more about the baby?

She might just have asked how Linda was this morning.

What did the girl say to that?

"If I asked, I suppose she said she was all right," Mrs. Plum said carefully.

"Did you ask?"

"I might have."

"You were a bit puzzled in your own mind about her, weren't

you? You were wondering whether you should come to see us to mention your suspicions."

"If I'd known all the fuss there was going to be, I'd have kept my mouth shut," Mrs. Plum said smartly.

"And let them get away with snatching the baby and possibly putting its life in danger?"

"Who said its life was in danger?" Mrs. Plum demanded.

"The parents are very wealthy people. The usual thing in these cases is a demand for money. If it isn't paid, the child's life is threatened."

"I'm sure that girl wouldn't do anything to harm it, poor little thing."

"What about the man?"

"I didn't see much of him."

"And you didn't like much of what you did see?"

"Well. He spoke very nicely, to me, he did."

"But not to the girl?"

He was quick, this one, Mrs. Plum had to admit. "I did think once or twice she acted as if she was frightened."

"What do you mean?"

She hadn't really meant to tell this part of the story, but it came out. "There was one night the baby cried and cried, and she went and sat in the toilet with it. One of my lodgers, a Mr. Bodman he's called, he found her there next morning. Asleep on the floor she was. When I asked her, she said she didn't want the baby to wake Johnny. That was what she called him."

"She never said anything to you about him? About how they'd met? Anything like that?"

"Only about her wedding. According to her they'd had a big wedding. But she did say not to talk to him about it, and I thought, that's funny. Why should a young chap mind having his wedding spoken about? If it really happened, that's to say."

"You think they weren't really married?"

"I didn't say so, did I?"

"So you were wondering about them even before your friends talked to you about the Wilmington baby last night?"

"I was and I wasn't. One minute I'd think everything seemed quite ordinary and the next I'd find myself really. . . ." She stopped suddenly and sighed. "I guess I better tell you."

"There's something else?"

"It was the way she used to contradict herself, sometimes. When I asked her where she'd been lodging in Birmingham, because I've got a sister there and I know some parts of it quite well. She told me the name of the street she lived in, and then the next time she said something different."

"What was the name she said, do you remember?"

"Funny name it was the first time. Second time she said that name, same as the baby's."

"Linda?"

"Wilmington. That's what she said."

"She said *Wilmington?*"

"That's right."

By the time they let her go home, Mrs. Plum felt as if she'd been put through a mangle. She felt that she hadn't any private thoughts, let alone private life. She also felt sorry for that poor girl, who wasn't bad, but hadn't a clue. The only thing that comforted her was thinking what a lot she'd have to tell Pat and Marge and Fred at the pub that night. It wasn't every day they'd pinned down a kidnapping between them. She was fair, Mrs. Plum was. She knew she'd never have done anything about it on her own.

22

When Maureen had got back into the bedroom that same morning with the bottle ready for the baby, Skinner was up and dressed and waiting for her.

"What've you been saying to that old bag?"

"I didn't say anything. She asked about the baby, that's all."

"I heard what she said. What I'm asking you is, what did you tell her about where we come from?"

"I said Birmingham, like you told me, Skinner." Maureen didn't want to have to look at his face, it frightened her.

"You said something else, you must have. Yesterday, was it? She was on at you just now about the street you'd been in."

Maureen said, "No, I never," but she hadn't finished saying it before Skinner hit her hard on the face. She called out, but his hand was over her mouth and he put his face right up to hers and whispered. "If you so much as squeak I'll do you in."

She couldn't help crying, her face hurt so much.

"Now then. Going to tell me? Or do I have to hit you again?"

She shook her head and he took the hand off her mouth.

"What did you say?"

It was difficult to talk out of her bruised mouth. Maureen said, "She kept on asking where we'd been. I had to say something."

"So you had to say Wilmington? You bloody stupid bitch! You yapping big mouth! You . . . you slobbering freak . . ." he swore at her horribly. Lots of words Maureen hadn't even heard before. She didn't say anything, partly because it hurt to speak, partly because she was hoping he hadn't heard the worst of it. It had been bad enough to say the baby's name, though it was a thing anyone might have done after seeing it in the papers such a lot. But if he'd known that she'd first said Brady Drive, Maureen thought he'd have killed her.

"Come on. Don't stand there like that. We've got to get out," Skinner said.

"Can't I just . . . the feed's all ready. . . ."

"Damn the feed. Don't you understand? We've got to go! We can't stay here. She's probably going around to the station to jabber about us now."

"No she hasn't. She was going shopping."

"Get moving, will you? Pack everything up and make it double quick or you'll get another on the other side of your stupid face. Hurry, can't you?"

Maureen hurried. She didn't understand, but she was frightened enough to do what she was told. They packed everything. Fortunately there wasn't much. When they'd got everything— except the diapers hanging on the airer in the scullery, and Skinner said they'd got to leave those—into the big blue suitcase, Skinner went around the room wiping everything with his handkerchief. He wiped the ends of the bed, the knobs on the chest of drawers, the electric light switch, the ash tray. Maureen said stupidly, "What're you doing that for?" but he only said, "Finished? Now don't touch anything, see? And keep the kid quiet while I go and see what's up."

The bottle was nearly cold, but Maureen didn't know any other way of keeping the baby quiet than giving it to her. She supposed that was wrong too, but there wasn't any choice with Skinner like this. He'd gone out of the door quite ordinarily, not especially trying to be quiet. Maureen had heard his steps along the passage and a minute later she heard the toilet flush. He came back and shut the door behind him and whispered again.

"She's back upstairs. You go down and back straight out. If she sees you, or anyone else, say you've got to go out this early to go to the doctor. Go along the street to the left and round the corner and wait at the bus stop. I've got to get the case out without anyone seeing. I'll bring the stroller down for you, you just put the kid in it and scoot. And mind! If you act stupid, or say anything, you've had it. You won't have to worry about what happens next, because there won't be any next for you."

They went down the stairs. Maureen could hardly see to get down, she was so scared. She went first, carrying the baby with the bottle still in its mouth, and Skinner came just behind her with the carry-cot and the stroller. Maureen could hear the whine of the vacuum cleaner from the second floor, and over and above its noise, Mrs. Plum whistling a tune off key. Maureen had noticed she always did that when she had the cleaner on, as if she couldn't bear not to be making more noise than anything else going. As they reached the bottom of the stairs the cleaner's whine stopped and Maureen stopped too, petrified. She felt Skinner's hand on her back, pushing her on, and the next minute the cleaner started up again. At the front door, Skinner opened the latch with his handkerchief around his fingers. Outside he opened up the wheeling part of the stroller and put the cot in it, and Maureen laid the baby in it. Skinner gestured one way, Maureen supposed it was left, like he'd said, then he went back into the house, and Maureen started along the street, looking back over her shoulder all the time as if she expected someone to come along and grab her any minute, which was how she felt.

The bus stop was only a little way along the next road. There were quite a lot of people waiting there, mostly on their way to work, reading newspapers and peering along the road to see if the next bus was theirs. Maureen waited in the line and presently found she was at the front of it, only of course she couldn't get on a bus because she didn't know which one Skinner meant to take. She had to shake her head when the lady behind her asked her if she didn't want to get on the number 917 and offered to help her with the chair, but she didn't say anything, she was too frightened of saying something wrong. She wondered what Skinner would do if, when he came, he found she'd got on a bus and just gone away. She'd have liked to do that, to get out of this mess. She didn't want to have to look after the baby any longer and now she was really frightened of Skinner, she didn't want to stay with him. She'd leave the baby in its cot and just get on a bus and never come back and never tell anyone what had happened. At this moment it seemed the most beautiful thing she could possibly ever do.

Another bus drew up beside her, and the man behind her waited for a moment to see if she was going to climb on. Maureen's foot actually went forward an inch, she wanted to go off so badly. But she didn't follow it. She knew that if she did that, Skinner would hit her again and harder. She didn't really think he'd do her in as he'd threatened, but then there was the baby. If she left the baby, what would Skinner do with it? He didn't mind what happened to it so long as he got the money he was after. Maureen thought he might quite easily do something really bad to it. Perhaps just leave it somewhere to die. Or hit it hard because it cried and woke him up. Maureen fingered the side of her face. It hurt a lot and it was coming up in great lumps. If Skinner hit the baby like that, he might kill it. Maureen stayed waiting at the bus stop.

Just then she saw Skinner. He was coming quickly along the street, carrying the big suitcase. He didn't stop at the bus stop but just said over his shoulder, "Come on!" and went on walking. Maureen hurried after him with the stroller.

"Aren't we going to get on a bus?" she asked, breathless.

"After you've been standing there for everyone to look at? 'Course not. Train," Skinner said.

"Where to? Where're we going to, Skinner?"

"Oxford Street."

"*Oxford* Street? What for? What for are we going to Oxford Street?"

"You'll find out," Skinner said, walking quicker than ever toward the tube station so that Maureen had almost to run to keep anywhere near him.

She didn't understand. She didn't understand why they left the stroller in the underground part of Oxford Circus station, and she had to carry the baby. Or why Skinner put the suitcase into one of the lockers there and dropped the key down a grating in the road when they came up. She didn't understand at first why they went into one of the big chain stores or why Skinner should be buying her clothes at all when he was mad at her. He bought clothes for the baby too. Then he bought two shopping bags and put the clothes in one, and told her to go to the Ladies and change. She was to change all her top gear and the baby's too. She wasn't to keep on anything that showed, not even shoes. She was to meet him by the ticket office back in the station in ten minutes. "And if you aren't there I'll come and find you. I know what you look like even if no one else will. If you know what's good for you, you'd better be there," Skinner said, pushing his face against hers and with that dreadful look that Maureen couldn't bear. She said, "Yes, Skinner," and went off with the baby to look for a Ladies where she could change.

It wasn't easy, changing in one of those little cubicles, and with the baby too. When she came out and saw herself in a mirror, she was surprised to see how different she looked. Before, she'd been wearing a green coat Skinner had bought for her and a red dress underneath and no hat. Now she had a brown sort of trouser suit, a bit too long in the leg, she'd had to turn over the elastic hem at the waist, and a big floppy brown hat she could hardly see out from under. And the baby was wearing a suit thing, blue with a cardigan over the top. She'd been all wrapped up in a shawl before. Maureen quite liked herself in the trouser suit, except that it didn't do anything to slim her down. But it was always nice to have new clothes. She felt better as she went back to the tube station to meet Skinner.

At first she hardly recognized him. He'd got on a denim suit, cut very tight, and he'd changed the soft hat he always wore for a cap with a peak. He'd got a pair of glasses too, with thin wire rims. They made him look clever somehow, like a teacher or something like that. He was waiting for her, she'd been slower than him, but then she'd had two of them to change, hadn't she? He didn't say anything, just started walking down the escalator back toward the trains. Maureen said, "Where'll we go now, Skinner?" several times, but he didn't answer. Maureen said, "What about the baby's feeds, Skinner?" and he didn't answer that either. In the train he sat reading a paper he'd got hold of and Maureen sat holding the baby, who'd been lulled into quiet by the motion of the train, glad of a chance to get some of the weight off her arms. While the train slid through endless dark tunnels, Maureen looked at her reflection in the window opposite. She wasn't sure about the hat, she'd never had one like it. She looked at Skinner's reflection too, and saw that the new clothes and the peaked cap hadn't changed his face. She looked at his mouth, and she shivered. It was hot in the tube train, stuffy, even, but Maureen suddenly felt cold.

23

That same Tuesday, late in the afternoon, Detective Chief Superintendent Price called, by appointment, at Kensington Walk. He didn't want to raise false hopes and the information they'd received didn't mean that they were going to be able to get the baby back safe and well, but at least he had some advance to report and something to go on, instead of endlessly having to say, No, he'd got no further, in answer to poor Mrs. Wilmington's questioning.

He was shocked when he saw her. In the five days since it happened she must have lost pounds. Her eyes were sunk in her head like an old woman's and her skin had no color at all, it was waxy gray. He could see that she'd tried to make something of herself, she'd had her hair done, she'd put on a little make-up this afternoon, and she greeted him politely as she would have any visitor. He could barely stand the flash of hope that came into her face when he told her, warning her that it mightn't be much, that they had got a step further. That was what he'd come to tell her.

She listened while he told her about the two identifications they'd had of a young man who'd been seen with a girl and a baby. He explained that they hadn't taken much account of the children's story except to check the whereabouts of the man

Purfitt that the young girl had picked out. They'd found he'd moved from the last address they'd had for him and as far as they knew he wasn't serving another sentence. But that didn't prove anything. But when this Mrs. Plum had come forward with her story, and she'd picked out the same man, then they'd begun to believe that they might really be on to something. And the couple had flitted that very morning, without a word. That looked suspicious too. Now they were getting out descriptions of both the man and the girl and circulating them all over the country.

"But you've got a photograph of him?"

"And we're getting an identikit picture of the girl. From the two descriptions, this Mrs. Plum's and the boy's. But these fancy pictures don't always help. Don't look like anyone. I often wonder whether they don't put people off more than help."

"Didn't anyone see . . . the baby?"

"This Mrs. Plum did. Helped to look after it, apparently. That was what made her suspicious in the first place, that the girl didn't seem to know what to do for it."

"What did she say about the baby?"

"The baby was all right. She thought the girl didn't know much about babies, but was really trying to do her best for it," Price said.

"What about the people who saw them on the train? Didn't they notice anything about the baby?" Sally Wilmington asked.

"Not a thing. Just heard the couple talking and thought he sounded a bit too offhand to be its Dad." Price hadn't told her the words the youngsters had repeated to him. He didn't like the sound of them himself, and didn't mean to frighten the poor girl more than necessary. He added, "They're quite young. Not more than sixteen or seventeen at the outside. Still at school, both of them."

He was astonished to see Sally Wilmington's eyes focusing on him with interest. "What are they called?"

"Stephen Rawlinson and the girl's called Vicky something or other. Stanford. That's it."

Sally Wilmington said, "I've seen them. They came around here."

"You didn't tell me. . . ."

"Andrew said it was all made up. . . ."

"Made up? They gave quite a good account of themselves to me," Price said sharply.

"Because of it all being . . . what d'you call it? Telepathy or something."

"That's not how I had it from them. They said they'd seen this precious couple in the train, as I told you."

"That's not what they told us." She'd started shaking again.

"Mrs. Wilmington. Don't let this upset you."

"Andrew didn't trust them. He thought they were in it for what they could get out of it. But I liked them. I liked one of the girls. . . ."

"One of the girls? Was there more than one?"

"There were two when they came here."

"Vicky, she was called."

"That's right. She was the one I liked. The other one was nice too. Pretty. But the Vicky girl. . . ."

"What?"

Sally Wilmington said slowly, "She made me feel she really wanted to help."

"She's the one who turned up on Sunday with the boy, with this bit of news about the tube train."

"And she said it really happened?"

"Yes, they both said so."

"You think they're lying?"

They stared at each other.

"Suppose they did it because they knew they wouldn't be believed?" Sally Wilmington said.

"How d'you mean, Mrs. Wilmington?" Price said, not understanding.

"They came here on Saturday and told us this story. And Andrew wouldn't listen because it was all supposed to have been second sight. Something like that. The other girl, the pretty one, said that these two could see what was going to happen. And of course . . . you know. It is difficult to believe. They might have thought you'd listen to them properly if they said it had happened in the ordinary sort of way."

"It would certainly sound better to me," Price said.

"And they wanted to help. I know they did. I just don't believe they wanted to get paid or anything. That girl . . . the Vicky girl . . . I could feel. She really minded."

"You say your husband didn't take much account of it?" Price asked.

"He got angry. He was terribly tired. And there's been a lot of silly stuff. People ringing up or coming round. Sometimes you can see they're frauds or that they're going to ask you to pay. But those two . . . I thought they were different."

"I'd better see them and find out exactly what is going on," Price said.

"But you said the girl picked out the same picture. Why shouldn't her story be true?"

"Mrs. Wilmington, I'm just a plain, ordinary policeman. I like facts. I don't like crystal balls and the stars telling you what's going to happen the day after tomorrow. In my experience it never does. . . ."

"But if they really could? If they could see where Caroline Ann is? What's happening to her? Then you could go there and stop them . . . get her back. It just might work, mightn't it?"

Price hated to have to take away any slightest thread of hope, but he knew his duty. "Look, Mrs. Wilmington. If I thought there was the smallest chance of these youngsters being able to tell us where to find your baby, you know I'd take it. But there's no reason to think they can. Whichever of the stories they told is true, they haven't said they can tell us where to look. And I'm short enough of men as it is. To my way of thinking it's better to use the force I've got going around London and asking questions, following up other leads, than sending men off on a harebrained chase set up by a crazy schoolgirl who thinks she sees visions."

"I know you'll do your best," Sally Wilmington said.

"You can be sure of that."

"Only . . . if those children do suggest anything. . . . You won't turn it down straight away?"

"I won't do that. And I'm certainly going to interview that precious pair again and get to the bottom of this caper," Price said. He left the house, disturbed, angry with himself for having been taken in by the precious pair, and yet unable to decide how they'd picked out Purfitt's picture if they were indeed impostors. It was too late to do anything more that evening, he'd have to leave the confrontation until tomorrow.

24

The next morning Detective Chief Superintendent Price was at the address the girl had given, bright and early. He knocked on the door and it was opened at once. Before he knew it, he'd almost come out with his thought—"So you're the pretty one," but he managed to check the words before he'd said them and he only asked, "Does Vicky Stanford live here?"

Chris said, "Yes," and stood looking at him.

"She's at home? Could I see her? Police." He showed her his card.

"She's out," Chris said.

"Know where she's gone to, by any chance?" Price asked.

"She's having coffee with . . . with a friend."

"Would that be Stephen Rawlinson?" He was amused to see her surprise. Show her that her sister and the boy friend weren't the only ones with second sight.

"How did you know?" Chris asked, not liking it.

"They came around to see us in the Criminal Investigation Department on Sunday with some information about a case I'm working on. There are one or two things I'd like to ask them about. We've had some further evidence we think they might be able to help us with."

Chris obviously hesitated.

"Could you tell me the name of the coffee shop?" Price inquired.

"It's in the High Street. The Witches' Cauldron. I'll show you, if you like."

"I'd like that, if you can spare the time," Price said. It was always useful to get some idea of the sort of background there was to a story as unusual as this was. He was still sure they'd been taken in by this Stanford girl and the boy because, although Mrs. Wilmington seemed to think they were genuine, the stories just didn't fit. Something must be wrong somewhere.

But he didn't get much further during the ten minutes' walk with Chris. The most interesting thing he picked up was the strong impression of normality. By the time they reached the High Street he'd have been willing to swear, against all his better reason, that this girl wasn't mixed up in anything shady, and was convinced her sister and boy friend weren't either.

He saw Vicky and Stephen, talking earnestly, before they saw him. Plotting something else his suspicious mind asked. But again when he reached the table and they stood up to greet him, they didn't look to him guilty. Vicky, in fact, seemed pleased to see him. She asked, "Is there any news?" at the same moment as he said, "I'd like to ask you a few more questions."

"What . . .? Do you mean here?" Stephen asked.

"Not here. Would there be a room at your house that we could have to ourselves for half an hour? Or at yours?" Price said, looking at Vicky.

Chris and Vicky looked at each other, and Chris said, "The front room. Mum's out anyway."

"You'll come?" Price said to Stephen. It was not exactly a question, more a statement.

They hardly spoke till they'd got back to the Stanford house and were sitting around the table in the small, seldom-used front room, Chris as well as the other two. Vicky asked again, "You haven't found the baby, then?"

"No."

"I thought perhaps you'd caught them."

"No such luck."

"Something's happened though, hasn't it?"

"Why do you say that? Seen the future in a crystal ball?" It was meant to take her off her guard, and it did. She flushed and looked quickly at her sister, "Chris! You didn't. . . ."

"Your sister never said a word. It was Mrs. Wilmington told me you'd been 'round there before you came to us, with a story about seeing what's going to happen before it takes place."

Vicky sat scarlet and silent. The sister urged her, "Tell him it's true."

She said, "What's the use? No one ever believes us."

"Is that why you told a different story at the Yard?"

She said, "Yes," defiantly.

"Which story are we supposed to believe? The one about the tube train or the other?"

She said, "Does it matter? If you want to get the baby back."

"So now you don't believe a word we've said?" the boy asked.

"I didn't say I didn't."

"What have you come here for, then?"

"To ask you which is the truth. The story you told us or the one you told the Wilmington couple?"

The boy said, "It seemed important to tell you what we knew. So I told Vicky we should pretend it happened on the train like we told you."

"But it didn't really?"

"No."

"How, then?"

Vicky was silent, Stephen tried to explain. Pictures, flashes. Unexpected, they never knew when or why. Like remembering, Vicky had thought, only working backwards. You didn't always choose what you remembered, did you? They didn't always get it exactly the same . . . Vicky interrupted.

"I'll tell you what it's like. It's like smells."

"*Smells?* Not for me it isn't. . . ."

"I don't mean in the flash. I mean how it comes. Don't you know how sometimes you suddenly remember something and you can't think why just then, and then you realize it's because of a smell? Like meths always reminds me of hospital, when I had my tonsils done. They used meths to clean the trolleys."

"That's right! Kippers make me think of Yarmouth . . ." Chris said, but Price wasn't listening to her. In his mind he was standing by a fruit and vegetable shop on a hot day last summer, wondering why he'd suddenly had a picture of the garden where his grandmother had lived in Kent. He could see her clearly, a little woman with white hair pulled back into a bun and the black apron with white spots that she always seemed to wear, laughing. She was laughing at him, Jimmy Price. Only Jimmy Price was a small boy who'd been caught eating the gooseberries before they were ripe. The sourness of them had made him screw up his face and spit them out. Then she'd picked a leaf from another fruit bush and told him to smell it, it would take the sharpness away, and he'd smelled black currant for the first time he ever remembered. A lovely distinctive smell, different from anything else. Funny! He didn't like the fruit much even now, but he did like the smell. It had been the smell of sun-warmed black currants on that fruit stall that had brought back his Granny and her country voice and the garden which had seemed to him, a London child, so big and rich. He wondered what had happened to that cottage and its garden now. Pulled down to make room for a council estate probably. Or worse, bought by some business man who'd be there only for week-ends. . . .

He came back suddenly to the Stanford front room and the other three at the table. Chris was still speaking. Funny thing too how all those memories and all that feeling could take no time at all. He'd lived through five summer holidays of exploration and content such as he'd never recaptured, and the girl hadn't come to the end of the sentence.

" . . . because they'd only been caught that morning," Chris ended.

"Only it isn't a smell that starts it off," Vicky said.

"And you've no idea what it is?" Price asked. He saw Vicky

look at him. She'd cottoned on to a change in his attitude. Whether this girl could see the future or not, she was certainly quick on picking up people's feelings.

"I think it's something that happens when we're together. We've never had flashes when we weren't," Stephen said.

"What about that first time? You weren't together then. We hadn't even met you," Chris said.

"But we were near each other. We were both waiting to cross the road," Vicky said.

"Was that when you saw the baby being taken?"

"No, quite different. We both saw an old lady being knocked down by a van."

"I don't see what. . . ."

"It hadn't happened when we saw it. . . ."

"I thought Vicky was crazy," Chris said.

"I said to Chris she was going to be knocked down and Chris said there wasn't an old lady on the crossing."

"But it did happen directly afterwards."

Price sat looking from one face to another, wondering. Could they possibly be such good actors? It sounded impossible and yet he found he'd begun to half-believe them.

"We weren't together the next time either," Vicky said.

Stephen, embarrassed by the recollection, said, "I was outside the café, though."

"We had different flashes that time. I saw the headlines in the paper and Stephen saw Mrs. Wilmington and the pram without the baby in it."

"How long before it actually happened? Just a few minutes again?" Price asked.

"Much longer. Must have been days. More like a week."

"Neither of you've ever had one of these flashes by yourself?"

"No."

"Can you get them when you want?"

"No. We've tried. It doesn't work."

"Have either of you ever had anything like this before? Visions? Heard voices? That sort of thing?"

"You make it sound phoney," Vicky said frowning.

"More like Joan of Arc," Chris said.

"Never mind what it sounds like. Have you?"

"I haven't," Vicky said.

"Nor have I. Thank goodness. I could do without them now," Stephen said.

"When was the first one? How long ago? When you saw the accident on the pedestrian crossing?"

"Right at the end of last term. So it must have been a Saturday or we wouldn't have been in the High Street in the morning. More like three weeks.".

"Is it always accidents you see? You didn't happen to see any Cup results? Or who won the National? You could make your fortune," Price said, just as Chris had done.

Stephen said, "Yes," just as Vicky said, "No, it isn't." She added, "Don't you remember when we saw Chris and Paul? And she said about him getting a place at York?"

"That's right! I'd forgotten."

"But that was the only time."

"And you haven't had any more since Sunday?" Price asked.

"No."

Price said, "All right. Now tell me what you saw that last time. When you heard the girl say that about hurting the baby. You did see something as well as hear them talking, didn't you?"

"Saw them. I saw him, sort of, and Stephen saw her."

"Anything else? Where were they? Was it in a tube train?"

They told him. But just a room, no indication where, wasn't going to be much use. "They never mentioned the place or anything?" No, all they'd heard was that one sentence of the girl's. Nothing about the room that they'd be able to recognize? No, it was just a room.

"Tell him about the picture," the boy said.

"How's that going to help?"

"What's that?" Price said sharply.

"Vicky saw a picture on the wall. Behind the girl's head."

"It was one of those mountains . . . a volcano. With fire and sparks and things coming out of its top."

"How big? What sort of frame, do you remember?"

"The frame was black, with gold bits. About that big," Vicky said, measuring with her hands.

Price said, "Well, I'm . . . blowed." In his mind he used a stronger word. Because how could the girl have known? It wasn't the sort of thing you'd invent. He'd been surprised himself, when he was looking round it, to find in Mrs. Plum's front first-floor double a print of Vesuvius showering fire down on the unaware, bustling city of Pompei. And the frame had indeed been black and gold.

When Price had left them, Stephen and the two girls sat around the table and stared at each other.

"He believes you! I knew he would!" Chris said.

"I didn't," Stephen said.

"He really does. He asked you to tell him if you had any more flashes."

"I wish we knew why we sometimes do and sometimes don't," Stephen said.

"It's when you're together."

"But not always when we're together."

"There must be something else, then."

"Perhaps it's the time of day?" Chris suggested.

"No, it isn't. It's been all sorts of time of day."

"Something to do with the moon? When it's full. Like people going mad."

"Thanks very much, Chris."

"Anyway, it can't be that, because you've been having them all this month, and the moon's only full every four weeks."

"I don't know, then."

"What's up, Vicky? You look moonstruck or something."

"You don't think . . . ? No, it's silly."

"What?"

"It's just that it never happened before."

"What didn't happen?"

"The flashes. They only started afterwards, didn't they?"

"After what? Do finish what you were going to say. After what?"

Vicky took her hand out of her pocket and put the piece of wood on the table between them.

"You mean . . . ? You mean, it's the egg that does it? My egg? But I don't see how. . . ."

"I don't either. Only it wasn't until you had it that we started seeing anything."

"No . . . Only that doesn't prove anything really."

"I just thought . . ." Vicky said, disappointed.

"I suppose it could be that."

"Did you have it with you when we had the flashes?" Vicky asked.

Stephen thought. "That first time, I did. And the next. I think I did the other two times too. It was in my pocket most of the time; I hadn't bothered to take it out."

"Did you have your bit then, Vicky? Vicky? Did you?"

"I think so. I can't be absolutely sure."

"That's it, then! You both have to be together, and you have to have the bits of the puzzle thing with you! That must be it. Mustn't it, Steve?"

"But it doesn't happen all the time even when we are and we've got the bits," Vicky said.

"Why don't you try? You might see something else about the baby, and then you could go straight off and tell that detective," Chris said.

Vicky and Stephen looked at each other.

"I think you ought to. Suppose something awful did happen to the baby?"

"You'd better come back to my place," Stephen said, remembering gratefully that his father would certainly be at work.

"You don't need me," Chris said.

But Vicky wanted her to come. Even with Chris there she

only half-liked being taken into the house by Stephen, and she was relieved when he said, after looking round the door of the kitchen, "Nobody here. Why don't you come in?" He sat them at the table and asked, "Had enough coffee, or would you like some more?"

"Can you make it like your Mum does?" Chris asked at once.

"No. But there's probably some here in the pot. Yes, there is. Would you like it?"

"Smashing. Tell you what, Steve. You go and fetch your bits of egg and Vicky and me'll put the coffee on to warm up."

Stephen left them and went upstairs. To his fury he couldn't at once find the plastic bag which held the bits of the egg. He didn't realize why, then saw that his mother had been on one of her tidying jags, and everything was in a different place. He searched, swearing softly under his breath, and eventually found the plastic bag in the pocket of his other coat. He'd put it there himself and forgotten. He laughed at himself and wondered how many other sins which were really his own he blamed his mother for.

As he went down the stairs he could smell the coffee, and when he'd almost reached the hall, he could see Vicky's feet as she stood with Chris at the stove. He was on the bottom step when the flash hit him. He grabbed the banister and stood still while the jagged edges of the frame jolted each other and the bright picture inside trembled into clarity. He just had time to feel surprise that what he was looking at wasn't the face of that fuzzy-haired girl with the baby. It was Chris's. He heard a boy's voice, a voice he should have recognized but didn't immediately. The boy was saying, " . . . didn't want to interfere . . . thought you were going out with him." He saw Chris's face change and she said a name. His. She said, "Stephen? He's really nice but there's never been anything. . . ." He saw her face light up and glow—she really was astoundingly pretty—as the boy said, "Then it's all right if I ask you . . ." and then the blackness closed in and he was stepping down the last step and crossing the hall toward the kitchen door, trembling.

In the kitchen-dining room, Chris was standing at the stove, with her back toward him, intent on pouring the coffee from the saucepan to a jug. Vicky was looking toward him. He saw immediately from her face that she'd had it too. She shook her head a fraction and he understood she meant that they mustn't speak of it in front of Chris. That was right. No one would want to think you could overhear bits of their private conversations. Funny, how he and Vicky sometimes knew without speaking what the other was thinking.

"There! Would your mother mind if I looked for some milk in her fridge? I don't really like mine without," Chris said, putting the mugs of coffee on the table. Looking at her more closely, Stephen saw that she hadn't got that extra flush of liveliness that added so much to her prettiness and which had so much struck him at their first meeting. It wasn't that she'd been remote or difficult today, she'd been warmly concerned for the lost baby, but she'd been somehow subdued. He felt he'd been ridiculously blind. He'd been jealous of Paul the first time he'd seen him with Chris. Why hadn't it occurred to him that Paul might feel the same about him? And what would he have done if it had? Paul had presumably just kept out of her way, and she minded. At which thought Stephen's jealousy renewed itself. He hadn't been thinking so much about her lately, but now for a moment he hated Paul for having the power to dim Chris's sparkle—and to light it up again. For that same moment he felt the unaccountable urge to snatch, the need to establish sole rights, which constitutes so large a part of sudden and overwhelming attraction to another person. He looked at Chris, still quite astonishingly much prettier than any girl he'd ever met, and resented the idea that she might prefer someone else, that he wouldn't have a chance if he really set about trying to win her. At the same time an uneasy cool thought slid into the back of his mind that she wasn't his sort of person. He dismissed it angrily. He didn't want reason here, he wanted simply to feel.

He was so far away, pursuing his reactions to Chris, that when Vicky said, "Did you find it?" he'd forgotten what it was he'd gone to look for. Then he remembered. The egg. For an answer he emptied the contents of the plastic bag onto the table. The separate pieces fell out, a jumble of crooked billets of wood, but so carefully carved, so lovingly shaped to fit into and hold each other, they had a sort of beauty, a look of purpose, even apart. Like Adam and Eve as God made them, each had its own symmetry, and yet was not complete in itself.

Vicky put her solitary piece on the table too.

"Why don't you put the whole thing together?" Chris asked. But Stephen hesitated, and Vicky stretched out a hand as if to draw her piece back again.

"Go on! Why don't you?" Chris urged.

Stephen said, "I don't know if . . ." just as Vicky said, "Suppose when it's put together it doesn't work?"

"You mean you mightn't get any more flashes?"

"That's right."

"But . . . ! You'd think it'd work better when it's like it was meant to be."

"I don't think so," Vicky said.

"Why not? How d'you know?"

"I didn't say know. I only think."

"What? Why shouldn't it work when it's all put together?"

Vicky said, "Something to do with it being all in one piece. Then it doesn't need anything else, it's got everything it wants . . . I know it sounds crazy . . ." she stopped, embarrassed.

"I don't see . . ." Chris began.

"I know what Vicky means. If it's complete, it sort of isn't anything to do with us. If it's all in separate bits, then it does need us, or someone, to put it together."

"But that's what I want you to do!" Chris exclaimed.

"But if we do, we've lost it. Or we've lost whatever we have as long as it's separate. Anyway I think Vicky is right. I think we shouldn't try to put it together until after we've found the baby. Then if we don't get any more flashes it won't matter."

"There might be something else you want to find out then," Chris said, and Stephen thought of wanting to know about girls, of discovering what they wanted; but was it Chris, he was thinking about? Or was it Vicky? Vicky thought about her father. She didn't really believe that the wooden egg would help her to find out where he was or what he was like. But if there was the smallest chance, she wasn't going to spoil it.

The front door opened and shut. Stephen had time to think, "Oh God, that's Mum," before Mrs. Rawlinson came in at the kitchen door. Vicky's hand had gone out for her piece of the egg, and Stephen had bundled the other bits back into their plastic bag and had transferred the whole thing to his pocket, before his mother had reached the table and put her shopping basket down. Not, however, before she'd started apologizing for disturbing them, as though, Stephen thought gloomily, she hadn't the right to be in her own kitchen. "One thing I'll never do when I'm married, is get my wife so frightened that she doesn't know what she's doing," he thought, and noticed with amazement that this hypothetical wife didn't look like Chris, hadn't the self-confidence of a girl who has always felt safe and loved and courted, but was a more complex character, who needed encouragement and the security of being wanted.

But Mrs. Rawlinson's hesitation didn't last. Reassured by Chris, finding herself in the position of having to forgive the raids on her coffee and milk jugs, she relaxed, she talked, more easily than Stephen often heard her. Once she even laughed at something one of the girls said; not the nervous, anxious-to-please laugh with which she so often greeted Dr. Rawlinson's barbed wit, but a real, open, belly laugh. She looked animated, younger. Stephen saw, for almost the first time, that she must have been pretty herself as a girl. He wondered now whether she'd have been happier and felt more at ease if he'd been a girl. The thought intrigued him, and when Vicky and Chris had left, he asked his mother, "When I was born, did you want a son? Or would you have preferred a daughter?"

She was anxious at once not to say the wrong thing. "No, of course not. Why ever should you think that?"

"I just thought you got on rather well with those two and I wondered if you minded not having any girls."

"I'd really have liked to have both. I always meant to have a big family. Well, four, anyway."

"Why didn't you?" It struck Stephen as extraordinary that in all his seventeen years he'd never asked this question before.

"Daddy—Roderick—thought one was as much as I could manage."

"I bet you'd have been better than you expected if you had had a lot of children," Stephen said.

"Do you really think so?" his mother asked. She sounded surprisingly pleased.

"You wouldn't have been able to spend so much time wondering whether you were doing it right or not. You'd have had to get on with whatever it was."

His mother said, "I suppose so. It would have been rather . . . fun."

"Never mind! You've got me," Stephen said.

"Only I don't think I'm much good to you. As a mother, I mean."

"If you mean you don't interfere with what I want to do all the time like Aunt Jean—I can't think how Luke stands it. Being asked every minute how he's feeling and what he's thinking about."

"I think some people tell each other too much," his mother said.

"I've never heard you say anything like that before, Mum."

"Oh dear! I didn't mean to say anything against . . . I mean, I know a lot of people really need to talk about their troubles . . . especially to a person who's trained. . . . I only meant. . . ."

"I know what you meant. You don't always have to say everything to be understood," Stephen said, and left, taking the fragmented egg with him. Mrs. Rawlinson sat for an unaccustomed two minutes' rest at the kitchen table, feeling an equally unusual warmth from Stephen's reassurance and from the obvious liking and appreciation shown by those two nice girls. And yet they hadn't actually put their feelings into words any more than Stephen had. She hadn't had to be told, she had known. She wondered if perhaps she could believe more in knowing and not so much in being told how by experts and whether everything she did wouldn't turn out better? Even her cooking, possibly? Fired by this thought, she decided to scrap the cheese soufflé she'd meant to make for lunch and instead to make toasted cheese on slices of fried bread, the way she and her sister used to do when they were children. With a fried egg on top, it had seemed the most delicious thing they'd ever eaten. With plenty of salt and mustard and a drop of Worcestershire sauce. She remembered those cooking experiments so vividly she could have done it blindfolded. After all, if Roddy didn't like it, he could always have more of the *coq au vin* which was for dinner. She just hoped the sauce would thicken properly this time.

"Chrissie!" Vicky said as they'd nearly reached home.

"What?"

"What's wrong?"

"I didn't say there was anything wrong."

"I know there is, though. There was on Sunday, wasn't there?"

"Sort of."

"What is it? It's to do with Paul, isn't it?"

"It's silly. It's nothing, really."

"Did he say anything you didn't like?"

"No. He hasn't said anything. Anything at all."

"But you know he likes you."

"I thought he did. And that made me like him more. You know how it is."

"He does like you. I know he does. What's happened, then?"

"We went out. Sunday afternoon. Only to the common. And everything seemed all right. Only when we came back, he didn't say anything about seeing me again."

"He is working for his 'A's'."

"Not all of every day. Anyway, if it'd been that, he'd have said."

"D'you think perhaps he thinks you're going out with Stephen?" Vicky dared to suggest.

"But I'm not! I don't . . . I like Steve. But I wouldn't go out with him. . . ."

"He's all right!" Vicky said, more fiercely than she meant to.

"He's really nice. Only I just don't fancy him."

"But Paul might think you do. We have been seeing a lot of Stephen this last week."

"Do you think he really might think that?"

"He could."

"Seen it in one of your flashes?" Chris asked, not meaning it. But Vicky was pleased she was able to tease again, and she didn't say no.

Thursday

Maureen had never been so thankful as she was when Skinner told her they were going to move on out of Fred's mother's house where they'd been staying since they left Edmonton. Fred didn't like her, never had, but then he didn't like girls at all. He called her Fatty, like Skinner did, and passed remarks about her figure and the slow way she did everything. He made Skinner worse to her than before, having the two of them on at her all the time was awful. She couldn't help crying sometimes, and that got them madder than ever. She'd thought, when she heard the house belonged to Fred's mother, that perhaps she, the mother, would be nice to her and talk to her like Mrs. Plum had, perhaps even help her to look after Linda. But Mrs. Stowe wasn't a bit like that. She was rather smartly dressed, though you could see she was quite old, with platinum blonde hair and a nasty short way of talking. She wasn't pleased to have Maureen and Skinner and the baby staying with her and she didn't trouble to hide it from them. She'd shown them the room they were to have, half down in the basement, it was, and given Skinner a key and told them they'd have to look after themselves, she had enough to do upstairs.

It was Fred who'd shown them where the toilet was and the kitchen, though he'd said they weren't to use it more than they could help, so they lived mostly on what Skinner brought in; warm beer and fish and chips and a loaf of bread and a pot of jam. Maureen wasn't fussy about her food, but she didn't think much of having just that and nothing else for two whole days, nearly three. After the first day, she felt she'd give her soul for a cup of tea, so she went upstairs into the kitchen and found what she needed and made herself one. Fred came into the kitchen while she was at it. He never said much, just looked, and then he said, "Did my mother invite you in here drinking her tea?" and when Maureen, frightened, said, No, but she hadn't seen any harm, Fred said, "If you want to leave here inside your greasy skin, you'll keep out of this kitchen until you're asked in." After that Maureen never went near the kitchen again. She made up Linda's feeds in the toilet and warmed them up as well as she could in front of the gas fire in the bedroom. One bottle she put too near the flame and it broke and the milky feed made a nasty mess all over the rug. Maureen mopped it up with toilet paper and never said a word. She made do with just one bottle, she didn't dare tell Skinner. The big black roaches which ran about on the floor whenever you hadn't got the light on were much interested in the remains of the feed on the rug, and congregated there hopefully, waiting for more.

The only thing that was a bit better than it had been at Mrs. Plum's was Linda. Now that Maureen knew about getting up her wind and giving her feeds more or less at the same times of day, she did sleep more and she didn't cry half as much. Which was lucky, because Skinner had told her that Fred's mother wouldn't stand for a howling kid, she'd got to keep it quiet or they'd both cop it. She made a mistake, though, the first day they were there; after she'd rinsed out Linda's rubber panties that she had on over the throw-away diapers, she hung them on the washing-line outside the back door. You'd have thought she'd committed a crime to hear how they went on at her, all three of them, Skinner and Fred and Mrs. Stowe. "Didn't he tell you not to go out of the house?" Fred said, looking at her with those cold eyes, and Maureen said Yes, but she'd thought he meant not out of the front of the house, she didn't know she wasn't to go into the garden.

"Anyone might have seen her," Mrs. Stowe said.

"Your neighbors nosy?" Skinner asked.

"Not more than most. But that Mrs. Bennett next door, she's always at home. She might've seen the kid's pants even if she didn't see your . . . girl," Mrs. Stowe said. Maureen had never heard a woman swear like she did.

"What'll you say if she asks?" Skinner said.

"Say I've got a niece staying with me who's not too bright."

"You can say that again," Skinner said.

"You certainly got a beauty when you found her. I don't know why you had to pick on one that was half-witted as well as fat," Fred said. And later, in the horrid bedroom downstairs, Skinner hit Maureen again several times, not as if he really cared or was even furious, but just as he might have swiped at one of the roaches that happened to be about. She cried and he hit her again. "You stay in here tomorrow. You don't so much as put your fat pig's snout out of the door."

"Have we got to stay here long?" Maureen asked.

"You won't stay anywhere long if you don't learn," Skinner said.

"Who'll get me the feeds for Linda? I haven't hardly got enough to last tomorrow."

The next day Fred brought in another tin of the stuff she had to make up for the baby's bottle and two packets of the throw-away diapers, and she stayed in the bedroom all day. Linda slept. There wasn't even a radio to listen to. Maureen was frightened and bored. She slept all the afternoon and only woke up when the front door banged upstairs and there was the sound of angry voices. She could hear Skinner and Fred and that peculiar high voice, almost like a girl's, which meant that Jakey was there too. Maureen shivered. She pulled the covers of the bed closer up around her chin as if that could keep her safe.

Steps came quickly down the stairs and Fred opened the door, without knocking or anything.

"Upstairs," he said.

"Who? Me?"

"Who d'you think I mean? The blasted kid? Get on with it. We're waiting."

Maureen dragged herself off the bed and up the stairs. Fred led the way into the front room which Maureen hadn't ever seen, and she followed him. Seated on the three-piece suite were Skinner and Jakey and Bus. Without realizing it, Maureen gave Bus an imploring look. After all he had pinched her bottom more than once and she half-hoped he might be more on her side than Skinner or Jakey seemed likely to be.

"There she is, the bloody cow. You ask her," Skinner said.

Fred sat down on one of the hard chairs by a table that had a big plant on it. No one suggested to Maureen that she should sit, so she continued to stand. Jakey began.

"What'd you say to that woman you been lodging with?"

"Nothing," Maureen said.

"That's a lie, and you know it. You told her about the kid."

"I didn't! I never!"

"Why'd she go to the coppers, then?"

"I don't know—I never told her anything."

"Skinner says you did."

Maureen was no match for this sort of game. Her mouth drooping open with terror, she said, "He doesn't! Does he?"

Jakey pursued his advantage. "You told her Wilmington."

"I said it was a street. She kept on asking. . . ."

"What else?"

Maureen looked at him too terrified to speak.

"Hit her, Fred," Jakey said. Fred said, "It'll be a pleasure," and hit her across the mouth.

"There's more where that came from. Go on. What else?"

Maureen's mouth shaped the words, "Nothing else." They didn't come out very clearly and Fred hit her again. She felt her lips swelling so that her mouth felt like cotton wool that had soaked up pain. She tasted blood too. It was lucky for her that saying anything after this hurt so much, because it saved her where her poor fuddled brain might not have. All she could think was how not to have to speak, and far away behind that was a sort of knowledge that she must never, never, never, if she wanted to stay in one piece, as Skinner said, and not get hurt too much, mention the name Brady Drive. She shook her head. That hurt too.

"What else?"

She tried to say, "Nothing," but it didn't come out right. She heard Fred ask, "What about another?" but she didn't hear the answer because this time Fred hit her in the stomach and she fell, gasping. She hadn't ever had such an awful pain. She heard the voices going on over her head but she couldn't understand what they said. Presently the pain went away a bit and she listened. Jakey seemed to be doing most of the talking. She heard him say, "Fair description they've got of you and Fatty. That old cow must've talked all night."

Skinner said, "Where'd you get that?"

"Radio this evening."

Skinner said, "We got different gear."

Jakey said, " Don't know how much that goes for."

"What does Smithy say?"

"Says you've got to get out of here by Friday. Keep on the move, he says and don't let that fat slob anywhere where she can talk, see?"

"Can't you grow a beard or something?" Bus asked Skinner.

"Overnight? Who d'you think I am? Tarzan?"

"Pad yourself out a bit, then. Look as if you'd got some weight about you. Tell you what. Bus can get you a wig."

Even in the state she was in, Maureen knew this was the wrong thing to say to Skinner. He minded people noticing the way his hair was. She heard him grunt, then Fred said, "What're you going to do about that cow?" and she knew he meant her.

"Get rid of her," Jakey said.

"We can't let her go now, she'd gab."

"I didn't say let her go, I said, get rid of her."

"Smithy wouldn't like that. You know how he is." That was Bus.

"Anyway, I got to have someone to see to the kid."

"You said she wasn't any good at that either."

"She's better than Skinner'd be," Fred said, giggling.

"She's useless, but I got to have someone."

"I reckon you're stuck with her then, Skinner man."

"Rather you than me."

"Once we got the cash we shan't need her any more."

"Or if we don't."

"Either way, she'd be better out of the way. And from what she says, no one isn't going looking for her. That's why I took her, see? Had to be a bird who hadn't got no one."

Maureen, lying on the floor and hurting, heard this talk but didn't take it all in. She knew they were talking about her and she knew it wasn't nice. Their voices were unkind. She wasn't sure what exactly they meant to do, but like an animal she understood the smell of danger. They were frightened, and frightened people are cruel. She did hear the last thing Skinner said and the words rang in her ears. A bird that hadn't got no one. That was her.

She heard Skinner say something else. He asked Fred, "Your old woman got any scissors?"

"What d'you want scissors for?"

"Just bring them. You'll see."

Then there was more talk she didn't listen to. She didn't think it was about her. She wondered whether she could get up and go downstairs and lie on the bed. Her head hurt badly. She moved, but someone kicked her in the side and she fell back on the floor and groaned.

"Stay put, I haven't finished with you," Skinner said. Someone was holding her chin and turning her head sideways, and pulling at her hair. He pulled it roughly and she cried out, partly because it hurt and partly because she realized what he was doing. Skinner was cutting it off. Cutting off her hair, the only thing she really liked about herself. She tried to stop him, but Fred caught both her hands and held them, and she was frightened to move her head too much with those scissors blades so near. Skinner wouldn't bother if he cut her neck or her ear, so she lay still, tears trickling down onto the floor. He was cutting off her hair close to her head, shorter than it had been since Maureen could remember. She could feel the blade of the scissors grazing her scalp, and she called out, "No, Skinner! Don't take it all off! Please, Skinner, no!"

No answer. Only the cutting went on. She could hear him sort of gasping, he was cutting in a sort of fury, as if he couldn't do it enough. Bus said, "Here, steady on, man. You don't want to make her look like a skinhead, do you?" Skinner didn't answer, but Jakey said, "Stop it, you! She looks like a scarecrow. No one couldn't forget what she looks like, now."

Skinner said, "She looks different, anyway." And to Maureen he said, "Get up and go downstairs."

She had difficulty getting up. Her stomach still hurt where Fred had punched her, and her mouth felt huge and awful and her head felt cold. She looked at the floor where she'd been lying and saw it covered with hair. Her hair, fair and curly, masses and masses of it. She started to cry again, she really couldn't help it. Skinner said, "Stop that, unless you want another lesson," and she tried to swallow her sobs. Bus, looking at her critically, said, "Why don't you put her into pants and pass her off as a fellow?"

"Who's ever seen a fellow with cheeks like that?" Fred said, sneering at her behind.

"Get out," Skinner said to Maureen and she went off and down the stairs to the roachy bedroom. She went over and looked at herself in the mirror by the dim yellow electric light, and what she saw made her cry more than ever. Skinner had cut her hair right off, jaggedly, close to the scalp which showed through in places. It looked terrible, and it being cut so close made her face look fatter. It was all swollen up anyway because of being hit and crying, her eyelids were red and there was dirt all over her where she'd lain on the floor and the tears had brought dust off on her. Jakey had been right when he said she looked like a scarecrow. And then Maureen heard Skinner's voice again. "A bird who hasn't got no one." Nor, like this, who ever would have anyone. Maureen sat in front of the speckled mirror and howled.

Her howls woke Linda, and Linda cried too, so presently Maureen wiped her sore eyes and got out the tin of baby food and lit the gas fire and went out to the horrid toilet in the basement area for water and made up the next feed. She didn't care whether it was time for it or not, she was going to give Linda something that would keep her quiet. She got it all ready, and she went over to pick the whimpering baby up. She picked her out of the carry-cot and felt that she was wet, so she changed her first and then sat on the floor with her back against the bed, the baby in her lap and the bottle ready to give her. This way she could rest her back and have a proper lap the baby didn't slide off all the time.

This was when the miracle happened. The baby, not really ravenous because it wasn't all that time since her last feed, took the bottle's teat in her mouth and took a few sucks and then she stopped. She pushed the teat out of her mouth and she looked at Maureen. Whether she saw the puffy, red-rimmed eyes, the ragged hair, the swollen mouth, didn't matter. She looked at Maureen for a moment and before she started feeling for the bottle and sucking again, she smiled. At Maureen. Pleased that Maureen was there. *Wanting* her.

During the rest of the baby's feed, great gentle drops fell over her face from Maureen's already overworked eyes. But they made her feel better, this time, not worse.

Coming back with Chris from the swimming-baths that Thursday afternoon, Vicky was caught by Mrs. Stanford and called into the kitchen, while Chris went upstairs to dry her dripping hair.

"Vicky! Come in here a minute."

Vicky came and her mother shut the kitchen door behind her. Something serious, then.

"There's been a policeman around here to see you," Mrs. Stanford said.

"What did he say?"

"You don't sound very surprised."

"No."

"You know what he came about, then? He didn't say."

"Yes, I know."

Mrs. Stanford waited a minute. Then she said, "If they say you've done anything wrong I don't believe it. But if you've been a bit silly, you'd better tell me. I'll have to know sooner or later, won't I?"

"I would have told you, Mum, only it's all so complicated."

"Is it something you've done?"

"Nothing like that. We . . . Stephen and me—we went to the police first."

Mrs. Stanford was struck by another idea. "Vicky! It isn't

what we were talking about the other day? You didn't go to ask them to find out about that?"

"Yes, I did. No, wait a minute, Mum. What were we talking about? I don't remember you saying anything about it."

"About not knowing who your father was. I thought you might have gone to the police to ask how to find out. Only— stupid of me. You'd have gone on your own. You wouldn't have told that Stephen boy too." She caught sight of Vicky's face. "You have! Then it was that you went to them for!"

"No, it wasn't. Honestly, it wasn't, Mum. It's something quite different."

"But you have told Stephen about . . . about you?"

"Yes." She knew that her Mum wouldn't miss the implications of this, but she also knew that she wouldn't make a song and dance about it. Mrs. Stanford said, "I see. Well. What was it then, you and he went to the police about?"

"About the baby. The one that got stolen last week. You remember?"

"That poor woman! I keep on thinking about her. Wondering how she keeps going. It's all of a week now, isn't it? Fancy not knowing where your baby can be for a week! What's it got to do with you, anyway?"

"You know there was that appeal on the radio? For anyone who'd noticed anything funny, to tell them. Stephen and me did hear something we thought was a bit funny, so we told them."

"I don't see why you couldn't have told me, too. Then I wouldn't have nearly jumped out of my skin when that policeman came here asking for you."

"I'm sorry, Mum." She really couldn't begin to explain.

"Did Chris know about this?"

"Yes. It was just we weren't sure they'd believe us, so we didn't want to say." It sounded a bit lame, but Mrs. Stanford appeared to accept it.

"Well. I suppose at your age I shouldn't expect to know everything you do. You have to have some secrets you don't want your parents to know, even if they're nothing bad. I know I used to be like that with my Mum. Silliest things I'd keep from her, just to prove to myself I was grown up. She used to get mad at me for it."

"We tell you a lot, Chris and me."

"You're both good girls."

"Is that all, Mum?"

"I suppose so. Only, Vicky. . . ."

"What?"

"Stephen's a nice boy. I can see that. Only just remember, you're still only young. Plenty of time to look around."

"Oh, *Mum*. You talk as if we were going out together. Serious."

"Sometimes things get serious before you know. Don't be in a hurry, love. It doesn't pay."

"I'm not in a hurry."

"Nor for the other thing. Your father, I mean. Later, if you really want it, I daresay there's ways of finding out. We could try. If it really bothers you, I would."

Vicky knew how much her Mum didn't want it. She must be frightened that if Vicky found her real father, she'd somehow lose her. But she wouldn't, not ever, not however much Vicky found anyone else, nothing would ever measure up better than what this Mum, that she'd known all her life, had given her. She said, "Thanks, Mum," and knew that her voice said what she meant. Then she asked, "Did that chap from the police say when he'd be coming back?"

"This evening or tomorrow morning. I said I'd tell you, so's to make sure you'd be here."

"I wonder if he went around to Stephen's place too?" Remembering Stephen's account of how his father explained everything so that it meant something different, she giggled. "I wonder what his father thinks a policeman means?" She had to explain this to Mrs. Stanford too, but there wasn't any difficulty about that.

What Detective Chief Superintendent Price had meant to Dr. Rawlinson, who had opened the door to him under the impression it was one of the patients he saw in his study at home, was made clear to Stephen when he came back later from a visit he'd paid by himself to the Chinese section of the British Museum, to see if he could find anything like, or that would give him a clue to the nature of, the egg. Just as Vicky had been called into the kitchen, Stephen was invited to come into his father's study the moment he let himself into the house. Dr. Rawlinson sat in his usual chair, behind the leather-topped desk and motioned to what Stephen thought of as the patient's chair opposite to him. It was lucky for him, he thought gloomily, that he wasn't invited to lie on the couch, which stood handy, and to say everything that came into his head.

"Why don't you have a glass of sherry?" Dr. Rawlinson inquired. The sherry decanter and two glasses indeed stood on the desk.

"No thanks."

"Well, I think I will. I can recommend it. It's not the very driest, but it really isn't bad. For the price. Are you quite sure you won't?"

"Quite. I don't really like sherry."

Dr. Rawlinson said, "Ah! Perhaps it is an acquired taste."

"And anyway, why? I mean, you don't generally offer me sherry. Why now?"

"I wanted just to have a quick word with you. Without your mother."

He was nervous, Stephen could see. He waited.

"You had a rather unexpected visitor this afternoon. Unexpected, that is, by me."

"Vicky!" Stephen thought, but he still didn't say anything.

"He told me his name was Price. Detective Inspector, I think he said."

"Detective Chief Superintendent," Stephen said.

"Yes. I gathered you and he had already met."

"I've seen him twice. Did Mum see him?"

"That's what I wanted to tell you. Fortunately she was out, so she doesn't know anything about it. I thought you and I could have a little friendly talk about this whole affair now, and decide what is best to be done."

"Talk about what?"

"About whatever the trouble is you're in. And I want you to remember, Stephen, that as a psychiatrist I've seen a number of people in trouble, and I think I can promise that whatever it is I shan't be angry and I shan't be shocked. The fact that you are my son will make no difference."

"Who said I was in any trouble? Didn't that detective chap tell you what it was all about?"

"He used the expression that you 'were helping the police with their inquiries.' I've seen enough police procedure to know that that generally means they have suspicions which they can't yet prove. The usual method, I understand, is to go on questioning the person until he gives himself away somehow."

"Is that all he said? Didn't he tell you that we went to see him first?"

"Who is 'we'?"

"Vicky. The girl you met here the other day. She and I went to see him."

"I certainly got the impression it was he who was looking for you rather than the other way about. But of course I'm delighted if you aren't in any sort of difficulty with the police. That's excellent news."

"I can't think why you should jump to the conclusion that I must have got into trouble," Stephen said.

His father's reply seemed, at first, to be just the normal jargon. "Repressed aggression against paternalistic figures . . . the need to demonstrate a negative reaction toward authority . . . normal masculine protest of the young human. . . ." He felt he'd heard it all before. And then suddenly he heard his father's voice saying, " . . . but I should like you to believe that if you had got on the wrong side of the law, I should have done everything I could to help . . . " and he realized that this was true, and that although his father was probably mainly relieved that the opportunity wasn't going to arise, at the same time he might have looked forward to being, for once, able to do something for him that Stephen would have to accept, acknowledge, even be grateful for. What was bad was that he didn't want his father's help. He felt intensely irritated by the idea alone. Why? Was it because of everything being wrapped up in all that language? Or because he feared he'd be drawn into the excessively complicated world in which his father seemed to exist? Or because it was all so stilted and unstraightforward, hedged around with offers of sherry and formal statements? "I think I can promise not to be angry . . . the fact that you are my son will make no difference. . . ." "But it bloody well ought to make a difference, he ought to be prejudiced, he ought to be able to be angry," Stephen thought, and felt sad and cheated and as if, like Vicky, he had a father so far away that he wasn't any good. Not understanding was almost as difficult as not knowing each other.

He did try, however, to explain about the Wilmington kidnapping and how he and Vicky were implicated. Dr. Rawlinson couldn't bring himself to ask him about it directly, but his assurances that he would never attempt to force Stephen's confidence or inquire into his private life became too pointed to ignore. Stephen gave him the overheard-in-the-train version and hoped he'd never have to embark on an explanation of any less ordinary way of gaining information. Trying to show a friendly spirit at the end, he asked, "Why do people snatch babies, Dad?"

"It's a sign of a very pathological state of mind. Always women, as far as I know. Often a young girl who's lost a baby of her own for some reason. Though there have been cases of quite young girls who act in that way for no apparent reason. An aberrant acting out of the repressed maternal instinct possibly. . . ." He was off again. Stephen stopped listening, but was then brought back to the present by realizing that his father had asked him a question.

"Sorry! What did you say?"

"I was asking if you were quite satisfied in your own mind that this girl you are . . . involved with, really has nothing to do with this baby's disappearance?"

"Vicky! Of course she hasn't! What on earth . . .?"

"It seems possible that the police may not share your conviction."

"But why . . . ? I mean, if she'd been mixed up in it, why would we go to the police and tell them about what we heard?"

"Mind you, Stephen, I'm not doubting your word. I'm only suggesting that to the police it might sound—suspicious. A clever red herring. You describe a couple no one else has seen, so there can be no confirmation of what you say. You see? To divert suspicion. You couldn't blame them if they feel that there are more questions to be asked before you're—what I think is called 'in the clear.'"

"But I'd have to be in it too! It couldn't be just Vicky. I was there when we heard them saying that about the baby!"

"Are you sure you were there? In the train with the girl? She didn't merely tell you this story and you agreed to make it sound more probable by saying that you had been with her at the time?"

It was all so horribly like the confabulations which had in fact taken place between him and Vicky, that Stephen was dumb. His father followed up his advantage by saying, "You know I'm not a snob, Stephen, but I have been wanting to have a word with you about those two girls you brought in here the other day."

Stephen said, "What about them?"

"Just be a bit on your guard. I only want you to remember that with a girl of that class the standards are different from ours. I mean, she might seem to be taking the same sort of attitude about certain things as yours would be, and then, when it was too late, you might find her expectations were quite different from yours. That's all."

"I don't know what you're talking about," Stephen said, rage rapidly boiling up inside him.

"I'm sure you do, Stephen. Consciously you may reject the idea that as your father I'm in a position to be able to advise you about certain aspects of life, but unconsciously you understand exactly what I'm dealing with. After all, your education in matters of sex hasn't been neglected, I think."

"You mean that if I got a working-class girl pregnant, she'd expect me to marry her?"

"Roughly, yes. I'm sorry it all has to be spelled out quite so crudely."

"I don't see it's any worse saying it straight out. And I don't see that it's any worse getting one girl pregnant than another, if I don't want to marry her anyway."

"I was just pointing out that in that class when a girl gets pregnant. . . ."

"And you can't say you aren't a snob. Class doesn't make any difference nowadays. You'll say next that Vicky or Chris is more likely to have taken that baby because they're not middle class like us."

"At any rate, the police are more likely to suspect her."

"That's no reason why you should."

"I suppose you realize, Stephen, that your springing so heatedly to this girl's defense is a very clear indication that you are far more deeply involved with her than you realize. . . ."

To Stephen's own surprise, his instant reaction to his father's disparaging reference to "this girl" was to see under attack, not Chris's pretty, flushed face, but Vicky's; bonier, plainer, alive with intelligence and feeling. He almost didn't believe what he saw. He still felt the stirring of rivalry with Paul for Chris's affections. But for Chris he didn't feel the need to protect, he didn't feel that spark of recognition which proclaims, "This is my sort of person, this is what I understand." He admired Chris, thought she was lovely and sweet and warm, but he realized, with the echo of a pang, that she was not for him. He could never feel completely at ease with Chris's direct view of life, he couldn't accept the black and white terms in which she saw her own and other people's actions. He remembered now Vicky's silences, Vicky's embarrassments, how she'd looked when she told him she didn't really belong to Chris's mother and father, the warmth with which she'd claimed a relationship, through appreciation and love, to Mrs. Stanford and Chris. All this, while his father's measured, cultivated voice sounded in his ears. He heard the end of the sentence, " . . . of course she is unusually good to look at, I'm not surprised you find yourself attracted, but . . ." and he interrupted, "Vicky's not the pretty one," and saw his father's astonishment and felt glad that he had broken out of the parental pattern and had committed himself to something that was justified only by feeling, and not by the logical clauses of cold reason.

On Friday morning Stephen rang the number Price had given him, and heard his voice, a little impatient, immensely weary, "Price here."

"It's Stephen Rawlinson. You said to let you know if anything happened. We've had another."

"When?"

"Just now. About an hour ago. And I think it might be urgent."

"Where are you?"

"In a callbox near the tube station."

"Is the girl there too?"

"She's waiting outside."

"Right. Don't tell me anything now. I'll send a car for you. Can you be at that coffee place I saw you in the day before yesterday? Both of you?"

"Yes, we'll be there."

"See you." Price rang off.

"What did he say? Did he believe . . . ?" Vicky asked as soon as Stephen was out of the callbox.

"He's sending a car for us right away. He sounded as if he believed it."

"He didn't on Wednesday. Not at the beginning."

"I thought he did by the end. It was something to do with the picture."

"Then why didn't he say? If he knows it was there, wherever it was. He doesn't tell us anything."

"That's just because he's police."

"You don't think really he thinks it was me, like your father said?"

"No, I don't. I think that's just my father being too clever by half. As usual."

"You don't talk about him as if you liked him much, Stephen."

Stephen said, "Come on. We've got to get back to the café, Price is sending for us there," and they started toward it. But Vicky wasn't going to let him get off without answering and as they walked, she said again, "Don't you like your father at all?"

"Well, you've seen him. Would you?"

"I only saw him for about five minutes. He might not be like that all the time."

"No, he isn't, exactly. But rather. Making things more complicated than they need be and criticizing my mother."

"I suppose he's very clever," Vicky said.

"He is, but it's all . . . I don't know how to express it. It's all thinking. He's stupid about people's feelings. And he pretends not to have any himself."

"Have any what? Feelings?"

"That's right."

"Perhaps he's frightened of them," Vicky said.

"Yes. You're quite right. That's what it is, he's frightened. How did you guess?"

"I know what it's like. You feel it's safer to work it all out by thinking. Then you won't be made to look silly. Or get hurt."

"Do you feel like that now?"

"How do you mean, now? Because of the police, do you mean?"

"No. I meant with me."

Astonished, Vicky turned to look at him. To his fury Stephen felt himself blushing. Immediately Vicky blushed too and looked away again. Neither of them spoke. The next thing Vicky said was, "There's the café. Let's get a table by the window where we can see when they come." Stephen, glancing sideways, saw that her color had returned to its normal smooth pallor. He followed her into the coffee shop.

Forty minutes later they were again in the Kensington police station, sitting opposite Price, and he was saying, "Now then. Tell me about it."

"It was another flash," Stephen said.

"Where were you?"

"In the café. Vicky and I were having coffee."

"Go on."

"I saw Mrs. Wilmington. . . ."

"Mrs. *Wilmington?*"

"Yes. It was dark. She was walking along a road."

"What road?"

"I'm afraid I don't know. It looked as if it might be in the country. There weren't any houses. Only trees."

"If it was dark, how could you see anything?" Price asked sharply.

"In the headlights of the car."

"So there was a car too?"

"There were two. She was walking away from one. I'm not sure what make it was. Smallish. Could have been a Fiat, that sort of shape. I could see that better than the other, because the headlights from the other car were brighter."

"Was there anyone else there?"

"There was a driver in the other car, I could see the outline of his head. And a passenger beside him. I couldn't see anything else."

"How was Mrs. Wilmington dressed?"

Stephen was uncertain. "I'm not sure. Trousers, I think, and a sort of jacket. But there was one thing. . . ."

"What?"

"She was carrying something in her hand."

"A handbag?"

"No. Smaller. Like a book."

"An envelope, could it have been?"

"Yes, it could easily."

"Did you see this too?" Price asked Vicky.

"Not quite the same. I saw more inside the other car."

"Tell me."

"I couldn't see much. It was dark, like Stephen said. Only I could see their heads against the light of her car. Mrs. Wilmington's. There were three of them. It was like as if I was looking in through the window at the back."

"Could you see their faces?"

Vicky shivered. "They had stockings on over their heads. It was horrid."

Stephen said, "But you heard them say something."

"I heard one of them say, 'Don't let her see the kid's not here.'"

"Could you see her? Mrs. Wilmington?"

"Not properly. I could see someone coming down the road. But their heads were between her and me."

"Do you agree with Stephen's description of what she was wearing?"

"I didn't notice. It all happened so quickly."

Price sat and looked at them.

"What did you think was happening? You," he said to Vicky.

"I thought she was going to give them money so as to get the baby back."

"But the baby wasn't there?"

"That's what they said."

"What did you make of it?" Price asked Stephen.

"I thought she was handing over the ransom money, too. I didn't know about the baby not being there, though. Not until Vicky told me."

"What makes you think this is urgent?" Price said to them both.

"Because she mustn't do it, must she? Not pay a lot of money and not get the baby back."

"How do you know it hasn't already happened?"

"Always before we've seen things that were going to happen. Why? Has it?" Stephen asked.

"Not as far as I know. Is that all?"

"I think so. Can't think of anything more. Can you, Vicky?"

"No."

"Would you recognize that man's voice again?" Price asked her.

"I might. I don't know. There wasn't anything special about it."

"The man you saw before—Purfitt. Was he one of the men in the car?"

"I don't know. It's difficult to tell through those masks."

"Not difficult, impossible," Price said.

"So I don't know."

"Did you see anything of the road? Notice what sort of trees they were? Bushes? Anything like that?"

"Not really. Big trees. They hadn't got many leaves on them, though."

"Not pines, then?"

"Their branches were sort of flat. Sort of like layers, not twiggy like some trees are," said Vicky, the town-bred child.

"Beeches possibly. Anything else? What about sounds? Owls? Traffic? Anything?"

"Terribly quiet. I did notice that. Did you, Stephen?"

"Yes. Now you say so of course that's partly why I thought it was country. I could hear her walking along the road."

"I did, too. Wait a minute. . . ."

Price waited.

"Her feet. The sound they made. It was different from London roads. You sort of go clop on the roads round here. She didn't. It was . . . gritty."

"Not macadamized," Price said.

"Pardon?"

"An unmade road. Loose stones, uneven. That's a very bright bit of observation," he said.

Vicky flushed slightly and said, "Is it any help?"

"Could be." He got up. "Have to get going. If you're right and it hasn't happened yet, there's a lot I've got to do."

"You mean. . . . You do believe we're not just making it all up?"

"If you are, and I catch you at it, God help you," Price said, suddenly stern.

"We're not. I know it sounds crazy. We didn't ask to get mixed up in it . . ." Stephen began.

"All right. I didn't say I didn't trust you, did I?"

"What were you going to ask us yesterday when you came around and we weren't there?" Vicky asked.

"Just a few more details. Only I think we'll leave them for the present."

"Will you tell us about this? I mean, when it's happened?" Stephen asked.

"You'll be hearing from me. And if you get any more flashes, you'll let me know. If you're really on to something, it means we've got a chance of being a move ahead of this little lot. Which would give me a great deal of pleasure," Price said, standing up.

"I'll ring you if there's anything," Stephen said.

"Do that. And I'll be in touch."

"He does believe us," Vicky said as they left.

"I can't think why. I wouldn't if I was him."

29

Sally Wilmington looked at her wristwatch for the hundredth time in an hour, and saw that she was still much too early. She mustn't be late, but also she mustn't be hanging around the place, wherever it was, for hours. She'd been warned against that. She moved over from the middle of the motorway to the slow lane and dropped her speed to just over thirty. Agony to have to do this, when what she wanted most was to go quickly, quickly, impossibly fast. But then yesterday and today had been an agony of impatience and frustration, of having to pretend and to keep a watch over herself and to appear to be as hopeless as she'd been all the last week. Of having to lie to everyone and at the same time set up a whole system inside which she could do what she knew she had to do without anyone guessing.

The worst thing had been getting the money. Sally had never realized how difficult it could be if you wanted a great deal of cash in a hurry. She'd been to the bank and asked the manager. Said she wanted to put down a deposit on a place in the country, but he'd told her it was impossible to let her have more than ten thousand. Ten, when she needed two hundred. She'd pleaded, but she hadn't dared to allow him to see how much it meant to her, because no one must know the truth. She couldn't risk his ringing Andrew and asking him to confirm the need for urgency. So she'd pretended to be satisfied. She'd gone home with ten thousand and had gone through her possessions to see what she could turn into cash. In the afternoon she'd taken her pearls, the diamond star, the gold collar and most of her rings to a place she'd heard of in Knightsbridge where they advanced money on the security of jewelry. Gwen had told her about it when she, Gwen, was being blackmailed by that horrible woman. But altogether she'd only raised just over fifty thousand. She'd almost broken down and cried. The man—he was surprisingly nice, quiet and businesslike and quite incurious—had suggested she might have something else at home which could go toward making up what was required, and she'd remembered the Picasso. Andrew had paid over a hundred thousand for it, it must be worth more now. She'd told this to Mr. Franklin and he'd agreed to look at it, if she could get it to him within the hour. She'd gone straight back, and, in what she thought was an inspiration, she draped her two mink coats over the arm that held the Picasso and directed the waiting taxi to take her back to Knightsbridge. In the end she'd raised just over a hundred thousand. She'd have to persuade them it was as much as she could get. She'd promise them the rest once she had Caroline Ann back. She must get her back, she must. The hundred thousand would show that she was in earnest. They must believe her. She'd make them believe her. She'd. . . .

She looked at her watch again. Only nine. She'd speeded up too much again. Ten o'clock the voice had said, and don't hang around before and don't be late. We shan't wait more than a minute for you. Take the Henley exit from the motorway and go on through Henley on the Oxford road, and just four miles outside the town you come to a stretch of road through woods. Take the turn to the right marked Mocking End. Drive a hundred yards and stop. Keep your headlights on and walk toward the car you'll see parked there. Hold up the money so we can see it.

The money was in an envelope, a big one. It made quite a bulky packet. She put her hand out and touched it in the glove compartment. Nearly all old notes. They must let her have Caroline Ann back, they must. She was doing everything they'd told her, wasn't she?

Don't tell your husband. Come alone. Don't tell anyone where you're going. And if you tell the police, you'd better start getting the next kid on the way as quick as you can, because you can count this one out. If you want any help, if your husband isn't too keen, one of us'll be happy to oblige. . . . Dirty sniggers. Hateful. If there's anyone with you or you've been followed, if you've tried to be clever, you'll see us do the kid in. Better be careful. No tricks. Just do as you're told. Do as you're told. Do as you're told. She was doing as she was told, wasn't she? They would see that she was.

She'd had to lie to Andrew. When he'd come back yesterday evening and asked at once, "Any news?" she'd said "No, nothing new." She'd lied to the nice Chief Superintendent when he'd come to see her. She'd told him, no more telephone calls; she'd asked if he had any more clues. He'd told her that he had one or two, that they had an address the Edmonton landlady had given them. The girl had mentioned Brady Drive as a place she'd stayed at in Birmingham. There wasn't such a road in Birmingham, but there was in Walthamstowe and he'd got a man going from door to door asking if anyone had seen a girl answering to the description. It didn't mean much to Sally, but he'd seemed to think it might lead to something. When he'd left he'd said, "You won't go doing anything on your own without telling us, will you, Mrs. Wilmington?" And she'd looked straight at him and said, "No, Superintendent, I won't." She hadn't known she could act so well.

Or had she? He'd been back again today. He'd come just when she was meaning to go off to the Knightsbridge place, and she'd been in a fever to get rid of him. He seemed as if he would stay forever. It had been almost as if he suspected she wasn't telling the truth. He'd asked her again and again, "Are you sure you haven't had another demand for money?" She'd had to keep on saying No. He'd said, "You know, if they asked you to take any action without telling anyone, say your husband or us, it could be dangerous. We're dealing with a very ugly crowd. I don't think there's anything they'd stick at." If he meant to frighten her for herself, he'd taken the wrong line by saying that. If there was nothing they'd stick at, what about Caroline Ann? What would they do to Caroline Ann if Andrew went on refusing to pay up? So she'd just said politely that she did understand and that of course she wasn't going to do anything silly, and would he excuse her, she'd got an appointment to keep. The moment she'd got rid of him she'd been on her way to Knightsbridge.

Damn! She was going too fast again. And the minute hand on her watch still only just after the hour. She was passing the Heston Services, she'd be at the Henley exit in another quarter of an hour. Fifteen minutes to get into Henley and out the other side. There was a fair amount of traffic on the road, you expected that on a Friday night, but it was too late for the rush hour at the end of the office day and too early for the theatre crowd. She might have to find somewhere in Henley where she could have coffee. She wouldn't drink anything stronger, she must have her wits as sharp as they could be. Would that count as hanging about? No, she didn't know a soul in Henley, and if anyone remembered afterwards seeing her there, it wouldn't matter because by that time she'd have Caroline Ann. Andrew was going to be late tonight, he'd got a business dinner out of town that didn't start till nine. That meant he couldn't possibly be back before midnight, probably later. She'd be back long before he was, and when she'd explained why she'd taken the picture and her furs and the rings and things, and shown him Caroline Ann, he'd see that she'd been right, he'd be glad. What did furs and pearls and pictures matter, anyway, compared with Caroline Ann? She'd get the picture back for him anyway if he wanted it.

She wouldn't think about the possibility that she might come back without either the money or the baby. Price had said to her,

"You do know, don't you, that with this sort of criminal you can't trust what they promise? They're quite capable of taking the money and not handing over your baby." But Sally wouldn't listen to this, except to say inside herself that it was a risk she had to take. If there was the smallest chance of getting Caroline Ann back she was going to take it.

She reduced her speed again.

But all those warnings had made her extra cautious. She didn't want to find she'd been followed. Price might have taken it into his head to have all her movements watched. So she'd told the man on duty outside the house that her husband was out that evening and she was going to drive out to her mother's outside London. She'd be back late. And when she'd set off she'd gone round-about, not straight on the M4, looking all the time to make sure no police car was following her. Several times she'd pulled up and watched the traffic go past. When she felt safe, she drove out west. She'd rung her mother and said she was on her way, but she was having trouble with the car and might not be able to make it. She meant to ring again later and say she'd had to stop in a garage and wouldn't be able to get there. Then if the police checked on the story, there'd be nothing to make them suspicious. The only precaution she hadn't taken was to change cars. She was driving her own little Fiat. But she didn't think Price even knew about it; it had been in the double garage each time he'd been to the house. She hadn't taken it out once in all this dreadful week. She couldn't think of anything she'd done wrong.

After she'd got off the motorway, there was more traffic and she had to slow up a lot. She didn't get into Henley until a quarter to ten. She parked in the space by the side of a hotel on the river and went in and asked for coffee, but when it came, she couldn't drink it, just the smell made her feel sick. She went to the loo and then got back in the car again. She was shaking so much she could hardly start it up and pull onto the road. It was dark, of course. She was terrified of missing the turning; she'd better leave and risk being a minute or two early. She was out of town, was driving on a country road again. No trees near at hand yet. Uphill, then the road straightened out between hedges. She must have gone at least three miles. The trees were closing in over her head before she realized. Her headlights lit up the silvery boles of smooth beech trunks. Above were the flat, layered branches, fat buds just beginning to leaf. She was going very slowly now, looking to her right all the time. A clock very far away tolled the hour, and she panicked. She was late, they'd have gone, she'd never see Caroline Ann again. She increased her speed and at that moment saw the sign. Mocking End ¾ mile. She turned, the trees closed out all light from the sky, the wheels crunched on stones and grit.

She saw the headlights of the stationary car ahead of her and drew to a halt. She took the packet in her hand and got out of the car. A voice called, "Dim your lights, can't you?" She reached back into the car and turned the headlights down. Then she started walking toward the stationary car, dazzled by the light coming from it, unable to see. She held the packet out in front of her. Her lips were forming words, she was talking almost out loud. "It's all I can get. I promise you shall have the rest. I promise . . . I promise. . . . Give me my baby!"

Whoever was in the car with the blazing lights sat very still, very quiet. She was coming near it now. The wood was very quiet.

Suddenly she heard something else. Very quiet, but unmistakable, the sound of wheels on the unmade road in front of her, beyond the other car. Immediately there was a tumult, the engine of the other car roared into life, someone shouted, there was a shot, two shots, and the other car came racing toward her. She jumped sideways and fell, scratching her face on a tangle of briars. The car flashed past, grazed her Fiat and roared out onto the main road. She heard another engine start up and go in pursuit. She got up shakily and began to walk back toward her own car. She was crying, gasping for breath, the packet was still in her hand.

A voice called out, "Mrs. Wilmington? Stay where we can see you, will you?" Not one of Them. Price appeared out of nowhere on the side of the track and came up to her and took her arm.

"Did they hit you?"

"No. I jumped. Just scratches, that's all."

"If it's any comfort to you, we don't think they had your baby there," he said gently.

"How did you . . .? I didn't tell anyone. How did you guess?"

"I'll explain everything. Now we'd better get you home. Do you think you can drive?" He looked at her. "No. I'll get one of my men to take your car back. You'd better come in the other one with me."

He was very good. He only once said, "I told you so," and Sally was too exhausted and too miserable to offer any defense.

Price blamed himself for the shambles the evening had been. There had been one serious mistake after another. If only he'd had more time, so that he might have set up a proper monitoring system to cover all Mrs. Wilmington's movements, then he'd have got his ambush posted on site before those bastards arrived and he'd have copped the lot. If only she, Mrs. W., hadn't lied to him when he tried to get her to tell him about a further ransom demand. If only—and he'd no one but himself to blame here—if only he'd believed those children and forced the truth out of her. But a policeman's natural skepticism and caution had obliged him to go around checking up and verifying. If only he hadn't been thrown off the scent by finding no record on the monitored telephone line of any such conversation. That had brought back all his doubts about the children's story. It was only late Friday afternoon that he'd seen the possible significance of one of Thursday's phoned messages: would Mrs. Wilmington ring a number, 148-394X at twelve o'clock midday. He checked and, of course, it was a callbox. How did they know she'd ring from outside the house? Because she had a standing appointment with her hairdresser at that time on Thursdays. Too easy to check that she was going that day.

Price groaned. There were brains behind this operation. It wasn't just an amateur effort.

By the time he'd worked that out, and got a grudging admission from the manager of her bank that though professional discretion forbade him to give any information concerning the private affairs of a client, if the Chief Superintendent stated that Mrs. Wilmington had inquired about drawing out a large sum in cash, he wouldn't categorically deny it—by the time all the tiresome, long-winded business of checking was done and he knew that the children were right, she'd given them the slip. Drove off in her little Fiat toward the middle of London·and was lost. He put out a call to every man on duty to look out for the car, but it was too easy to miss. If only the children's account could have given him some idea of what direction she'd be heading for! But a quiet road with beeches could describe a hundred places within driving distance of Kensington. Even when they'd had their first piece of luck and had a report of the car on the M4, there were too many exits to guard with no time at all to get the men there. Then she'd been spotted coming out of Henley and they had a car following her as soon as possible, but not soon enough. They'd lost her on the Oxford Road, it was only chance that Potter had seen the headlights blazing through the trees and thought it was worth having a look. Of course, coming in without proper precautions like that they hadn't a hope of surprising them, it was just a question of catching them in the resulting chase, and they hadn't even succeeded in that. Potter had said they drove like devils and someone in the car must know the country round there backwards. Probably lived there as a kid. Twisting roads, high hedges, everything to make it as difficult as possible for even an experienced police driver who didn't know the roads. They'd got clear away, and he was no nearer getting them. Nothing. Not a bloody thing to go on. He just hoped the girl Vicky had been right too about their not having the baby with them. If they had had, he wouldn't give much chance for its hope of survival. That sort of crowd weren't too particular what they did when they got frightened. And they'd missed getting the money as well. It looked black for the Wilmington baby. What the hell was he going to do next?

It was ten o'clock. He'd only had a couple of hours' sleep before coming to the office, and he was dead tired, but he couldn't rest.

He read a report from the woman who'd been investigating the Brady Drive angle. A girl answering to the description given by Mrs. Plum had lived at number 26 but had left a few weeks before. Name, Maureen Hollingsworth. Had been living with a father and young stepmother. When interviewed, the step-mother said that Maureen wasn't very bright. As far as she knew she'd never been in any sort of trouble with the police. She and Maureen hadn't got on too badly. They didn't have much to say to each other, that was all. She thought Maureen hadn't liked her father marrying someone who wasn't all that much older than she was herself. Maureen hadn't left as the result of a quarrel, she'd just said one day she was going to share a flat with a friend and she'd walked out. No, she hadn't thought it was all that funny. Maureen was eighteen, she had a right to go where she wanted. She'd thought the friend was probably a boy friend, because Maureen suddenly started getting a lot of new clothes, things she'd never have bought herself. Also she stopped moan-ing about never being asked out by boys. Before she'd left she'd been out most evenings, sometimes not come back all night. Maureen's father had said he wasn't worried either. Maureen was old enough to look after herself. The policewoman had got the impression that both of them were glad to have the place to themselves and weren't anxious to try to find the girl or even to know what had happened to her. The father explained that she was a bit slow and that Kitty got impatient with her sometimes. He'd kept on saying that it wasn't natural for a girl of that age to want to stay at home. He seemed to think it quite natural that she should go off and not tell them where, or ever come back to see them.

A name, that was all. She'd worked in Woolworth's but no

one there knew anything about her. She hadn't made any friends there. One girl had heard her boasting about a boy friend who had plenty of money, but she hadn't believed it. "She wasn't the kind of girl who'd get a fellow with lots of money." A photograph of Maureen, a poor snapshot taken some years earlier, provided by her father, seemed to confirm this.

Price picked up the telephone and dialed the number of the Rawlinson house. It was a woman who answered. He asked for Stephen and heard her calling his name. Then Stephen's voice. "Hullo?"

"It's Superintendent Price speaking. I want to ask you a favor."

He could hear Stephen's surprise. "What?"

"Could you and Vicky Stanford come to the Yard?"

"I can. I could find out about Vicky. When?"

"As soon as possible. This morning if you can."

"I'll go 'round to Vicky straight away. If she's not at home, do you want me alone, or . . .?"

"No. I want the two of you. I'm going to ask you to do some of your magic."

Stephen didn't care for the word magic and said stiffly, "Did anything happen about the last one?"

"It certainly did. I'll tell you when I see you. And. . . ."

"What?"

"I shall be really grateful if you two can help me."

It was an apology for his past disbelief.

"I'll have to take the egg with me. Vicky must have her bit too," Stephen thought.

Price recognized that they were touchy, uncertain of their status as young adults, embarrassed by their inexplicable power of seeing forwards as well as backwards, suspicious of him as an expert and an authority. He also felt today a shift in their own relationship; something not firmly established, perhaps not even conscious, but there was a solidarity of purpose, an awareness of each other that hadn't been there, he'd swear, the first time he'd met them. In no time at all they would know they were in love, he thought, and he envied them a good deal and pitied them a little. He wondered how they'd deal with it when they knew. Judging by the general opinion of how young people went about things nowadays, he supposed they might be in bed with each other within hours of the discovery, and he hoped if it happened like that, they'd be good for each other and that no one would get hurt too much. Both of them were sensitive and intelligent, love for boys and girls like this was a dangerous game. The odd thing was that however much you ached, you didn't wish it had never happened. What an old cynic he was, thinking first of the pain and ignoring the sudden irradiation of joy which could accompany the realization that you were loved in turn! Like a rocket exploding out of the dark night. The feeling of being, for the first time, alive down to the most insignificant cell of your body and to the shadow of every thought. You were weightless, you flew, your feet skimmed the ground, you were so blesséd you felt you had only to look at a sick person and you would heal them. He himself had felt all that when Laurie had said she loved him. And when she left him, he'd been through the consequent hell.

He came back to the present. He was treating them with extreme seriousness and a politeness which he hoped wasn't exaggerated. They'd arrived in his office just before midday, and after telling them about the events of the night before—the events which had so completely proved them right—he took them out to lunch in the snack bar portion of a Westminster pub much patronized by politicians. There weren't many of those around on a Saturday, but he was able to point out one well-known face and to tell a few anecdotes about other figures in the public view. He could feel that his methods were succeeding. Both the boy and the girl became more relaxed, let down the barriers they'd put up. By the end of the meal they were both talking naturally about ordinary things; they asked him about his job, and he was careful to answer seriously. He told them about the slog that goes into detective work, the detailed, boring drudgery that has to be put in behind every brilliant guess and intuitive response. "That's where I went wrong yesterday. I should have accepted your story and acted on it straight away. Instead of which I went around checking, like a mole burrowing underground when what he's in search of is daylight," he said. He knew that to admit that he'd been in the wrong would reassure them and make them more accessible for what he wanted them to do.

Back in the office he told them what this was.

"We're stuck. Those devils got away last night and they'll have been properly frightened off. We've no idea where to look, even. If they're in London, they could be anywhere and there's nothing to prevent them just sitting tight in the house of one of their friends who won't give them away. They won't risk going into lodgings again. We've got their descriptions and the pictures, but a change of clothes or of hair style could make them virtually unrecognizable. There must be hundreds of thousands of young couples with babies. We can't check up on them all."

"What do you want us to do?"

"Will you try if you can see them? If you could just tell me what they look like now, it'd be an immense help. If you knew where they are, of course, that'd be even better. And I want to know about that baby. I haven't told its mother but I'm seriously concerned about its safety. After last night they might do anything. I don't know, you see, whether they'll risk another demand for money. And if they aren't expecting to get the money now, the baby becomes a liability. They don't need to keep it alive."

Stephen and Vicky looked at each other.

"I know you don't like being asked to do it. I know it must seem as if I was expecting you to perform some sort of trick. But don't think of it like that. Think of it more as if you had some special kind of scientific instrument which I can't get hold of. An electronic microscope, something like that. I'm asking you to use that instrument to give me information I can't get on my own," Price said quickly.

"I will if Stephen will," Vicky said.

Stephen said, "All right."

"Any idea how long it will take?" Price asked.

"No. We've never done it like this. Tried, I mean."

"Suppose I leave you here in my office for the next hour? I've got to go along to look up something in the files. You can stay here. I'll tell the switchboard to put my calls through some-where else, so you won't be disturbed." He picked up a couple of files and left.

"I'm glad he left us alone," Vicky said.

"I wouldn't have tried if he'd been going to be sitting there watching us, would you?"

"Don't know. If it was the only way I might've."

"I feel stupid," Stephen said, going over to the window and looking down at the road beneath.

"So do I. Some ways it's better when we don't know what's going to happen."

"I don't feel as if anything would."

"It's got to! If they really might hurt that baby."

"Perhaps he said that just to make us keen."

"I thought he really was worried."

Stephen continued to look out of the window.

"Do come and sit down, Stephen."

"Why? It hasn't ever mattered before what we were doing. You don't have to be sitting down and concentrating."

"You aren't trying."

Stephen said, "Oh, all right!" and sat down on one of the hard chairs opposite Vicky.

"Do you think we should hold on to the bits of the egg?"

"We can if you think we ought to."

"And not talk."

Twelve immensely long minutes passed. Vicky was sitting with her eyes shut most of that time. When at last she opened them, Stephen said, "It's no use. I didn't get anything and I'm sure you didn't."

"No I didn't."

"Well, then!"

"There's still three-quarters of an hour left," Vicky said looking at the synchronized electric clock on the wall.

"I can't go on like that for that long."

"I don't think I've got the right sort of mind. I can't go on thinking about anything all the time. I keep on thinking about other things. Silly. Like what we had for lunch," Vicky said.

"I'm like that too. I kept on thinking about my Ma's shopping this morning. She'd gone out to get some steak, and the butcher persuaded her to have pork instead, and she spent hours trying to decide how she could cook it so my father wouldn't know the difference."

"Why should he mind?"

"I daresay he wouldn't if only she'd just tell him she'd changed her mind. Only she always starts by saying, 'I'm sorry, but. . . .' You know. So then he thinks there's something she ought to be sorry for and starts telling her off. Not exactly telling off, more explaining to her why she's done the wrong thing again."

"She ought to say she did it on purpose," Vicky said.

"That's what I'm always telling her."

"Oh! I'd forgotten," Vicky said, remembering.

"So had I."

"Shall we try again?"

"I'll tell you what I think, Vicky. I don't think we ought to try. I think what's wrong is, we're looking at it too hard."

"How do you mean?"

"When I first got the egg, it was all in pieces. I went on and on and on and I couldn't even fit two pieces together. And then I stopped trying like that and just sort of sat and didn't think about it, and it began to get into one piece again. I mean, it was my fingers doing it, of course, but I wasn't telling them what to do, and it worked much better. I think that's what we ought to be doing now. Not making it happen. More like letting it."

"I know if you say we should sit still and make our minds a blank I won't be able to. I tried once, when Chris wanted to do Yoga with one of her boy friends and they tried to teach me. I kept on thinking of the most awful things. I wasn't blank at all."

"We won't try to go blank. We'll just not think about that."

"How?"

"We could talk to each other."

"What about?"

"Or, I'll tell you what! We'll play a game."

"A game?"

"Animal, Vegetable and Mineral. You know, like they do on the radio. Twenty questions. You think of something and I have to guess what it is."

"All right. If you think that'll work."

"You weren't thinking about what was going to happen the other times, were you?"

"No . . . No, I wasn't. I was talking to Chris."

"Then?"

"All right."

"You start."

Vicky thought and then said, "Vegetable and mineral. I don't think it's got any animal in it."

"Can you wear it?"

"Not exactly."

"Have you got one?"

"I've got half a one."

"What do you do with your half? I mean is it useful?"

"Half isn't. I mean, Chris and me have got one between us. Then it's useful."

"Where do you keep it, indoors or out of doors?"

"Indoors."

"Can you carry it, or is it too heavy to lift?"

"Not heavy at all."

"Do you use it in the kitchen?"

"No."

"In the bathroom?"

"No."

He went on asking. Vicky had forgotten to keep a count of his questions but finally they agreed he must have had more than twenty and he gave it up.

"An umbrella. That's why we keep it indoors, but we don't use it there."

"What on earth made you think of an umbrella on a day like this?"

"Don't know. Now you think of something."

"Vegetable," Stephen said.

"Can you eat it?"

"No."

"Is it made into something? Or is it just a vegetable, like a tree?"

"It's made into something."

"It's the egg!"

"You're too quick. Yes, it's the egg. . . ." He didn't finish what he had been going to say because at that moment the flash happened.

Vicky was looking out through the windscreen of a car. Rain was lashing outside with such fury that she couldn't see out at all. She heard a girl's voice say, "Stop, Skinner, I'm frightened!" She was aware of two heads between her and the streaming windscreen, then suddenly the wipers came into action, the water cleared and she saw that the car was driving along a road that lay between chalky walls on one side, and on the other an angry gray sea, whitened with the storm of raindrops hitting up little spouts of spray as they struck its surface like arrows. The car swerved and Vicky shut her eyes. Then she opened them again and saw Stephen opposite and knew he'd been there too.

"It was the same girl. But, the back of her head looked different," Stephen said.

"How different?"

"The one I saw saying that about the baby had a lot of hair. This one didn't."

"Short hair?" Price suggested.

"Almost as if she hadn't got much. Sort of straggly, all ends and bits sticking up."

"As if someone not very expert had cut it?"

"That's right!"

"That's probably just about what did happen. How about him?"

"I didn't really see," Vicky said.

"Did you get the impression from what you did see that it could be the same man?"

"I suppose so. He was the same sort of shape. Only this time he was wearing a hat."

"That fits Purfitt. He doesn't like showing his hair. The landlady in Edmonton said he wore a hat whenever she saw him."

"She calls him Skinner."

"It's one of his nicknames." She hadn't known that. A further confirmation of this extraordinary story.

"Does it help?" Vicky asked.

"It could. This means they've left London for the coast. It's a pity, of course, that such a lot of English coastline is chalk, practically the whole of the south from Kent to Weymouth. Still, it does give us something to go on. You didn't happen, either of you, to notice anything else about the road? Whether there were street lamps? Was there a pier? An esplanade? Houses? A bus stop? Anything like that?"

"I don't think there were any houses," Vicky said.

"There wasn't a pier or a proper esplanade. I don't remember a bus stop," Stephen said.

"Any cliffs in the distance? A lighthouse?"

"No. Just sea, I think."

"Notice anything about the car? The dashboard, for instance? Any indication of the make?"

Stephen hadn't, but Vicky said, "I don't know if it helps, but I was sort of surprised how high up it was."

"You mean the road? High above the sea? I thought you said. . . ."

"Not the road, the car. You know how when you're in a car you don't feel very high above the road? Well, this one was. You couldn't have thought you could touch the ground with your feet."

Price puzzled over this, half-inclined to write it off as a piece of over-elaboration which he'd in a way invited, by asking too many questions, till Vicky said, "More like a bus."

"That's it! Ever been in a Land Rover?"

"Yes, like that! Only this wasn't open at the sides like a Land Rover."

"A van. A Commer Van. Or a Volkswagen. That's what they've gone off in. Of course. That makes sense."

"What are you going to do?" Stephen asked.

"Take your hint about the girl's hair and change the description. Get them alerted all along the south coast. We'll get them somehow, even if it means stopping every van between Axminster and Dover. Which side of the car was the sea, by the way?"

"On the left."

"That means they're heading west. Doesn't tell us a lot, but it might give us a lead."

"And the rain," Vicky said.

"What about the rain?"

"It isn't raining here."

"You're quite right. Now that might really tell us where they are. It was a sudden storm, you thought?"

"Because he hadn't turned the wipers on. As if he hadn't expected it and then couldn't find the right switch."

Price dialed a number on the telephone and asked for the meteorological reports for the south coast.

"You've forgotten something, though," Stephen said.

"What?"

"I'm afraid the rain may not help. Because all this hasn't happened yet."

"You're sure of that?"

"We've always seen it before, not after."

"But it could happen any minute," Vicky said.

"It was daylight, wasn't it?"

"Yes. Only not very light because of the rain."

"So they might not have left London yet," Price said, wondering whether it was worth putting a watch on all the exits to the south of the city and deciding that as a precaution he'd have to. Though what was he to tell his men to look out for? Any van driven by a young man in a hat? He didn't know the make, the color, the size. The girl very likely wouldn't be visible either, she'd probably be kept in the back with the baby. At which point in his thoughts, Vicky asked, "Do you think the baby's still all right?"

Price said gravely, "I hope so. One thing I'm thankful you've told me is that the girl's still around. As long as they've got her, I think it's probable they've got the baby. She's just there to look after it for them, obviously. She's not the sort of girl they'd take around otherwise."

"But if she wasn't there?"

"Then I would be very much afraid they might have decided the risks were too great and that they wouldn't keep either of them, the girl or the baby."

"But not give it back?"

"No."

"But they want the money! They've got to have the baby to give back if they ask for the money again, haven't they?" Vicky cried.

"It has been known that the ransom has been asked for and paid and the child hasn't been returned. I don't trust this lot. Especially after last night's caper. That's why we've got to find them. Before the baby comes to any harm."

"What do you want us to do?"

"Keep me informed of any . . . messages you get. I'll leave it to you to get in touch with me, I shan't keep bothering you. I'd only ask you to ring me fairly regularly—say twice a day, just to say you have or you haven't anything to tell me."

"Don't you take any time off?" Stephen asked, surprised.

"Not when I've a case like this on my hands. I daren't," Price said, thinking of James Henry Purfitt, whose record showed he'd as soon use violence as not, careering along the south coast with a dim-witted girl and a baby, either of whom he might at any moment decide would be better out of the way. It wasn't a pretty thought. He only hoped that at least the bastard knew how to drive.

32

They drove on and on. Maureen's eyelids kept on dropping, then she'd wake up again with a start as the car jerked and Skinner muttered bad words. She'd had a terrible night. Skinner had been out and not come in till it was nearly morning. Then he hadn't been to bed, he'd told her they'd got to get off as soon as Bus brought the van around. Maureen said, "What van?" but Skinner didn't answer. He almost never did. When Bus'd come with the van, she'd heard him say to Skinner, "Smithy says to keep going. He's going to have another try and you've to be ready to hand over the goods." It meant nothing to Maureen. She'd just put the carry-cot in the back like she was told to, and got into the front seat, when she saw Bus wasn't coming with them. And here they were, hours later, still going through endless streets, all looking to Maureen just the same. Once she said, "Where we going, Skinner?" but he didn't answer until she'd asked a lot of times. Then he said, "You'll know when we get there, won't you?" Another time she said, "I didn't know you could drive, Skinner," and he'd said, "Anyone can drive." But from the way the van jerked about and other drivers leaned out of their cars and swore at him, Maureen didn't think he could have learned very long.

Presently they started seeing more trees and things. Fields, houses with big gardens. It was like country. The sun was shining very bright and Maureen cheered up a bit. She was glad to be out of the basement with the roaches, and Fred and his mother. Perhaps they'd go to lodgings again and there'd be someone to talk to and the telly to watch. She'd like that. She felt a bit braver and she asked, "We going to stay in rooms again?"

"No," Skinner said.

"Where'll we stay, then?"

"In the van."

"How can we? At nights and everything? Where'll we sleep?"

"You'll see."

"We don't have to stay in the van all the time, do we, Skinner? We'll go out for our meals, won't we?"

"You won't," Skinner said.

"I'll have to get Linda's feeds warm," Maureen said, feeling that no one could deny this.

"You'll do that in the van, too."

"Won't I ever get out?"

Skinner didn't answer that and Maureen asked it again.

"You won't if you want to stay alive," he said then.

"Won't there be anyone else? Only you and me and Linda all the time?"

He imitated her voice. "Only me and you and Linda. That's all. And if you aren't careful it'll end up only me. Got it?"

It wasn't even so much the words that made Maureen really frightened. She'd felt, like an animal, the threat of people under pressure, frightened themselves and therefore dangerous, while she'd been in Fred's mother's house. Now, from Skinner she could almost smell fear and violence. For the first time since she'd taken over the baby, she felt mortally afraid. Not just afraid of being hit, but afraid for her life. For the first time since they'd left London she dimly began to think about escape.

But Maureen's brain wasn't the sort which occupies itself with plans for anything, even at such a moment. Anyway, what could she do now, in the van, with Skinner right beside her and the baby in the back? And she was very, very tired. Before they were more than ten miles outside Greater London, Maureen slept.

She woke once or twice, generally when the car pulled up abruptly and she was thrown forward with a jerk. Once her head fell sideways onto Skinner's shoulder and he pushed it off. Once when she couldn't see in front of her, the windscreen looked like the window in a bathroom that you weren't meant to be able to see through. When she'd realized the car was still moving, she'd said, "Stop, Skinner, I'm frightened!" But he hadn't stopped, though she could feel the van skidding about. He'd pulled at the knobs in front of him and then the wipers began to sweep across the windscreen and she could see out again. To her surprise they were right away from houses, there was just a big white sort of wall on one side, and on the other something gray and white and heaving and a whole lot of it. It took Maureen a minute to realize that this was the sea. She'd seen the sea several times when she'd gone with the school on day's outings, but she'd never seen it look like this before, so restless and angry it made her own stomach heave to look at it. She said, "Are we going to the seaside, Skinner?" but as usual he didn't answer, and after she'd looked at it for a bit they came to some houses and he turned away from the sea. They drove through a sort of town and past a church that had a clock on the tower and Maureen saw it was nearly four o'clock. This reminded her about the breakfast she hadn't had, and now the lunch. She'd have to give Linda her feed too. Skinner must have been hungry, because without her saying anything he drew up just past the shops and got out of the van. He said, "I'm getting something to eat. You stay there. If you move or say anything I'll do you." Maureen sat quite still and didn't speak to anyone, and in five minutes Skinner was back with fish and chips and bottles of fizzy stuff and some chocolate. He drove a bit farther till they were out of the town on a road that went a long way up a hill, and then he pulled up in a side road and they ate the food, and he let Maureen go out to go behind a bush which she needed terribly. The awful rain had nearly stopped by now.

When the van stopped moving Linda woke up. She seemed to have liked the movement, she'd been ever so quiet all the way, but now she started to cry.

"What'll I do about Linda's bottle?" Maureen asked Skinner.

"Give it to her if you have to. We can stay here for a bit."

"But I'll have to have water to make it up. And warm it up."

He showed her the inside of the van which she hadn't seen properly. Slightly comforted by the meal she'd just had, Maureen was quite interested. There was a paraffin stove, and a cupboard with crockery in it, even a tiny washbasin. Two bunks and a flap table you could pull out from the wall. It was like a little house. If she hadn't been so scared, and if she hadn't had to be there with Skinner, she could even have enjoyed it. There was water in two big bottles. She was able to feed Linda and change her, and after she'd been put back in the cot, the baby didn't go to sleep again, but lay and talked to herself. Maureen had heard her do this before, after she'd got better at knowing what to do for her, getting her wind up and that. She'd woken one morning in the roachy basement and heard at first what she'd thought was pigeons, and then she'd realized it wasn't birds, it was the baby making that cooing murmur. It sounded as if she was happy. How could she be happy in this van, with Skinner so nasty and not knowing what was going to happen to them? But, of course, being a baby, she wouldn't know about that. All she knew was that she'd had her feed and she hadn't got a pain because Maureen had brought her wind up for her, and she was clean and warm. It didn't take much to make a baby happy, then. Only things that she, Maureen, could do. It was wonderful, Maureen thought, to be able to make someone, even only a baby, happy so that she sang that funny, tuneless, wordless song to herself. Fancy being able to do that for anyone!

"Stop snivelling. You don't know when you're well off," Skinner said.

She hadn't realized she was crying. But she couldn't explain to Skinner that it wasn't because she was miserable she was crying, it was thinking about the baby and being able to make her happy. Even though she herself wasn't happy at all.

They stayed quite a bit in this place. Maureen rather liked it, there were big green hills all around, very smooth. If only the rain hadn't started again she wouldn't have minded staying there, but presently Skinner said they'd got to move on, they'd got to find somewhere to park for the night before it got dark.

"Where'll we park for the night, Skinner?" Maureen asked.

"In a street where there's other cars," Skinner said.

"Why not stay here? It's quiet," Maureen said.

"And have some nosy cop come up to ask us why?"

He made her get in the back of the van after this. She lay down on a bunk and dozed, while the van drove on, she hadn't a clue where. Once or twice she woke up properly and felt the van sway and shake, as if some giant hand had nudged it. She tried to look out of the little windows at the back, but it was raining again and she couldn't see anything. They stopped once or twice, and she heard the wind roar around the van and push it sideways, so then she knew what had nudged it before. They seemed to go up and down hill a lot, and then they went slowly and she could just make out through the windows that they were in a town. Presently the van stopped and didn't start up again. Skinner opened the door between the driver's seat and the back and said, "We're stopping here. I'm off for some food. You keep quiet."

"Where are we, Skinner?" Maureen asked.

"Brighton."

Brighton! Maureen was amazed. She'd heard of Brighton. Kitty had been there with Maureen's Dad. She'd said it was all lights and lots to do. She'd liked Brighton, wanted to go back. But all Maureen could see out of the front window was a long street of small houses, with lace curtains in the windows and cards stuck up on the frames. She read the nearest one with difficulty. It said VACANCIES. She didn't know what that meant.

"Isn't there sea at Brighton?" she asked.

"Enough to push you into so you wouldn't come back," Skinner said.

There were lots of other cars parked in front of them, and some people walking along the street. Maureen felt glad there were people. It occurred to her now that perhaps she wouldn't have liked to be out in the country alone with Skinner with no one else who'd hear if she called out.

"Linda's asleep. Can't I come out too?" she asked.

"Didn't you understand? I said, No. You stay here. All the time. And if you've got to do another lot for the kid, you'd better do it now while you can see, 'cos you aren't going to get any lights when it's dark. The van's got to look empty, see?"

"But Skinner. . . ."

"What now?"

"I'll have to go to the toilet some time. How'll I manage that?"

"You'll have to manage with the street when it's dark," he said and left, locking her in. He didn't come back till a lot later, when she'd been asleep for a long time. She'd fed Linda, but there wasn't anything for her to eat. He'd brought her a cold meat pie when he came back, and she was grateful even for that. She was grateful too that he got into the other bunk and went to sleep at once. He'd had something to drink, she could smell it on his breath. She lay awake for a little, still hungry and very frightened. But she still hadn't made up for the broken night she'd had before and presently she went to sleep too.

Sunday

There was an appeal on the nine o'clock news on Sunday for information from anyone who had noticed an unfamiliar van, or car, possibly with a London registration number, parked anywhere in the South of England. The description of the driver was detailed, but less was said about his companion. "Crazy. A couple with a baby and a London registration number! At this time of year! We can't possibly follow up every car near the coast. Fine weekend like this one, half the population of London's on its way to the sea," one of Price's colleagues grumbled. And it seemed that he might be right. Information poured in and the force was overwhelmed and angered by the number of useless leads they'd been given. If they'd also been told the source of Price's knowledge of the van they might have been angrier still. "Crazy. I can't understand how an intelligent officer like you can be taken in by that couple of school children," Andrew Wilmington said.

"We'd never have known about the ransom demand your wife tried to meet if it hadn't been for them," Price said, sitting stiffly in the handsome library in Kensington Walk.

"And that wasn't much help, was it?"

"She might have handed over the money and not got the baby back."

"There's no proof that they didn't mean to give her the baby back. And since your men frightened them off, that's something we shall never know."

"There's also the possibility, which seems not to have occurred to you, that she was in a very vulnerable position herself. If she'd really been there entirely alone, in that fairly lonely spot, what was to prevent them taking her off with them and asking you for double the amount?" He saw from Andrew Wilmington's face that this was a new idea to him. He added, "And in the children's account of this scene in the car by the sea yesterday, they told me there was a violent rain squall. It was windy, too. Now when they told me that yesterday afternoon, the day in London had been bright and sunny. A bit of wind, not much. But along the Sussex coast yesterday afternoon there were gusty winds and some quite heavy rainfall. It's details like that I find convincing. Against my better judgment, mind you."

"I must remind you that there are such things as advance weather forecasts. They only had to listen to one of them to have a pretty good idea of what might happen."

"You put more faith in these weather forecasts than I do. They're as often wrong as they are right. I checked on the forecasts yesterday up to midday, after which they certainly didn't hear one, because they were with me. The rain was quite unforeseen. The forecast for the whole of Southern England was dry and bright with moderate winds. The experts were taken by surprise, as they so often are."

Andrew Wilmington said, "So. What next?"

"I would like to say emphatically that if there should be another ransom demand, I must be told. At once."

"Certainly."

"Since this lot obviously know that the phone in this house is monitored, they wouldn't come through to you here. Probably ask you to ring a callbox number again, as they did your wife. In that case you will let us know all the details so that we can take the necessary steps."

"I'll do that."

"Meanwhile all we can do is to go on looking. I shall let you know any news we have as soon as possible."

"Do you mean the news your psychic pair give you? Or what is so realistically called 'hard news'?"

"I'll let you know anything I can," Price said discreetly and left. Andrew Wilmington felt vaguely dissatisfied. He went into the little sitting-room and found Sally sitting, as she usually did now, with a book in her hand. Not reading. Not doing anything. Just sitting. If she wasn't doing nothing, like this, she'd be engaged on some activity which she worked at feverishly. Turning out cupboards, going through old letters, rearranging books. Always looking lost and drawn and haggard. He'd hardly have recognized the girl he'd married.

"No news, darling," he said quickly, before she could look at him with that awful questioning hope which made him feel so sick.

"Couldn't we go there, Andrew?"

"Where, darling?"

"Down to the coast. If that's where they think she is?"

"Darling! What use would it be us going? We haven't any idea where to look. Even if this ridiculous story of Price's were true, he hasn't a clue which bit of the coast it might be. What could we do there?"

A day or two ago she'd have argued this. Now she said, "No. I expect you're right," and sank back into silence and immobility.

"I promise you if there's any reason to think one place is more likely than another, I'll go there straight away. I promise," he said again, trying to engage her attention by any statement, however rash.

"Where would you go?"

"I said. Anywhere it seemed possible we might find . . . Caroline Ann."

"If those children told you, would you? You mean you'd believe what they said?"

He hesitated.

"You see? You wouldn't do anything. I would. I'd do any-thing. I wouldn't care if it seemed stupid, I'd try it. It wouldn't matter if I felt silly doing it. That's why I went with the money. It seemed just a chance."

"It didn't help," Andrew said.

"But it might have."

Andrew remembered what Price had said. He might have lost Sally as well as Caroline Ann. He said, "I'd do anything too."

"Anything those two said?"

He said, "Yes. Now. I'd do anything, even if there wasn't anything more than their story to go on."

Sally said, "Thank you, Andrew." Her frozen face quivered and she tried to smile at him. He sat down beside her and put an arm around her. She leaned her head on his shoulder and they sat there, side by side, not speaking, for a long time.

Walking on Hampstead Heath that Sunday afternoon, Vicky and Stephen were playing Twenty Questions. Stephen thought of the sea. It was mineral, he thought. Or was it abstract? Not manufactured, something that no one owned. Vicky floun-dered, she couldn't get it at all, she gave up. Stephen told her.

Her turn. She thought of St. Paul's Cathedral. Stephen got it in sixteen.

Stephen thought of something that was animal. Vicky got it in five. A wren. Too obvious.

Vicky thought of a prince. In her mind's eye she saw him, a fat elderly prince, she didn't know why. She'd said "Animal" and Stephen had started as usual asking, "Can you eat it?" when the flash came. The flash stopped their walking, and when Stephen could see Vicky again she was shaking.

"What is it? It must've been different from what I saw. . . ."

"Something's gone wrong. They couldn't have. . . ."

"What? I saw the girl and the baby. . . ."

"I saw a place. It wasn't England," Vicky said.

"You mean . . . ? When we saw them yesterday they were leaving? Of course! The sea! They were going to get the cross-Channel ferry."

"We must tell the Super. Now. At once."

"But Vicky! How do you know it wasn't England? Did you see a signpost or something? Or hear . . .?"

"Come *on*! I'll tell you while we go. There's a callbox in South End Green."

Price picked up the telephone before the second ring.

"Stephen? News? I can't tell you how much we need it."

"We had another just now. About a quarter of an hour ago."

"Tell me quickly, and then if need be perhaps you could come over."

"We didn't see the same thing. We don't always."

"Go on."

"I saw the girl. The Maureen girl. You were right, her hair's been cut. She looks awful. Someone's been punching her on the face."

"Where are they?"

"I'm afraid I don't know. Inside a sort of room. Very dark. I could only just see her."

"Night was it?"

"I don't know. It's all so quick. I just saw her in this tiny room."

"Anything else? What about Vicky?"

"That's what's so extraordinary. Vicky saw a place."

"Go on," Price said impatiently.

"She says it wasn't England."

"How does she know? Language?"

"By the buildings. She says."

"You mean she recognized some place abroad?"

There was a slight pause.

"Go on. Did she recognize it?"

Stephen said miserably, "She said it looked like pictures of Moscow."

Price's voice changed. "Is this supposed to be a joke?"

"I knew you wouldn't believe it."

"Is Vicky there? I'd like to speak to her."

Vicky said, "It's me," in a small voice.

"What's all this about Moscow? Do you realize you're playing with a child's life?"

"I'm not playing. I did see it."

Price sat at his desk and faced the horrible possibility that Andrew Wilmington and the others might be right and that the whole thing was a put-up job. That he'd trusted in these two and now they'd let him down. That he'd wasted precious time and taken a risk which was turning out unforgivably high. Vicky had never heard his voice as grim as when he said, "What exactly did you see?"

"It was a sort of palace. Green and blue and goldy. With a round thing and spires. No, not spires exactly. It was like that building you see in pictures of Moscow. Not a bit like England. Truly."

She sounded distressed. Price saw suddenly in his mind's eye her bony, pointed, intelligent face. He'd liked the child. So had Sally Wilmington. He groaned.

"You'd better come over at once. And Stephen. Take a taxi. We'll pay here." He rang down and gave the order. Another hope fading. And no time at all. If it had all been play-acting he'd flay them so they'd never do it again.

When they arrived he was prepared to grill them. But again they didn't feel like impostors. Perhaps his intuition was all wrong. Perhaps they had just that quality which he'd met once or twice in a long career of dealing with criminals, of persuading themselves of their integrity. There was nothing so misleading as that; the story then came out with the clarity of truth because for the moment it was the truth to the teller. He was tired, too, and he couldn't be sure whether through dulling the edge of his intellectual processes the fatigue heightened his perception, or if all his faculties were less acute. Whatever the reason he found himself again believing Stephen, from whom he'd demanded the first story. He took him through it, asking about every detail. The ragged hair. The swollen face. The size of the tiny room. Where the light was coming from. What was she wearing? What color was the jumper? What color were the trousers?

"I couldn't see very well because she had the baby on her lap."

"The baby! The baby was there? You saw the baby?"

"It was on her lap. I told you, she was sitting on a sort of. . . ."

"Why didn't you say at once you'd seen the baby?"

"I don't know. I just thought if she was there of course the baby would be too."

"You mean you think it was there? You didn't actually see it?"

"Yes, I did."

"Are you absolutely certain? What was it doing? Was it . . . alive?" He heard Vicky gasp.

"She was giving it a bottle."

"You're sure? You couldn't have mistaken a bundle of clothes or anything else for the baby? Did you see its face?"

"No, but I saw its hand."

"Moving?"

Stephen thought, then said, "Sort of waving about."

It had to be true, Price thought. He turned to Vicky.

"Now then, let's hear exactly what you saw."

She told him again what she'd said on the telephone. Price put her through some sort of third degree too. At the end of twenty minutes she was on the edge of tears, but her story hadn't varied by a hairsbreadth. She'd seen a street, people, all quite ordinary, then this fantastic palace, floodlit. It didn't make sense. Price began to wonder if one of them was hallucinating. Even if the couple had somehow managed to evade the watch that was being kept on all ports and had slipped across the Channel, how could they have possibly got as far as was suggested by the Eastern look the girl had described?

The telephone rang. Price said into it severely, "I told you not to disturb me unless there was something really urgent."

"Inspector Drinkwater thinks you ought to hear about this one, sir."

"What is it?"

"Description of a van seen parked last night in Brighton, sir."

The duty sergeant was surprised by the roar with which the

Chief Superintendent greeted this. "Brighton! My God, what a fool I've been! Yes, send it up, Sergeant. It could be important." To Vicky he said, "Here's a pencil and there's a pad. Draw what this building was like."

"I'm not much good," Vicky said.

"Never mind. Just to give me a rough idea."

While she was drawing, the message came in. A Mr. Mackenzie had found the parking space outside his house in Messenger Street, Brighton, occupied when he'd got back from the pub on Saturday night. It wasn't one of his neighbors' cars, he knew them all. It was a van. He couldn't be sure of the registration, he hadn't bothered to look. It had gone now. He thought it was a green van, but he couldn't be sure of that. He'd gone out to look at tea time because of hearing the police notice on the radio, and his wife said he should. Why had his wife said he should? Because she said she'd heard a baby crying early in the morning and there weren't any babies near that she knew of. He hadn't heard any baby, but then he was a bit on the deaf side.

"Follow it up. Ask all along the street if anyone put up a couple with a baby last night. And the two streets next to it. Anywhere near where they could have lodged. House-to-house inquiry. Put out notices for a green van, probably going west from Brighton. Say the girl has short hair and has the marks of injury on her face. Get someone to examine this Mackenzie chap and see if he can't remember a bit more about the van. He'll probably come out with the make, even if he didn't notice anything else. And hurry. The baby's still there. We've got to get to it soon."

"It's nothing like it. I told you I can't draw," Vicky said.

Price looked.

"Have you ever been to Brighton, Vicky?"

"No. Been to Eastbourne, though."

"Wait a minute," Price said. He rang downstairs again and made an unlikely request. Five minutes later a grinning sergeant brought in a handful of picture postcards, sent back to the staff-room by officers on holiday to excite envy in those left working. They came from all over the world. Many from Spain, several from France, one or two from America, a sprinkling from Italy, Germany, Scandinavia, some from neglected England. The first one from the south coast was the usual fat-lady-knickers type. The next showed a pier, the third chalky cliffs. The fourth Price laid in front of Vicky, covering the place name with his hand. "Is that your Kremlin?" he asked.

The Pavilion jumped at Vicky with its impossible pale un-English colors, its ridiculous, frilly, superb, extravagant form. She said, "Where is it then?" and Price said, "Where it should be. Where it was built, for a prince. And the baby's still there. We might catch them yet."

Sunday evening

Vicky didn't get home 'til nearly nine. Her mother would certainly ask questions too difficult to answer if she stayed out any more of the day. But she was possessed by a sort of feverish impatience which made it impossible to sit still, to eat, to talk normally. She wanted all the time to be doing something. While she tried to conceal from her Mum's quick eye the fact that she had hidden most of the tinned salmon under her knife and fork, while she tried to listen to the others' conversations and to make appropriate replies, she wasn't really in the kitchen at home at all. In her mind she was scanning the southern coast of England for the van. She was cowering with the girl away from being hit all over her face. She was remembering Sally Wilmington and the way she'd said to Mr. Wilmington, "You won't let them hurt Caroline Ann?" and then that girl's voice saying, "You said you wouldn't hurt her." She remembered the Super saying to Stephen this afternoon, "Was it . . . alive?" It had been alive in Stephen's picture. But they didn't know just when that was. It could still be tomorrow, it could be today. She had caught Price's fear and she shivered. Mrs. Stanford saw it.

"Vicky! What's the matter? And you've not eaten anything either!"

"I'm just not hungry, Mum."

"Do you feel ill? You've hardly said a word all through tea."

"I don't think so."

"You don't feel well, though?"

If she said No, it would get her out of having to explain. But then she wouldn't be allowed to go out and meet Stephen tomorrow, and if they couldn't meet they might not be able to save the baby. She said, "I'm all right. Truly, Mum. I'm just tired, that's all."

Mrs. Stanford waited until she and Vicky were washing up alone, then she said, "There's something wrong, Vicky. Want to tell me?"

Vicky shook her head. She found she was surprisingly close to tears.

"Have you and Stephen fallen out?"

Vicky shook her head again.

"You're seeing a lot of him, aren't you? Considering you told me it's nothing serious."

"I did tell you, Mum. We keep on having to see the police about that kidnapping."

"I thought you'd told them what you'd heard. Why do they want to go on and on about it?"

"There's lots more questions they think of to ask us all the time."

"It isn't they think you had anything to do with it?"

"Oh *Mum*! Of course not."

"I can't see why you and that Stephen boy have to be at their beck and call all the time for all that."

Vicky said, "They're frightened about the baby." Her voice broke.

"Is that what's worrying you, love?"

It was such a relief to say, "Yes," and to allow the tears to come. Mrs. Stanford abandoned the washing up. She sat herself down and took Vicky, great grown-up, nearly sixteen-year-old Vicky, onto her lap. Vicky cried wetly and almost enjoyably. It was wonderful to sit on Mum's lap like this as if she was six, and simply let go. She cried with great choking sobs, not trying for the stiff upper lip or being a big girl now. She didn't think. She melted.

Mum was fantastic. She simply held Vicky and allowed her to cry. After a time Vicky lifted her head from that comfortable shoulder and said, "I must look awful."

"If you're thinking that you must be better."

"It was just . . . Mum, that baby!"

"I know. Only I keep thinking of its mother. What must she be feeling?"

Vicky said, with difficulty, "Mum! Did my Mum—you know. Did she . . . Did she feel like that when she knew she wasn't going to go on living? About me?"

"I don't think she knew she was going, love. Thing was, she got so weak she didn't hardly know anything."

"Did she know you'd be taking me home?"

Mrs. Stanford knew when a whole truth was not called for. She said, "She knew if anything happened to her I'd look out for you."

Vicky said, "I don't think anyone ought to take babies away from their Mums and Dads. I think it's cruel. I think it's the worst thing anyone can do."

"She's only young. She could have another one," Mrs. Stanford said, seeing the picture of young Mrs. Wilmington in the paper.

"But it wouldn't be the same, would it? She'd always want that one. Wouldn't she?" Vicky said.

"'Course she would. I shouldn't have said that. When I think how it would be if you or Chris had got taken and I'd thought I'd never see you again. . . . Knowing I could have twenty more wouldn't make me feel any better," Mrs. Stanford said.

Vicky dared to ask the question she'd often thought, never said. "Mum! Do you feel different about us? Because Chris is yours and I'm not? Would you . . .?" She couldn't finish. But Mrs. Stanford understood, and knew that only the truth would do here.

"I've often asked myself the same. Do I feel different about

Chris being mine? I don't know, Vicky, and that's the truth. Thing is, I'm so used to having the two of you, I can't tell what it'd be not to have you both. 'Course it isn't the same. Not for me any more than it is for you. I'm like you; sometimes I wonder about what your father was and how it all came about. But it doesn't worry me now. It used to, right at the beginning. I'd think, Suppose I don't do the right thing by the child, when she wasn't mine to start with? And then—I don't know. It seemed so sort of natural to have the two of you, and I'd have felt so bad if I'd had only the one, I stopped feeling like that. I just felt pleased. And Chris wouldn't have been so happy as she is if she hadn't had a sister. I've seen it with onlies. It isn't right."

"Chris'd have been all right anyway."

"I don't know about that."

Vicky yawned.

"You ought to go to bed, my lass. You're tired out."

Vicky realized, astonished, that this was true. She got up off her Mum's comfortable lap and stretched.

"I will. 'Night, Mum."

"'Night, love."

So much you didn't say. Stephen's father would have wanted to have it all spelled out or he wouldn't know it was there. Vicky felt drained. Better for all that crying, guilty because it hadn't helped to find the baby. But she had to sleep. She'd meet Stephen again tomorrow. Tomorrow. Would the baby see tomorrow? If she hadn't been so tired she'd have lain awake worrying, but as it was she was asleep five minutes after getting into bed.

Sunday

Skinner slept late that Sunday morning. Maureen had crept around the van, getting feeds ready and looking for something to eat herself. She was starving. If she didn't eat something soon, her inside rumblings might wake Skinner, and then, where'd she be? She made herself tea and put in some of the baby's dried milk. It was ever so nasty, but it did make her feel a bit better. She badly needed to go to the toilet, but although Skinner was so fast asleep she didn't think he'd have woken if she'd been able to open the back doors and slip out, she couldn't risk disturbing him by searching for the key which was in his pocket, and he'd gone to sleep in his clothes. She had to make do with the bucket, which she knew wasn't nice, but she couldn't choose. Then she must have dozed off again, because the next thing she knew, Skinner was saying he was going out for a bite of lunch, she was to stay there and he'd bring her back something. She didn't like that, she'd begun to say, "Why can't I come too, Skinner?" but he'd gone and shut the door very quietly behind him. She heard the key turn in the lock. She sat there then, with Linda, crying a bit and feeling really bad, stuck here in this nasty van, and hungry again. Linda was awake, so she gave her another feed, but after it the baby wouldn't go to sleep. She didn't cry, just lay there waving her hands around and looking at them as if she'd never seen hands before. Maureen supposed that she hadn't, at any rate not as often as people who were grown up like Maureen, who'd had time to get used to having hands and doing things with them, so that she never really looked at them and wondered where they came from or why they were that shape. Presently Linda went to sleep, sucking her thumb, and after what seemed a long time, Skinner came back with a bit of cold pie for Maureen and a tin of coke. He lay down on the bunk and went to sleep at once, and Maureen had another long afternoon trying to keep Linda quiet. That wasn't too bad. She found that she could talk to her very soft and Linda liked that. It was almost like the way Mrs. Plum had talked to her, and the funny thing was that when Maureen cuddled her and spoke silly baby language to her, it was comforting for Maureen too.

Before it had begun to get dark, Skinner woke up and went off again. To the pub, Maureen supposed, though he didn't say. He came back almost at once, angry. She could tell by the way he looked as he climbed into the van, even before he hit her, hard, on the face. She cried out and said, "What you hitting me for, Skinner?" and he said, "You been talking."

"I haven't! How can I talk to anyone, shut up like this in the van?" Maureen said, but then she remembered she had been talking to Linda and perhaps Skinner hadn't really been asleep, perhaps he'd heard.

"Don't ask me how! If you haven't been talking, how do the fuzz know where we are?" Skinner said, looking as if he might hit her again any minute.

Maureen supposed that the police must have somehow overheard that soft, silly talk she'd given Linda that afternoon. She said, "I'm sorry, Skinner, I didn't know."

"Who was it? Who'd you tell? Did you say any names?"

"I didn't, Skinner. Not any names. Only just to keep her quiet, so she wouldn't wake you, Skinner, that's all."

"Who was it?" Skinner said, and she saw his hand go to the knife he always carried in his belt.

"It was only her. Linda. When you were asleep and she wouldn't. . . ."

She didn't understand why he swore again. He said, "For Chrissake I picked a winner when I got you." Then he went out to the driver's seat and started driving away from the street they'd been in for so long. They seemed to drive for quite a time. Once, just as it was getting dark, she looked out and saw that they were still in streets with a lot of houses and a great big building with funny bulging tops to it, all lit up with lights, rather pretty. Quite different from anything she'd ever seen. She wondered if perhaps it was a circus. She'd have liked to see that. But later the lights disappeared and they drove ever such a long way through roads without any lights at all. Before they stopped for the night Maureen was too sleepy to notice where they were, except they seemed to be back in a town, parked where there were a lot of cars and trailers. There was a toilet here too, and Skinner let her out to visit it. That made Maureen's day.

Monday morning and afternoon
The ransom note fell through the letter-box with the rest of the post. It came in a long commercial envelope and was written on an electric typewriter on a sheet of plain white paper. Andrew Wilmington found it by his breakfast plate and read it.

"This is your last chance of seeing your daughter again alive.

Bring £200,000 in used notes to Bank tube station at five-thirty tonight, Monday April 25th. Stand by the top of the Central Line escalators. You will be contacted there. If you follow these instructions exactly you will be told where you can find your daughter 24 hours after the money has been handed over.

If we find that you have informed the police, handed over marked notes or taken any other steps to trace us, your baby will be the first one to suffer."

He had his instructions from Price. The first were easy to follow. He picked up the paper and the envelope in his napkin, went into his study and put them into a large envelope. "Not much hope of any prints, but we ought to try for them," Price had said.

The next step was more difficult. He had to decide whether or not he was going to play along with Price at all. Or was he going to agree to the conditions laid down by the letter? Was he going to tell Sally? If he did and she pleaded with him to do as they said, to trust that Caroline Ann would be returned, could he refuse? Suppose he stood out against it and they never saw Caroline Ann again, what would Sally feel toward him? Wouldn't it be the end of their marriage? Even if he didn't tell her and the baby was not returned because he'd stepped out of the line these bastards wanted to impose, wouldn't he always feel guilty? Wouldn't he have for the rest of their lives together to hug this horrible secret that he hadn't done everything he could to save their child?

He couldn't eat any breakfast. It was a good thing that Sally was having hers in bed or she'd have noticed something wrong. After half an hour of agonized indecision, he went up and kissed her good-bye, got out of the house without any questions and drove to the office. He would telephone from there. Price would have to decide how to handle this, he couldn't tackle it alone.

Price rang Stephen.

"Anything for me?"

"No. But I'm meeting Vicky in half an hour. We'll try."

"If you could get a look at the outside of the van. Its number for instance."

"Trouble is we don't seem to be able to choose what we get."

"I know. Try. Anything might help."

He rang off and considered. The van had been in Brighton yesterday up to tea time on Mr. Mackenzie's showing. If the Vicky girl was right in thinking that what she'd seen was what the couple with the baby might have been looking at, they'd still been there after dark. Evening, she'd said, but she thought not yet night. That put it somewhere between eight and nine. God, why hadn't the Brighton force been able to get it? He must have got through to them by eight at latest, they'd had over thirty minutes with the bloody thing there in the middle of the town and no one seemed to have noticed it. And they'd drawn a blank in Messenger Street, where nearly every house let lodgings. Not a single baby anywhere near the Mackenzies' house. No one had seen a baby. But a neighbor volunteered that he'd heard a baby crying too. If that was the right van the old chap had noticed, they must have slept in it. That was the tiny dark room Stephen had seen.

Price groaned. He wondered again if he was right to trust these stories. But he had nothing else to go on, he had to take help wherever he could find it. There'd been another appeal to the public on the eight o'clock news this morning. Perhaps someone would come up with something that would help. It was at this point that he was told that Andrew Wilmington was on the telephone, asking for him.

"How's it going to work?" Jakey asked.
"Supposed to be getting the cash tonight," Fred said.
"Who's collecting?"
"Me. Bank tube in the rush hour."
"What's your getaway if he's split?"
"Change of gear in the Ladies."
"You in the Ladies? That's rich!"
"I went in on the way back just to see. It's dead easy."
"It's the jeans and the hair. Suppose you could easily be a bird."
"No one looked twice."
"What's the gear you got to put on?"
"Blonde wig. Long dress. He'd got them all ready. Timed me. Took twenty seconds."
"Clever! Then you flush and walk out?"
"That's right. There's two exits, see? I come out of the other."
"Smithy's got brains," Jakey said, appreciating the joke.
"I'll say so if he pulls this one off."

"What about the kid?"

"That's nothing to do with me."

"Is he going to hand it over?"

"He's going to make bloody sure we're clear first. If there's anything goes wrong, the kid's had it."

"What about if things don't go wrong? Does Daddy get his precious back?"

Fred looked at Jakey and Jakey looked at Fred. Then Jakey smiled. Not an agreeable smile.

"You know Smithy. He does like to keep his hands clean," Fred said.

"But he doesn't like taking chances either."

"That's why I was careful not to ask," Fred said.

"What did you see?" Stephen asked.

"I saw him. In a shop. Buying bottles of fizzy drink."

"I saw the van."

"Inside? Was the baby there?"

"No. Outside."

"Is it green?"

"No, it's blue. And it had a great dent and all the paint taken off the rear fender."

"Doesn't that mean they'll find them quickly now?"

"I should think so. I'll ring up the Superintendent straight away."

"I don't think my flash is going to be any use at all. He won't want to know about them buying bottles of lemon or whatever it was."

"Didn't you see anything that would say where it was?"

"Don't think so," Vicky said.

"No names or anything?"

"No. Honestly, I can't think of anything."

"Was he taking the bottles off a shelf?"

"Out of a sort of wire basket. There was a big notice over it said Special Offer This Week. You know how those shops do.

Mum always tries to get those special offers if it's something she buys anyway."

"I'll tell Price. I suppose it might help."

"Not unless he asks; he'll think it's silly. Your seeing the van's what he'll want to know."

"I don't want this put out as a general appeal. I want every man in the country looking out for the van; it's got a badly scraped rear fender by the way—but I don't want the driver alerted. If he's desperate he might do anything. We've got to reach him before he harms the baby. I'm not too happy about the girl either. I suspect he means to get rid of them both. And I want you to find out if any self-service grocery shops in the area have had bottles of fizzy lemon or orange on special offer this week. If they all have, then forget it, it's not going to be any help to us. But if there's just one or two, then step up the search for the van in that locality. That's where they're going to be."

"Going to be! What's he got, a ruddy crystal ball?" the Brighton Chief Superintendent said with disgust. He didn't consider it a part of his duties to search out bargain offers of groceries even for a brother officer.

Skinner and Maureen and Linda in the van stayed in the trailer site all Monday morning. At midday, Skinner went out cautiously to prospect and to ring Smithy to find out what the plans were for the day. He'd got to keep out of harm's way till 19.00 hours, he was told. One of Smithy's peculiarities was this having the time in double figures so there shouldn't be any mix-ups with whether you meant morning or afternoon. Then he was to ring again to hear whether the bread had been delivered as arranged and if there'd been any trouble. If everything went through easily, then it was up to Skinner to cope with Maureen and the kid.

He decided to get out of the trailer site outside Eastbourne and go inland for a bit. Lucky the police seemed to have got it into their thick heads that he was still going west. Skinner took a couple of sausage rolls to keep Fatty quiet, and backed out of the corner where they'd spent the night. He found backing difficult, and scraped his off-side fender badly on another parked car before he got out. Then he drove off inland, making for small, unfrequented roads in farmland, where they could rest up in lanes or fields off the road. Lucky that Smithy had thought of getting the plates changed to a Midlands number. Lucky no one knew about that scrape. In the early afternoon he stopped at a little grocer's shop way out nowhere, in the back of beyond, and bought some packets of sandwiches and some bottles of fizzy drinks. Then he found another trailer site not too far from the coast, behind a lot of pebbles but not too near anywhere else, and he pulled into a corner where you couldn't see the van from the road. There were other vans of the same sort anyway. They'd stop there till it was time to call Smithy and find out what happened next. Skinner knew what he hoped the news would be. He couldn't wait to be rid of the snivelling kid and Fatty, with her endless questions and her useless mind. The sooner the better, was what he thought. He didn't sleep that afternoon. He lay and planned how he'd do it.

Stephen found lunch, after he'd got back from what now seemed a habit of coffee with the two girls in the coffee bar, uncomfortable. He'd been aware that his father was looking for the opportunity of another frank talk ever since that last embarrassing conversation four days ago, and he'd been carefully avoiding it. Today Dr. Rawlinson ostentatiously did not ask him where he'd spent the morning, but carried on an almost one-sided conversation about the liberty allowed the young people of today. How wonderful it was, how much he wished he'd had the same freedom for self-expression, how heartily he approved. How much healthier this new, liberated climate must be for the psyche. The wash of rounded phrases and technical words flowed on; in the significant pauses Mrs. Rawlinson said,

"Yes, dear," and, "Do you really think so?" while quite obviously thinking about something else. When his father had gone, Stephen drew a breath of relief. He looked at his mother.

"Dad does go on and on, doesn't he?"

"I think he wanted to say something," his mother obliquely replied.

"He said a lot. But not really what he wanted to, isn't that it?"

"I liked those two girls," Mrs. Rawlinson said, as if this were an entirely new subject.

"They're all right," Stephen said casually.

"The pretty one's nice. Friendly."

"Yes."

"But I really liked the other one best, I think."

"Did you?"

"She's more interesting. But I did like them both."

Alone in his room later, he thought about Vicky and Chris and remembered, with a twinge of self-reproach, that he'd hardly given a thought to the problem with Paul. He'd been so much engrossed in his own feelings that he'd forgotten Chris. She had been silent this morning; perhaps she too was heart-sore. Stephen wished he could do something to help her, then realized suddenly that he could. She'd said something, days ago, about Paul working for the school holidays in the local newsagents-cum-bookshop, and since no one's term had yet begun, he'd presumably still be there. After his first impulse to go straight away, Stephen's resolution wavered. What was he going to say to Paul when he found him? How could be plunge into a conversation about anything as private as Paul's feelings for Chris without any apparent excuse? Then he remembered the conversation he'd had with Vicky about Hamlet and about not acting on ideas because of thinking too carefully about them first. He went out of his front door and made for the High Street, without giving himself further time for daunting thought. He was supposed to be meeting Vicky again at the coffee bar anyhow, at three o'clock.

The same fear that his resolution might leave him, made him go directly to Paul, whom he saw at the back of the shop, in the book section, and say, "Hullo!"

Paul looked at him without smiling. "Do you want something?"

"Not really. I wanted to see how you were getting on. I was just walking past."

"I'm all right," Paul said.

"Is it interesting?" Stephen made himself ask.

"Not very. I didn't expect it would be."

"Aren't there any . . . I mean, there's plenty to read."

"Assistants in the shop aren't supposed to read while they're on duty."

"Can't you ever? When there aren't any customers?"

"It isn't the customers who are the trouble. It's the assistant manager," Paul said with a faint smile.

Stephen said, "Oh!" The conversation wasn't going well. If a genuine customer appeared Paul would have to serve him and he'd have lost his chance. He said, quickly, "How much longer are you staying in the job?"

"Till Wednesday. Term starts then."

Stephen said, without thinking, "Oh yes, Chris told me," and saw Paul's expression change from neutral to wary. He said, "Why don't you come and meet us at the coffee bar after you've finished here? Vicky and Chris and me."

Paul said, "I might," without enthusiasm.

"Chris'd be pleased."

"She say so?" Paul asked.

"Not Chris. It was something Vicky said."

At this Paul looked directly at Stephen. A long, questioning look. He said, "You're trying to say something, only I don't know what it is."

Hideously embarrassed, Stephen said, "I'm sorry. It isn't any of my business, I know. It's only that when we're together, I think Chris feels a bit left out sometimes. It'd be nice if there were four of us. Instead of three. That's all." To his immense relief he saw a couple of women enter the shop and make for the book rack where he and Paul were standing. He said, "Be seeing you," and went out. It might not make any difference; Paul might well just write him off as an interfering idiot, but he was glad he'd at any rate tried. He remembered that if Paul came around to the coffee bar tonight, he probably wouldn't find any of them. He'd got to go home after meeting Vicky this afternoon in case Price telephoned, and Mrs. Stanford had been threatening to keep Vicky in bed for the rest of the day. Well, he couldn't help that. He couldn't engineer a meeting between Chris and Paul. He'd done all he could. And at least he hadn't allowed a stupid fear of making himself look a fool to strangle him into inactivity.

Monday afternoon and evening
Andrew Wilmington had had exact instructions. He collected
the cash in the early afternoon and went, as he occasionally did
in the ordinary way, to his club. Anyone might have seen him
strolling in and ordering himself tea in the library. Various other
members, mostly elderly, retired gentlemen, sat about in the
vast padded chairs and slept, or studied the papers or wrote
letters on the club notepaper. Presently Andrew went downstairs to the newly established sauna baths. No one could have
found this extraordinary, there is always a first time. Anyone,
half an hour later, could have seen Andrew, in his light gray
suit, dark shirt, and pale, elegant tie, emerge from the club and
make his way back to his office in Lombard Street. And an hour
and a half later, just after five o'clock, anyone could have seen
this eminently recognizable Andrew Wilmington emerge from
his office and make his way along Lombard Street toward the
Bank tube station. Walking slowly, showing signs of anxiety in
his hesitation at the traffic-light crossings, in his intense preoc-
cupation which made him walk face turned down toward the
pavement, hands in pockets, as if fingering something there.
Anyone sufficiently interested in his movements to pursue him

further could have seen Andrew take up his position at the top of the escalator in the Bank Station. Looking around constantly, obviously on edge, expecting something. A clear case of nervous tension.

While his double blazed the necessary trail across the heart of London, the real Andrew sat in one of the cubicles of the sauna bath and found he could not concentrate on the books and papers so considerately provided for his entertainment. Horrible to have to leave all the action to everyone else. Horrible to have to stay in this hot, sweaty, claustrophobic little hole, while other people played with Caroline Ann's life. Horrible to know that it was all going on out there, but not to know just what had happened. Not so much horrible as galling to have to submit to orders, to be told what one could or couldn't do and to feel obliged, by Sally's misery and by the hope for Caroline Ann's safety, to agree. God, how his skin itched in this hot, humid atmosphere! Andrew scratched and endured. As soon as he received the signal he'd be off. Meanwhile he couldn't concentrate on anything at all.

By half-past seven he was home. He'd taken the precaution of warning Sally that he might have to go out again later. She said, "Did that detective tell you anything?" and Andrew said, "No."

"It's eleven days," Sally said.

"I know, darling."

"Does he think they'll ask for money again?"

"He thinks they quite probably will," Andrew said, loathing the necessity to lie.

"Andrew. If we don't get her back. . . ."

"Don't upset yourself, dearest."

" . . . I just don't want to go on living."

Yes. Living can be hell.

At the end of the long, long afternoon, which had been all the worse because Skinner hadn't slept, but had lain on his bunk staring sometimes at nothing, and sometimes, in a way she didn't like, at her, Maureen was pleased when he looked at his watch for the last time and said, "Now for it, Fatty," and made for the door.

"What're we going to do now, Skinner?" Maureen asked.

"Find out whether Smithy's got the cash," Skinner said, and Maureen couldn't ask him anything else, because he was gone and she heard him swearing as he tried to get the engine going again. Maureen looked out of the windows and saw the piles of pebbles disappearing. They were driving along a road which must be somewhere near the sea still, as she could see little houses on one side and bathing huts all stacked together on the other, but she couldn't actually see the sea. Then there were houses on both sides and the van kept on turning this way and that, and then it stopped in a small street, and she heard Skinner get out. It was a street with little shops in it and there were people walking about with shopping bags, although it was quite late. Maureen knew that, because one shop had a big old-fashioned clock face in the window and it said after seven o'clock. Maureen was hungry again as usual. She wondered whether Skinner might have good news about the money when he rang up Smithy. If he did perhaps he'd be nice to her again and take her out to a posh place for a meal like he'd done when they first got to know each other.

He was in a good temper when he came back, she could hear that, because he was whistling. When he was pleased he used to whistle "Shenandoah" under his breath. He didn't say anything to her, just got back into the driver's seat and started up with the usual crashing of gears and difficulties with the brakes. Maureen looked out and saw more streets and more streets, and then gradually they came out into country, lanes with high hedges and green fields and trees. Maureen didn't like this, she'd felt safer in the streets with people around, and besides, where were they going to get their supper out here?

She had, however, a more pressing need than hunger. After a

time she couldn't hold out any longer. She rapped on the front partition and she went on rapping until Skinner pulled up and called out, "What's the matter?"

"Please, Skinner, I've got to get out. Quick."

He drove on for a minute, then stopped and let her out. They were in a narrow lane on the side of a hill, right out in the country, not a sign of any houses or anything. Skinner pointed to a gate, and Maureen climbed over and went behind one of the tall hedges which were just beginning to get leafy and thick. From here she could see the slopes of green hills all around and right in the distance the spire of a little church. It should have been pretty, but somehow it wasn't, partly because it was a gray day, the sky, hanging very low, and no wind at all. It made you feel shut in between that dark sky, all of a piece, no clouds to be seen, and the empty countryside. It was funny; Maureen felt she'd almost rather be back in the van, though she'd wanted to get out badly enough before.

She climbed back over the gate into the lane and saw that Skinner was sitting waiting for her in the driver's seat, and he'd already started revving up the motor. She had a horrid feeling then that he meant to drive off and leave her there all by herself, not knowing where she was and with no money. She began to run toward the van, calling out, "Skinner! Skinner! Don't go off and leave me!"

But what happened was worse. He didn't drive past her, he drove at her. He came right up to where she was standing by the hedge. He came five yards, accelerated and there was the grinding of gears. Maureen screamed and tried to flatten herself against the prickling twigs of the hedgerow, but she'd have got hit if the engine hadn't stalled just as it so often had before on their journeys. Maureen got herself back to the gate and over it, before Skinner had the chance to get the motor started up again, and she stood there, shaking. Skinner leaned out of the cab and called to her. "Come back! What'd you think you're doing?"

"You tried to run me down!" Maureen said, hardly able to speak for shaking.

"Don't be crazy! Bloody thing got a bit out of control, that's all."

"You came straight at me!"

"'Course I didn't! What would I want to do a thing like that for?"

Maureen didn't know. Could he be right? Or if she came back over the gate would he try to do it again? While she stood there undecided, she heard the sound of some other car coming up along the road. She could see that Skinner had heard it too. It came into sight slowly, a red farm tractor. As it got near she could see it was driven by quite a young boy. It came right up to them and stopped and the boy leaned out and called, "You having trouble then?"

Skinner said, "No. Thanks all the same." But the tractor didn't move away.

"I said, we're not having trouble," Skinner said again.

"I'm going into that field," the boy said, pointing at the gate where Maureen stood.

"Open the gate for him, can't you?" Skinner said to Maureen. She wasn't very quick at finding how the catch worked, but she did manage it in time and the boy said, "Thanks," as he drove the tractor past her. Maureen watched him go on down into the field and wanted to say something to him, but she didn't know what.

"Come on! Don't stand there all day!" Skinner said.

She didn't know what else she could do, so she did as she was told. He came up behind her as she was climbing back into the van and locked her in as usual, then the van started going on its endless way. Maureen took Linda onto her lap for comfort, and sat there still feeling shaky. She wondered if perhaps she had made a mistake and Skinner hadn't really meant to hurt her. She couldn't see why he should want to do her in. She'd done everything he told her, hadn't she? But she hadn't liked the way he'd been looking all this afternoon and she didn't feel safe. She wished she could think of what she could do to get away from the van and Skinner and all. Poor stupid Maureen. She knew just enough to know that there was danger about, but she hadn't a clue how she could get away from it.

Another failure. Price was mad with himself, couldn't find enough bad words for his own ineptitude. Everything had been set up with immaculate care. The young man they'd got to stand-in for Andrew Wilmington had been superb—looked like him, walked like him, even managed to speak like him. It had all looked to be going so well. The switch in Andrew Wilmington's club made so discreetly, the notes handed over exactly according to instructions. The young fellow who received them, observed as he walked away along the exit passage. Then that sudden unexpected dash into the women's public lavatory, and Price's realization, too late, that the fellow must have made a lightning change in there, and left by the exit on the other side, where the man on duty hadn't yet been alerted. He/she had got away. They were almost no further on. The number of the notes had all been taken, of course, but checking them would take time and time was exactly what they hadn't got. Every half hour that elapsed was a further threat to the life of the baby. Very possibly the actual handing over of the notes had signed the baby's death sentence; it might even have been better to risk an arrest on the grounds that if they were caught they might not want to add murder to the charge of kidnapping and extortion. What had actually occurred was probably the most disastrous thing possible. Price wondered why he'd ever gone in for this soul-destroying, disillusioning, heartbreaking job. He knew the answer, of course. If looking for the truth is what matters to you, even if it's the mundane awkward truth of whodunit, rather than the philosopher's stone, this is the only life you can contemplate. He'd rather, perhaps, have been an academic, sitting at a desk and playing with words, looking in books instead of into back streets; he would rather have conferred with professors and learned doctors than with impostors and criminals. Or would he? Wouldn't he have got impatient with theory and words, and have longed for the excitement of searching out facts instead of theories, of saving the innocent instead of confounding someone else's speculations? But was he, this time, going to save the innocent? Hadn't he today, by gross incompetence, put the lives of a girl and a child at the mercy of a psychopath roaming around the Sussex coast? Price got a line to the Brighton police station for the twentieth time. No news. No news.

Monday evening

At six-thirty on Monday evening, Price rang Stephen.

"Stephen? Anything for me?"

"I'm sorry. We did try this afternoon for a bit, and then Vicky had to get back home. She wasn't terribly well yesterday and her mother's anxious about her. I'm not sure that mightn't have been why nothing happened this afternoon. She's in a state about the baby. I think she's trying too hard or something."

"Is she really not well? I was going to ask. . . . But it won't work if we can't have her, too."

"I beg your pardon?"

"I'm sorry. I'm not being at all clear. I don't feel it either. I was going to suggest taking both of you down with me to Brighton. I've got to go down there myself, and if I could have had you two with me, it might have been a help. But we've got to have Vicky, you're no good on your own."

"I don't think she's exactly ill. . . ."

"You think her mother might let her come? If I went to see her and asked?"

"I suppose she might. For you."

"I shall be 'round at your place in twenty minutes."

In fact it was twenty-five. He'd called first at the Stanfords, since if he couldn't have Vicky, there wasn't much point in taking Stephen. Vicky looked pale and shadowed, smaller and younger than he'd remembered. Price simply said to her mother that he was short of time, that he had to take every chance there was of catching the gang before they harmed the baby. He thought Vicky might be able to help since she'd seen the couple who'd made the snatch. He'd take every possible care of her, might he borrow her? Mrs. Stanford hadn't liked it. Vicky was to be taken off to the neighborhood of a gang who might be violent? But no, Price promised, she wasn't going anywhere near them unless all danger of violence was over. He needed someone who could identify one or more of them after they'd been taken into custody.

"She wasn't well yesterday. I'd have liked her to get to bed early tonight," Mrs. Stanford said.

"Mum! I wouldn't be able to sleep!"

"I wouldn't ask it if I wasn't desperate about this baby. And the girl whom we think is with her. I think they're both in danger," Price said.

"You'll see Vicky's kept safe?"

That meant Vicky could go. Having given way so far, Mrs. Stanford couldn't refuse to let Chris go too. It would have looked. . . . But she wasn't easy about it, would have refused if she could, if it hadn't been for Chris's pleadings. When she looked at her Mum like that, it was difficult to say no. She did say, "I thought you and Paul were going out tonight. I thought that's why he came around this evening, to ask you." But Chris said, "He'll understand, I've got to be with Vicky. I'll see him tomorrow." So Price arrived at the Rawlinson house with Chris and Vicky in the back of a very unofficial-looking car, driven by a plainclothes man. Price sat in the front passenger seat and during the drive south no one spoke much. Once Price said over his shoulder, "If anything I ought to know occurs to you, you'll let me know." He didn't want to embarrass them by referring to their flashes in front of a third party.

Because it was such a gray day, the light had begun to fade early. Inside the van, Maureen sat and nursed Linda in the near dark. She was scared. If the doors hadn't been locked, she thought she'd have tried to jump out and make a run for it. The van wasn't going all that fast and she guessed they were still in little country roads. They kept on going uphill and downhill, and turning corners and twisting about. She could have jumped out very quick and hidden behind a hedge before Skinner would know she'd gone. She might have been able to get right away and never see him again.

But the van doors were locked. She'd tried them. When she looked out of the little windows she could just see the black branches of trees against the heavy sky. Sometimes she saw a twinkling yellow window in a house some way away; when she saw this, it disappeared too soon; she'd have liked to feel that there were people about, that she wasn't alone with Skinner. He'd really frightened her just now when the van came right at her, and whatever he said about it being a mistake, she didn't feel sure he mightn't do it again. His face had looked really bad, as if he meant to hurt her and was sorry he hadn't managed it.

Suppose the next time they stopped, he tried again? He might just be waiting till it was really dark and there wasn't anyone else about, and then he'd go for her and do her in. He might be driving like this, what felt like round and round, away from streets and shops and people doing ordinary things, because when it was the middle of the night he'd have her all alone, away from everybody, and then he'd do it. Maureen remembered the knife and the way his hand had gone toward it when he'd been asking who she'd talked to yesterday. Once, what seemed like a long time ago, when she'd seen the knife for the first time, she'd asked, "What d'you want a knife for, Skinner?" and he'd said, "Everywhere I go, that knife comes too. And it's been used. It's not just for show." Maureen found she couldn't stop thinking about that knife and what he'd do with it if he was angry with her. She made a little whimpering noise in the dark.

And now it was really dark. It was almost black inside the van, she couldn't see anything. If she had to give Linda another feed, she'd have to turn on the little light in the roof so as to see to make it up. But Skinner wouldn't like that. He'd told her she couldn't have any light. It was a good thing she'd given Linda a bottle before they'd left the last parking place, while there was still enough daylight. Now she might sleep till the next morning, if only Skinner kept quiet. But he might not keep quiet. He might come in and go for her. Maureen couldn't stop thinking about that knife, with its long thin blade. She wished she had a knife too.

She thought about this. She wondered if perhaps there might be a knife somewhere in the van. She put Linda down carefully in her carry-cot and began to feel about. But though there was crockery and some spoons in the little cupboard, there was no knife. She went on feeling about. Pillows and blankets on the bunks, that wasn't any good. Matches. She could start a fire and burn the van. But with her locked inside it, that wasn't going to help her, she'd just get burned to death, and she wasn't at all sure Skinner would trouble himself to let her out. She had a picture of Skinner standing looking at the van all alight with flames coming out of the windows and laughing because he knew she was choking and burning inside it. The thought made her more frightened than ever. It was the worst thing that had ever happened to her, being trapped in this nasty bumpy van, with Skinner waiting to kill her as soon as he thought it would be safe. She wanted out. More than anything ever in her whole life, she wanted out.

Price arrived at the Brighton police station just after eight-thirty. Superintendent Cole met him with, "I don't know who told you about the special offer, but we've got it."

"Where?"

"Little one-man grocery shop on the Eastbourne Road, five miles this side of Eastbourne. Chap called Jerningham, always has one or two special offers, and this week. . . ."

"That the only one in the district?"

"That's right. . . ."

"My God, and we've been thinking he went west all this time! Switch your men to the Eastbourne area, anywhere between there and Brighton and further still, Pevensey, Hastings, the lot. No notices to the public, he may have a transistor and it's vital not to alarm him. If anyone spots the van—it shouldn't be too difficult with that great dent on the off side—give strict instructions that he's not to be rushed. As long as he's actually driving, they can intercept and get him, but if the van's parked it's got to be done without him seeing, if possible. Surround him, take him by surprise. And hurry! If we can't find him within the next two hours. . . ." He remembered Stephen and Vicky just behind him and checked himself.

"When was the van seen outside the grocery shop? Do we know how long ago? Yesterday? Today? If we knew that, we'd have a better idea how far east to look," Cole said reasonably.

"We don't know. You've just got to get on with looking in an easterly direction."

"He might have turned around. Or gone north."

"Look north as well, then, only get on with it!"

Price took Vicky, Stephen and Chris into the station and ordered coffee. He was shocked at Vicky's appearance, she looked drawn, pinched, gray. If she was going to crack up on him now, not only would she be no help, he might find himself responsible for more than the deaths of a small baby and a moronic girl. He was surprised that he felt a quick personal pang at the idea. He said, "Coffee's coming, Vicky. You'll feel better after that. I've got to be off. I've told Superintendent Cole that if you give him any messages for me he's not to ask where they come from, he's to communicate with me by radio telephone immediately. Understand?"

Stephen said, "Can't we come with you?"

"No you can't. One, I promised Vicky's mother I wouldn't take either of you anywhere near what could be a nasty situation. Two, if you're with me it takes just that much longer to get whatever news you have around to all the patrol cars, whereas if you're here it can go out to every single one and that might mean saving precious minutes. Three, I don't think Vicky's fit, I want her to stay here with you. Now, I'm off. Wish me luck, I shall need it. And . . . I know you'll do your best."

The coffee arrived, hot and sweet and nothing like Stephen's mother's coffee, but welcome for all that. There were biscuits too, and Vicky was surprised to find that she could swallow mouthfuls of crumbs washed down with coffee and that she did feel better afterwards. But she still felt tired. So tired she ached all over. She'd have liked to be able to lie down, but in the little room which, by Price's orders, they had to themselves, there were only chairs, hard, wooden, and a table equally hard. So she just sat beside Chris, leaning both elbows on the table, and looked across at Stephen who looked back at her.

"Howd' you feel?" he asked.

"I'm tired," Vicky said.

"You look it," Chris said.

"Stephen. He really thinks . . . doesn't he? That they're going to . . . that he mayn't be able to get there in time?"

"He's doing everything he can," Stephen said.

"I wish we could do something."

"I suppose we ought to try," Stephen said.

"But I was trying. All the way down. And absolutely nothing happened. You were too, weren't you?"

"Yes."

"It's hopeless. It's no good trying, you said so. You've got not to try, like you did before," Chris said.

"You didn't expect us to start playing Twenty Questions in the car in front of that other chap? The driver. I couldn't have. Anyway I don't believe it would have worked."

"It wouldn't have," Vicky said with unusual decision.

"But you can't just sit here! You must do something! That's why he brought you here," Chris said.

"I know."

"Steve! You *must*! Don't you see? He said every minute counted. You can't not!"

"I suppose so," Stephen said again.

"Why don't you then? Vicky, why don't you? Oh, I wish it was me," Chris said impatiently.

"Chris! You don't understand. . . ."

"What don't I understand?"

"It's because. . . . What we see hasn't happened yet. You know that."

"That's why you've got to do it quickly."

"But we might see something that isn't going to happen for hours. . . ."

"Then it's all the more important to do it *now*."

Vicky looked at Stephen.

"What is it, Vicky?"

Vicky said, "I'm frightened." She shivered.

"But Vicky. . . ."

Vicky said, "If the Super's right . . . and they're too late. . . . Don't you see, Chris? I don't want to see . . . what he finds . . . the baby. . . ."

There was a silence. Neither of the others had thought of this.

"Vicky, I'm sorry! I do see. Only I still think you ought to. I know it'd be awful. But if there's a chance of saving it . . . Vicky! you must!"

Vicky looked across at Stephen. He said, "Chris is right, Vicky."

"I didn't know it would be so . . . bloody awful," Vicky said.

"But you will?"

Vicky nodded.

Stephen said miserably, "I suppose we've got to play that stupid game?"

"We don't know any other way of doing it, do we?"

"It seems all wrong somehow. As if we didn't care."

"Of course you care," Chris said.

Vicky said to Stephen, "You start."

He thought. He couldn't fix his mind on anything. He looked around the drab, pale green-distempered room and at the dirty concrete floor. He looked at the high window and saw that outside the light had almost faded. He looked at the flyspotted single lamp hanging from the ceiling. He said, "It's no good. I *can't*. I absolutely can't."

"Vicky?" Chris said.

Vicky shivered again. "Suppose I can't either?"

"Try!"

She shut her eyes. Stephen and Chris watched her, Stephen aching for the turmoil which he knew must occupy her mind, Chris with unquenchable hope. The room was very quiet.

Suddenly Vicky cried out. She threw out a hand and cried, "No!" She said, "I don't want. . . ." and stopped. She opened her eyes and saw Chris and Stephen. She said, "It wasn't a flash. It was like. . . . You know when you're just going to sleep sometimes you dream . . . you're falling. . . ." She shivered. "It was . . ." Chris, busy putting an arm round Vicky and making comforting noises, didn't realize that it was at this moment that the flash hit both Stephen and Vicky. She felt Vicky shiver again. She looked at Stephen and saw that he was coming back to the present at the same instant as Vicky's exclamation, "It's dark. I can't see. . . ."

"Headlights," Stephen said.

"I didn't see any. It was all dark. Someone was running . . . she was crying . . . it's horrid. Something really bad. . . ."

"A flash! You'll have to tell that other Super," Chris said.

"What, though? I didn't see anything. Just the dark . . . and the person crying."

"Stephen saw headlights. He must have seen where it was."

"I didn't. Just a road and grass. Only for a moment, then the headlights went off."

"What sort of road? Steve! What sort of road?"

"Nothing special. Not a big road. With grass verges. I'll tell you what, though! It was on a hill. Quite steep. Looked like an edge."

"There must have been something else!" Chris said, impatient.

"There was a sound," Vicky said.

"You said. Someone crying."

"Not that sort of sound. Not a person."

"What then? Steve, did you hear anything?"

"I think I did. I know! It was the sea."

"There's sea everywhere around here."

"Only this wasn't like you hear it on the beaches. It was a long way off."

"Down below," Vicky said.

"Of course! It was up on a cliff!"

"That's why I had that feel about falling."

"There must be thousands of cliffs around here," Chris said, disappointed.

"Not all that many. Brighton's got a flat beach," Stephen said.

"It could help them, then. They might be able to guess where it is. Which way was the van moving, Steve?"

"It wasn't moving. What I mean is, the headlights weren't moving. If it was the van, it was parked on a road somewhere."

"We'd better tell them. Quickly."

"If only they'll believe. . . ." Vicky began.

"What is it?"

"It could happen any minute now and they wouldn't have time to get there."

"No it couldn't! You said it was quite, absolutely dark."

"Look out of the window."

Stephen and Chris looked. The sky, which had been overcast and gray when they'd first sat down in the room, was now an inky black. Vicky said what they all three thought, when she said, "It could be happening now. He's going to kill her. And the baby." Neither Stephen nor Chris contradicted her.

Monday night

8:35   Price rang Andrew.

"Mr Wilmington? We've got a lead. Van's possibly been seen half an hour ago on the road between Hastings and Eastbourne. Back of Pevensey Bay. Unfortunately we lost it again after that. We think it may be in Eastbourne itself. Trouble is there are too many blue Bedford vans on the roads, and all we've got to identify this one is the damaged offside fender. However, we shall carry on searching."

Andrew said, "I'm coming down," cautiously because he didn't want Sally to hear. She was supposed to be in the living-room, but she was so restless, he couldn't be sure how near she might be.

"There's really no need, sir. In fact . . ."

"I'm coming," Andrew said. It was only after he'd rung off that he realized he didn't know where he was coming to. Price had gone down to the Brighton station, he'd go there. He went in to tell Sally that he'd been called out to see an American business associate who was in London on a flying visit, he'd got to drive out to see him at Heathrow. "I'll ring from there to tell you when I'll be back," he said. Sally accepted it as she did everything now in her numbed misery. He kissed her hair and said, "Go to bed, darling, and take a pill. No point in staying up for me, I don't know when I'll be back." She might have said, "No point in taking a pill, I'm beyond that," but she didn't. She just let him kiss her. When he looked back from the door of the room she was still sitting there, not looking at anything, her hands idle in her lap.

9:15   No further sign of the van. Price, in a control car driving around Eastbourne, searching the back streets like the one in Brighton where the van had parked the night before last, sending men on foot to investigate parking lots, dead-end streets, deserted warehouses, was getting desperate. It was now a dark overcast evening with a fine drizzling rain. Somewhere around here, within perhaps twenty or thirty miles' radius, that young thug might be quietly getting rid of the girl and the baby. Price's anxiety made him extraordinarily short-tempered. When his driver suggested going out and having a look on the front, he bit his head off. Then apologized. Immediately did it again.

9:30   Chief Superintendent Cole couldn't understand it. Since he was a conscientious officer and obeyed orders, he'd transmitted immediately the extraordinary, garbled message produced by the three youngsters. A story of a road on the side of a hill, grass, headlights, a cliff, the sea. He didn't understand what it was supposed to mean. He wondered if these three were in radio contact with the kidnapping lot. It seemed unlikely. In spite of his knowledge of the need for urgency, it took him a little time to sort out what he was being told, to add it up in his mind, and when he spoke over the radio telephone to Price, his voice told how much value he placed on information got this way. He repeated what Stephen had told him. Said doubtfully that there were quite a lot of cliffs between Brighton and Eastbourne, but the obvious one would be Beachy Head. Well-known place for suicides. Sheer drop at one point, two hundred feet to the rocks below.

"How close is the road to the edge there?" Price asked.

"Fifteen feet? Right on top you can drive off the road right up to the verge, drive the whole thing over if that's how you feel."

"There's a police rescue post there, isn't there?"

"That's right."

"Doesn't sound so likely then. How far away is this other place where the road's so close to the edge?"

"Five hundred yards? On the descending road, going toward Birling Gap. There's a dip in the coastline, then the ground goes up again this way toward the old lighthouse."

"Popular area? Many people about?"

"In this weather? No one at all."

"I'm going there. I want six more cars as reinforcement. Take anyone you can off the flat ground and concentrate those I'm not wanting on other cliffs that have roads reasonably near. We've got to do this quietly, I want the van, if it's there, surrounded and surprised. Hurry. We haven't any time to waste."

Cole issued the instructions. He had to. "What does he mean, no time to waste?" Even if the place is right, it's ten minutes since those three told me what they knew. Whatever was going to happen up there must have happened by now. "Crazy," he thought. But with Jim in this mood, he, Cole, wasn't going to ask questions. He was going to obey orders and wait till it was all over for explanations.

9:45   Andrew, having exceeded the speed limit wherever possible, arrived at the Brighton police station, introduced himself and asked for Price.

"He's out looking for the van, sir," Cole said.

"Where?"

Cole hesitated, then said, "The thing is, sir, if he finds it he's hoping to get it surrounded and then surprise the driver. He thinks that way there'd be less risk of violence."

"Where is he?" Andrew said again.

"I'm afraid I can't tell you that, sir. Instructions, sir. Sorry, sir."

"God damn it, I'm the child's father!"

"I know, sir. I know how you must be feeling, but it's impossible for me to tell you anything more. If you'd like to stay here for a while, I'll see to it that every piece of news that comes through to us is passed on to you directly, sir."

With a very bad grace, Andrew sat. But he was too restless to remain here, just as he'd been too restless to stay at home in London. He got up and prowled. He went outside and looked at the dark wet night. He came indoors again and was going back to the room he'd just left when he saw a boy coming out of a door ahead. He said, "You!" and saw on Stephen's face just the look of surprise and dislike that he knew must be on his own.

"What are you doing here?"

"Superintendent Price brought us," Stephen said.

Andrew's immediate response was one of violent anger. His baby's life, Sally's sanity, lay in the hands of a gullible, incompetent policeman who was staking them on a story which sounded like the inventions of a fortune-teller looking into a teacup. If the worst happened he'd make sure that Chief Superintendent Bloody Price lost not only this case but his reputation as well. For a moment he couldn't speak, then he controlled himself and said, "I suppose you know exactly what's going on and where he is just now? Or doesn't your second sight tell you anything as practical as that?"

Stephen flushed, but he didn't turn away. He said, "I think he'll have gone toward a beach somewhere."

"Since we're on the south coast and there are several hundred miles of beach here, that's safe enough."

Stephen said, steadily, "I don't know the country around here. We thought it was high. Cliffs. But when we told Super Cole in there, he said beach, or something."

"What do you mean, you thought it was a cliff? What was?"

"Where the van is. Or where it's going to be. But the Superintendent had gone and we had to tell Cole in there what it looked like. I wouldn't have thought it was a beach, but he did say something about one."

Andrew suddenly saw himself as a small boy in gray flannel shorts on a school expedition. He said, "Beachy Head!"

"That's it! That's what he said!"

"That's where Price has gone? You sure?"

"I think he must've."

"On your recommendation? Another of these glimpses of the future?"

"He asked us to try to see. . . ."

"And you conveniently did?"

Stephen didn't answer this. He said, "Have you got a car?"

Andrew raised his eyebrows. He answered, "Since you're interested, yes, I have."

"Will you take us there? Cole says he won't, and we can't get there by ourselves in time."

"Take you there?"

"To that place. The place you said. Either the van's there or it's going to be. Vicky and I, we've got to be there. We just might. . . . *Please*. It wouldn't hurt you. Even if you think we're making the whole thing up, you can't afford not to take the chance. Don't you see? Vicky and me—we're the best hope you've got."

If he'd been angry, or if he'd been apologetic, Andrew wouldn't have listened for a second, but his quietness was impressive. Even so, he remained furious, skeptical, at this moment hating everyone, including himself. He opened his mouth to tell Stephen that he hadn't come to Brighton to give him and his girl friend rides about the country, when he remembered Sally. Sally had asked him if he'd do anything to find Caroline Ann, and he'd said he would. Even if there was nothing but these children's stories to go on. He'd meant it at the time. Did he mean it less now? He stood looking at Stephen without speaking, so that Stephen thought he couldn't have heard, but at last he said, "All right. Come on."

"Vicky'll have to come too."

"I said, come on," Andrew said and walked out of the station. His MG was parked just down the street. He unlocked it and saw that there were three of them, the two girls who'd come to his house as well as the boy. But it didn't seem to matter. The whole thing was so crazy anyway, what did it matter if he turned up on the top of Beachy Head with a crowd of school children? He said, "You'll be very cramped in the back," as the girls climbed in. The boy sat beside him and he started up. Stephen, even in the heat of the moment, noticed how quickly the speedometer needle climbed. He'd never been driven so quickly.

10:00   "Any sightings of the van? Anything seen of it on the road leading up toward Beachy Head?"

"No reports of a sighting, sir. Will keep you informed."

"Thanks, over and out."

"Over and out. What a horrible expression just now and just here," Price thought.

10:00   Maureen hadn't thought she'd ever be able to sleep when she was as frightened as she was now, but what with the dark and the movement of the van, she did doze off from time to time. Presently the van stopped and she woke right up, sure that Skinner was going to come in and do for her. She stayed for minutes, listening, with her hand on the paraffin stove, the only thing she'd found that she thought she might be able to hit Skinner with if he started coming at her with the knife. But there were no movements and Skinner didn't unlock the door or speak to her through the front partition, and after a while she felt a bit better and dozed off again.

When she woke, with a start, the van was moving again, faster than before and more as if Skinner knew where he was going. Nothing to be seen outside, but after a time Maureen could feel that they were going uphill again. Because she was sleepy, and because of nothing awful having happened the last time they stopped, Maureen was taken by surprise when the van pulled up with a great jerk, and she heard Skinner's voice from the cab in front.

"Ready to snack?" he said, and he sounded friendly again, like he used to be, so that Maureen said, "Yes, Skinner," joyfully, forgetting all the bad things she'd been thinking about him in the last few hours, and looking forward to chips and steak or fish and a big ice cream, and lights and people and music from the discotheque like they'd had before all this fuss with Linda. Only she wouldn't look very nice with her hair all short and raggedy. She heard him get out of the cab and come around to the back doors. But when he opened them it was all dark and quiet, except for a sort of sighing noise ever so far below, almost as if it was under the ground beneath. And the ground was just grass. Maureen had been badly frightened before and she began to be frightened again. She said, "I can't see any restaurant. Where is it?"

"Other side of the van," Skinner said.

"Why aren't there any lights, then?"

"Come on, and I'll show you. Round the next corner, that's all."

Maureen looked at all she could see, the dark shape of Skinner, and hesitated.

"Come on! You must be hungry. You aren't still sore at me because of that mistake I made this evening, are you?"

If he hadn't said that about the evening, Maureen might have believed him. But when she heard him say it, she remembered again the way he'd looked at her and the way the van had come straight at her. She drew further back into the shadows of the van and said, "No, Skinner. I don't want to."

"You've got to, you stupid bag. Come on! D'you want me to come and get you?"

Maureen, terrified, squeezed herself against the side of the van. The only advantage she had against Skinner with the knife, which she imagined as well as if she'd seen it, was that she was looking out of the more intense darkness. She could just make out his shape against the sky. He was looking in and couldn't see anything. She saw him wait for a moment before he put his knee on the van's floor, ready to hoist himself up. In that moment, Maureen put out her hand and felt the paraffin stove. She got it in both hands, and just as Skinner began to pull himself up into the van, Maureen brought the stove down on his head as hard as she could. She heard him cry out, and he must have fallen. The stove, which she'd let go of, fell too, with a loud metallic noise, and went rolling away downhill.

Maureen waited. She couldn't hear anything, except that sighing noise below, coming and going, now louder, now softer, but never giving up. It couldn't be the wind, because there wasn't any, the air was cool and damp and very still. It sounded almost like a huge animal with rattling uneven breaths waiting at the bottom of the hill for the van to come down again. Like Skinner might be waiting down there, just out of sight, so that when she got out he could run her down again or go for her with the knife.

She waited a bit longer, and then, too frightened to stay, she began to climb out. She let herself carefully down. One foot touched the ground, the other touched something softish, that gave, and she drew it back, shaking with terror. It was Skinner, she was sure of it. But no hand came out to grab her ankle and nothing moved. Very slowly she got herself right out of the van. She could just see Skinner's huddled shape lying on the ground. He lay very still. If he was waiting to jump on her, the sooner she got out of the way the better. Maureen backed away down the road and the darkness closed in on her.

She'd gone perhaps twenty paces, feeling with one foot in front of the other, sobbing loudly and stumbling, often, when she stopped.

She'd remembered Linda.

She'd left Linda behind.

Into Maureen's confused, feeble mind came a series of pictures. Of Linda with her bottle. Of Linda crying. Of Linda on Mrs. Plum's comfortable shoulder. Of the way Skinner looked at Linda. Of Sharon throwing the baby onto the bed and saying, "It's all yours." Of Linda smiling. Of Skinner coming after the both of them. Of Maureen hiding somewhere with Linda while Skinner roamed around with his knife out, all ready to use it again, and of Linda crying just then, so that he found them. Of the picture she'd been to with Skinner once, where a fellow and his girl had gone around killing people mostly for fun, and of the blood and the car full of bullet holes and the girl sitting dead in her seat with blood running down all over her nice white skirt. That's what she would look like if Skinner got at her with his knife.

There was something else. Out here in the dark it was scary, frightening. Maureen had never liked to be alone in the dark. If she had Linda with her, it would be some sort of company, it wouldn't be as awful as it was being here all by herself.

But suppose Skinner had woken up by now and was just waiting there for her to come back?

It was the most dreadful thing Maureen had ever done. She went up the road slowly, seeing the bulk of the van in front of her up on the grassy slope. Her foot kicked against something hard that rattled and made her jump. Then she realized it was the paraffin stove. She picked it up. It made her feel a little braver to have it with her. She'd hit Skinner with it once, maybe she could hit him again. He was still lying where she'd left him, but when she'd climbed back into the van, she heard him move and give a sort of snore like he did sometimes when he was asleep. She had to be quick. She felt around the van and found Linda. It was difficult to get down again without losing hold of Linda's clothes so that she wouldn't roll away down the sloping van floor, but she managed it. Skinner was making more and more horrid snoring noises and moving a bit, and she'd have liked to hit him again to keep him asleep a bit longer, but she couldn't do it without losing hold of Linda and she didn't dare do that.

She held Linda tight in her arms and started off along the road. Then she thought she'd better not stay on the road, because when Skinner got better, that's where he'd come and look for her. She went off onto the grass and felt her way along that, not knowing in the blackness where she was or where she was going, only wanting to get as far away from the van as she could. Only Linda was more of a weight to carry than she'd reckoned on and she couldn't go fast. She was frightened of Skinner and she was frightened of what might come at her out of the dark. She was frightened that in this cold, drizzling rain they might both get so wet they'd die. But most of all she was frightened that Skinner would get up and come after her. In a panic, Maureen wandered along the grassy verge of high chalk cliffs, listening to the sea worrying the shingle at their distant feet, clutching the baby and asking God all the time to please, *please* not let Linda scream.

10:00 "Where's this?" Stephen asked.
"Newhaven. Heard of it?"
"How far from where we've got to get to?"
"Far enough."

10:15 The van stood solitary and dark, barely visible against the low sky. When it came into sight, Price heard the man on his stomach in the grass next to him, sigh. "Do you think we've a chance, sir?" he asked, and Price could only reply, "A small one." But his heart sank. That devil had fooled them. Must have been somewhere inland all afternoon ever since the lunch-time purchase, and had then made for Beachy Head from the west, through Birling Gap, while they'd been searching East-bourne, Battle, the Hastings district. When they'd had the message about Beachy Head being a possible location, and had sealed off all the approach roads, he must already have been inside the cordon. Price didn't like the look of that solitary van, stationed so near the cliff edge, no one moving. He was thankful he'd refused to allow Andrew Wilmington to come here with him. He hated to think what that van might by now contain.

"We've got to get right up to him, and then rush him," Price said.

"He's very quiet," the man next to him said.

"That's what I don't like."

"Look!" the officer said, and Price looked. His eyes by this time were more accustomed to the dark, but even so it was difficult to make anything out. He felt his age as he said to the young man at his side, "What's going on?"

"The van's moving."

"He hasn't any lights!"

"Crazy bastard! He's driving, though."

"It isn't just the brakes slipping?"

"He's all over the road, but there's someone there."

"Then we move in. Call up the others."

The road in front of Skinner was suddenly ablaze with lights. A car across the narrow road. He pulled up with a screech of brakes and felt for his knife. But the blow on his head, though it hadn't incapacitated him for long, had slowed him down. He found himself out of the driver's cab, standing on the road, his arms held, surrounded by policemen. Price hardly looked at him, he was at the back of the van immediately. Unlocked. His heart dropped as he flung the doors open. As he'd feared. No sign of the girl or the baby.

"Where are they? What did you do with them? You. . . . Did they go over the cliff?" he asked Skinner, pushing his face right up to that mean one, feeling the need to hurt back, to repay violence with violence. Retribution, an eye for an eye. But if you are a respectable Chief Superintendent, you can't allow yourself the luxury of these human reactions, so he took his face back again and said to the officers, "Take him back to the car. I'll question him later. The rest of you cover the area for a mile around. There's just a chance they got away." Though knowing what her father and stepmother had said about Maureen Hollingsworth he couldn't believe that that poor girl could conceivably have outwitted·this young devil.

10:30   "Where's this?" Stephen asked.

"Birling Gap. We'll be up there in a minute or two. What's *that?*"

That was the road blocked by police cars, lights blazing, the van standing empty and unlighted among them. Stephen said, "That's it! That's the van!" Andrew pulled up. He asked, "Where? Have they found her?" But he knew from the silence with which they made room for him that they hadn't, that he'd have to go back to Sally with the news that they'd arrived too late, that her baby wasn't ever going to be found.

Price was there suddenly, his grave face confirming Andrew's fears.

"I thought you were going to stay . . ." he began, then saw Stephen.

"What are you doing here? I told you to stay in Brighton."

"I brought him," Andrew said.

"Vicky isn't here, is she? I promised her mother. . . ."

"We had to come. We're the only ones who've seen them . . ." Stephen began.

"All that's no good now. Purfitt's over there in custody. There's been some sort of fight, he's only half-conscious. . . ."

"The baby?" Vicky said.

"I'm afraid. . . . If only we'd got your news five minutes earlier we might have saved them, got there first. He must have got them out of the van and. . . ."

"I saw someone moving about in the dark. When Stephen saw the edge of the cliff before the lights went off."

"A struggle? Were people struggling in the dark?"

"Don't think so. Just one person. Crying. She might still be up there."

"I'm afraid she isn't, Vicky. We've got men up there looking around where the van was when we spotted it first. Even if Purfitt didn't push her over, she might well have gone over the edge herself. It's pitch dark up there, and she wasn't very bright, poor girl."

"But the baby?" She saw from the way Price glanced at Mr. Wilmington that he thought the baby had gone too.

"I want to go and look," Vicky said, persistent.

Price looked at Andrew. Andrew, incredibly, looked at Stephen. Stephen said, "I think she ought to go. We ought to try everything."

Andrew said, "Get into the car. I'll take you up there."

Vicky said to Price, "What's her name?"

"Maureen."

Stephen got into the back of the car with Chris.

They climbed two hundred yards. Vicky said, "Here. Stop."

Andrew stopped.

"Could you turn off the lights?"

"You won't be able to see anything."

"I know. Only, don't you see? She could be hiding from that horrible man. If she sees lights she won't know it isn't him; she'll hide. Also if I call, she'll know it's only a girl."

Standing on the damp grass near the summit of the great cliff, Vicky put one hand on the hood of the dark car, to remind herself she wasn't alone. She wasn't surprised the girl was scared. Nothing but blackness and the waves beating on the chalk hundreds of feet below. She called into the still air, "Maureen! Maureen! You needn't be frightened anymore! No one's going to hurt you. Won't you come out?"

No answer.

"Maureen! Please! You don't know me. I'm Vicky. I'm a girl like you. There isn't anyone else here except me and . . . friends. We've come to look for the baby. Maureen! If you're there, please come out."

No answer. Vicky's heart sank. She made herself say what she hadn't wanted to.

"Maureen! Please bring us the baby. Her father's here. He's come to look for her."

She'd begun to give up hope. She was prepared to turn back to Andrew and say that she'd failed, when a voice surprisingly near her said, "You sure Skinner's not there?"

"No one's here except me and my friends and the baby's father."

Maureen sobbed as she crawled out from under the gorse-bush next to the hummock where she'd been hiding. Vicky couldn't see anything except a dark bulky shape. She knew Maureen was fat, but was she as fat as that? She said, "Is the baby there?" and Maureen sobbed, "Here, take her," and Vicky found her arms full of a cold wet bundle which squirmed and fought and finally yelled. Andrew was out of the car in a moment. So it was, in fact, Vicky who put his daughter back into Andrew Wilmington's arms.

38

"Now!" Chris said.

Vicky took the piece of wood out of her pocket and put it, doubtfully, on the table of the coffee bar, between herself and Stephen.

"Steve? You have brought the rest of it, haven't you?"

Stephen pulled out the plastic bag and spilled the contents out in a jumbled heap of angles.

"Put it together! Make it a whole egg again," Chris breathed.

Stephen looked at Vicky.

"You sure?"

She nodded.

"What good's one bit of it to Vicky? I don't know why she ever wanted to keep it in the first place," Chris said.

"I told you. I liked the way it looked."

"Do you still want to keep it?" Stephen asked.

"No. You can have it."

The two girls watched Stephen's fingers taking up the pieces one by one. Delicately, gently, half-knowing and half-unknowing, Stephen pieced the egg together. His own pieces he knew now. He put them against each other, balanced them so that each supported its neighbors against gravity and was in turn held in its own position in the whole. At last, with something of a flourish, he took up the remaining piece, Vicky's, and fitted it into its predestined place.

It fell in easily. Too easily. It did not fill the space left for it.

Stephen looked across at Vicky and she looked back.

"Then mine wasn't the last bit!" she said.

"I thought when I'd got yours, it'd be whole," Stephen said.

"Won't the egg hold together now?" Chris asked.

Stephen released his finger-tip hold. The egg remained for a second poised, almost the shape of a perfect egg. Then it fell apart, littering the table with its spillikins of finely grained wood.

"There's still something missing," Vicky said.

"What a shame!" Chris said at the same moment.

"One piece. We can find it," Stephen said. He looked again at Vicky and knew that he was glad the egg wasn't whole yet. He didn't want to stop looking. He wanted the search to go on.